GET BACK

imagine…saving John Lennon

By
Donovan Day

Park Slope Publishing
Brooklyn, New York

Park Slope Publishing
Brooklyn, New York

www.parkslopepublishing.com

Copyright © 2015 by Donovan Day

Manufactured in the United States of America

ISBN (print): 978-0-9837963-9-8
ISBN (e-book): 978-0-9837963-8-1

For all the people and places I remember . . .

ONE

I love New York—the sophistication, the swagger, the cool, the bounce—but sometimes it can also be a trying place. Like today. At this very moment. I am standing in the Columbus Circle subway station, and it feels like every inch of my skin is soaked with sweat. It's something like three hundred degrees in here and there's a lot of humidity in this concrete jungle. Breathing requires effort and the rush hour commuters know it. These are horrid conditions for just about anything, yet here I am, guitar in hand, singing an acoustic version of the Imagine Dragons song "Radioactive" for the few coins and bills some kind-hearted souls will drop in my guitar case.

I'm not crazy about performing at this particular station in the unbearable August heat, but a lot of commuters pass through here. More people means more money, or at least the *possibility* of more money. I'm trying to bank some spending money for my last year of high school. I go to a public high school, not one of those fancy private schools where all the kids jet off to some Caribbean island for Christmas break. That's not me. I just want enough cash to go out on the weekends without hitting up my mother and maybe, just maybe, I'll be able to bank enough to buy an electric guitar. That would rock.

No one knows I'm down here. My mother is taking a leave of absence from her job so she can help care for an elderly cousin in Akron, Ohio. My dad is AWOL, divorced from my mom for a few years now and living with his new wife and family. So my mom arranged for me to stay with my grandfather and his husband in their two-bedroom, rent-stabilized apartment in the West Village. If you're confused, so was he. He says he didn't understand that he was gay when he knocked up his high school girlfriend, who insisted on having the baby—my mother. The girlfriend wanted to put my mother up for adoption. Grandpa refused and kept his baby daughter. Later on, after he graduated high school and his sexuality became, as he says, "obvious," he entered adulthood as a single gay father, a rarity back in the day. He eventually got some help when he met the guy who is now his husband. Both are named Joe if you can believe it. They're pretty cool, and they let me have a lot of freedom. They get it. I'm a city kid who's been riding the subway alone since I was twelve. As long as I make it back to their apartment by midnight, the Joes are okay with not knowing where I am every minute of the day.

The Columbus Circle station is one of the most popular in the city for musicians to perform. You're supposed to have a license, but my friend Marlon has a friend who forged one for me. Marlon doesn't care much for rules, and when I asked him how he managed to get it, he shot me a withering look and said, "Look Lenny, when you know the people who know the people . . . don't worry about it, okay?" So I'm taking his advice. I'm not gonna worry about it. Besides, it looks plenty real to me.

I admit to a serious case of nerves. I've only played in the subway one other time. It wasn't a disaster—no one booed, I didn't get mugged—but it wasn't a raging success, either. I hauled in a grand total of $12.35 for two hours of work. Not great, but enough to make me try again. As my mother says, I've got the performing bug, and I figure if I can play down here, I can play anywhere.

I finish up with "Radioactive" and a couple of people clap. I try to look cool while considering what to play next. That's when I feel something hit my leg. I look down to see a Peanut M&M bounce across the platform. When I look back up, one hits my guitar. A giant kid with a peach-fuzz mustache is laughing along with his friend. "Almost got it in the hole," he tells the friend.

The M&M thrower looks a little younger than me, but he's a head taller and more than a little intimidating. "What you looking at?" he says when I make eye contact.

I smile even though I'm more in the mood to smash my guitar over his punk head. A few years earlier I would have, but now I rein in my bad impulses—most of the time. A train pulls into the station, but of course, Giant Annoying Kid ignores it and begins throwing M&M's with more frequency. I am royally pissed off so I play the angriest song that comes to mind, Bob Dylan's "Positively Fourth Street."

I sing the opening lyric with gusto: "You've got a lot of nerve . . ."

The kid nudges his friend and points to my guitar case. There are about ten single dollar bills in it. I can tell people are watching and waiting to see what's going to happen next. A couple of them even hold up their cell phones, and I know they're about to hit "record" on their cameras. My heart is thumping, a stream of sweat rolling down my side from my underarm. I'm not going to let Giant Annoying Kid take my hard-earned cash, that's for sure. It may be time to revert to an earlier version of Lenny. I gotta show this overgrown child that I won't be pushed around.

As soon as he reaches down to grab my money, I slam the top of the case down with my foot. "Oops," I say. He jumps back a foot and his friend laughs at him. The would-be thief is not happy and takes a few steps toward me.

"Hey, punk," he says. "You got a problem?"

I keep singing, heading toward the verse where I tell him "what a drag it is to see you" when I hear a voice singing along with me. It's a girl's voice, and she is clearly enjoying spitting out the angry Dylan lyrics right in my tormentor's face. I glance over and see a tall Asian-American girl who looks about my age. She's wearing a very short skirt and high platform heels that show off her long, toned legs. Her hair is long, straight, and black. She's wearing a Ramones T-shirt, her entire outfit designed to show off her rocking body. We catch each other's eyes; I blush and immediately hate myself. Why does my dumb face have to give away my every thought? But we keep on singing, and my tormentor suddenly ignores me so he can stare at my singing partner. He grabs his crotch suggestively and gives her a big smile, trying to impress her from what I can tell. I wince, but I keep on singing. There's not much else I can do at this point. Nothing's going to happen as long as we're singing, but of course, the song is about to end.

As it does, my tormentor ambles over to this gorgeous girl standing next to me. "Hey, baby, you sound nice." He elongates the word *nice* so it means anything but.

"Thanks," she says.

"You should come downtown with us to Loisaida and forget this loser. We'll show you a good time."

"No thanks. I'm having a good time right here."

Whoever Miss Black Hair is, she's cool. Me, I'm still a ball of anger, and I'm waiting to see what comes next. I'm glad Miss Black Hair showed up, but now I have to defend both of us. It's part of the Guy Code.

"Come on, baby. I ain't never had an Asian girl before," Giant Annoying Kid says.

I open my mouth to tell him to cut it out, but she beats me to it. "You never had a girl before?" she says loudly so everyone around us can hear. "Is that what you said? You're a virgin?"

He blanches. "No, I . . ."

"Hey, everybody," she says out loud. "We have us a real, live virgin here! This dude has never had a girl before. You all heard it, right?"

She's laughing and so is everyone else, laughing and pointing their cell phones squarely at Giant Annoying Kid. Even his buddy is laughing at him. "Oh, shoot, Tony, she's got you pegged, man," the friend says.

The kid is desperate to regain the upper hand, but he doesn't know what to do because 1) it's not cool to hit a girl, and 2) he's clearly outmatched in the wit department. So instead, he settles for pulling up his pants in a "macho" way and spitting in the direction of my guitar case. "Bitch," he says and storms off. The cameras follow him as he holds up two middle fingers.

"Well," Miss Black Hair says to me, "that was fun."

All I can manage is, "You think?" I don't normally get tongue-tied around girls—they're just people, after all—but this girl is maybe the best-looking female to talk to me. Ever. She's way prettier than any of the girls in my school and that puts me off-balance. Very attractive girls can do that, at least to me; it's like a superpower.

As I'm stuck in neutral, Miss Black Hair extends her hand for a shake. "I'm Yoko."

"Yoko?" I say in an exaggerated way.

Her face changes ever so slightly. It's like a curtain has fallen. Her body stiffens. I've offended her. "I'm sorry, but I've never heard of anyone with that name . . . except for, you know, Yoko Ono."

"Gee, I never heard *that* before."

Uh-oh. I need to recover fast because she's eyeballing an arriving train.

"Hey, I'm sorry," I say. "I didn't mean anything by it. You have a beautiful voice, and it was fun to sing with you. And it was awfully nice of you to come to that guy's rescue because who knows what would have happened to him. You saved one of us a trip to the ER. I'm not saying who . . ."

She laughs. "Yeah, okay." She makes a move to leave. "I gotta go."

I step in front of her, which I immediately realize is a really dumb thing to do, because her entire body flinches for a second. I step back just as quickly. She smiles and her body relaxes.

Lenny, be cool.

"My name's Lenny, by the way," I say, sticking out my hand.

She doesn't take it because, at that second, she looks down at her purse. I put my hand back at my side. Then she finds whatever it is she was looking for, sweeps her hair back and ties it into a ponytail. "It's so freakin' hot down here," she says.

"It is hot, but people still want to be entertained. Did you see what happened after that song?" I say.

"What's that?"

I point to the guitar case. "People were dropping

some real money down there. I think maybe we should keep going."

"You want me to keep singing with you, like a duet?"

"Well," I say, "I can just play guitar and you can sing if you don't like my voice."

She considers me for a moment. "I think you have a nice voice, Lenny, but . . ." She pauses and bites her lip. I think I'm in love. No, I *know* I'm in love.

"But . . . ?"

She nods to herself, like now she can tell me what she was gonna say in the first place. "Okay, Lenny, I hope this doesn't hurt your feelings, but you sang the Dylan song way better than that lame version of 'Radioactive.' That song is played out."

"No problem. I like the oldies better anyway. So do we have a deal?"

"A deal?"

"Yeah, if we sing more oldies, you'll stick around and sing with me?" I say. I'm pulling this stuff out of thin air, but something must be working because she's still here in front of me, a real, live gorgeous girl. "How about 'Melissa' by . . ."

"The Allman Brothers. Yeah, I know that song. In fact, I love that song," she says.

"So you'll stay."

"Don't know. Let me hear you play the intro."

An audition? Whatever. I strum the opening chords and make the song as true to the original as I can. And then Yoko starts to sing the opening lyric, and her heavenly voice transforms this ugly, bleak subway platform into a much better place. Even the most jaded of commuters can't ignore a beautiful girl singing her heart out. People stop and hold up their phones again to record her.

A crowd of people stop and stare, including a group

of teenaged boys, who'd been watching Yoko closely. Now they have an excuse to size her up. They're all about my age, seventeen or so, and are trying to look as cool as possible. I doubt a single one has ever heard this quiet ballad by the Allman Brothers, but they close their eyes and nod along like it's one of their favorites. I know I'd be acting exactly like them if we switched places.

I admit to feeling a certain power over them simply because I'm the one with the beautiful girl by his side. That commands respect always. When the song ends, we get a healthy round of applause. Yoko takes an exaggerated bow that makes the boys clap harder. A flood of singles cascades into my guitar case. We play for another half hour, hitting classic oldies from the Beatles, and Van Morrison, and then "Stand By Me" before finishing up with "Dead Flowers" by the Stones. At that point, people are cheering. Yoko grabs my hand and motions for me to take a bow with her. I thank the crowd, put down my guitar, and turn to her.

"So how do you know all these songs?"

"I could ask you the same question," she says.

"Fair enough. My grandfather and his husband are baby boomers and nuts for music from the sixties, with a heavy emphasis on the Beatles. So's my mom. Lenny is short for Lennon so the Beatles are my favorite of course."

"Of course. But wait . . . your grandfather and his husband?" she asks, raising one gorgeous eyebrow.

"Yeah, they're gay."

"Well, duh." She laughs. "What about you? Are you gay?"

It's my turn to laugh. "Uh, no."

She smiles. "Joking!"

The blush is back. "So anyway," I say, trying to keep

the conversation going. "My Grandpa played all the oldies for me as I was growing up. What about you? How do you know all these songs?"

"My grandmother was a singer back in the day."

"And what day was that?"

Yoko looks at me but says nothing, as though she is trying to decide if I'm worth the bother of telling me the story. I see that thin veil fall cross her eyes again. She's not upset, only guarded, protective. "Maybe if I get to know you better, I'll tell you the whole story, but not today."

"Well, another day is cool. What's your number? Maybe we can get together for another gig?"

She looks me up and down. "How old are you?"

"I'm seventeen."

"Too young. I only date older men, sorry."

"I'll start shaving soon, I promise."

She laughs. "Well, you are funny, I'll give you that. And you play a pretty good guitar for a lefty, but, no, too young. I'm over young dudes. Too needy."

"I'm not needy, I promise, only dashing, handsome, and, uh, left-handed. Don't hold that against me."

She laughs again. "Now you're getting corny. But we'll see. Put your phone number in here," she says, handing me her phone.

"So you'll text me?"

"What did I say about not being needy?"

"Wait, how old are *you*?" I say.

"Sixteen."

What? "Oh, well, then forget it. I never date girls my age. Too sassy."

She laughs and looks at me, eyes narrowed in a way that seems to say she's along for the ride. Her tongue darts out to lick her lower lip and I think I might die. "Okay," she finally agrees. "You'll hear from me."

"Great," I say, trying not to sound as excited as I am. "Then we'll play again sometime, make some money."

Yoko looks down at my guitar case. "Oh, I get money from all this?" she asks, batting her eyelashes in mock surprise.

Idiot! Why didn't you offer before now? "Yeah, of course." I kneel down and scoop up the money without even counting it. I offer her half. "Here," I say, holding out a fistful of bills. "Thanks."

"Is that enough?"

"Enough for now," she says. "But if there is another performance, I get top billing and a dressing room."

What is she talking about? A split second too late, I realize she's joking, but by then she's punched my arm. "I'm kidding."

"Oh right, I knew that."

I'm so painfully slow on the uptake that it hurts.

At that moment, a downtown A train pulls into the station. "Okay, I'm outta here. Goodbye, Lenny with the gay granddads. I have a feeling we'll be seeing each other again."

"Are you on Facebook?"

She doesn't answer the question. "Bye," she says, squeezing into a crowded car. The doors close before I can think of anything else to say, and before I lose sight of her, she blows me a kiss. Damn!

My eyes follow the train all the way out of the station. Did that just happen? Did a beautiful girl my own age take a sudden interest in me *and* my music? It was all so quick. I want to relive every second, analyze it, and then do it again. Yes, I made some mistakes, but I think it went okay. *You're not delusional. You got her phone number, stupid! She liked something about you!*

I hate the way my self-doubt eats away at my confidence. *Never doubt yourself,* a favorite teacher of mine once told me. *Because there are plenty of people who want that job.* It's so true. I pack up my guitar and wait for the next downtown train.

While I wait, I pull out the bills I had stuffed into my pocket after giving Yoko her share and begin counting, my guitar case by my side. Thirty bucks. Not enough to buy a Fender, but better than I would have done on my own for sure. And there is the promise of a lot more if I can convince Yoko to sing with me again, which is definitely the top item on my agenda.

The train I'm waiting for roars into the station, and as it's rattling by, someone bumps into me—hard.

"Hey," I say, turning around.

My stomach tightens when I see who it is: Giant Annoying Kid.

"Where's your mommy?" he asks, smirking.

I pick up my guitar and head for the open train door. I'm not going to engage this dope anymore. Round one went to me. End of story.

But he doesn't seem to get it. "Where you goin'? Not so brave without your momma, huh?" He pushes me hard in the back, and I whip around.

"What's your problem?"

"Ooh," Giant Annoying Kid says to his friend. "Look who grew a pair."

I ignore him and take another step toward the door, but I feel a hand on my belt, and I'm pulled back out. "No one laughs at me," he says. He turns me around and pushes me in the chest with both hands. I drop my guitar, and push him back hard. He stumbles, nearly falling over. That does it. He rushes me twice as hard, putting his head down and aiming for my stomach. But this is not my first rodeo; I've had a few fights in my young life. I step aside and he goes flying past me across the platform, hitting a wooden bench where a homeless guy has set up camp for the night. Giant Annoying Kid and the homeless guy fumble around for a second before the homeless guy pushes the kid off him, back in my direction.

"I'm gonna mess you up!" the kid screams at me.

I don't have enough time to sidestep him again. He connects and I go flying backward, crashing into a subway beam. My head hits the iron beam hard and I go down, the kid on me immediately. He's punching me in the face as I struggle to get him off, flailing my arms and legs, using every ounce of strength. I feel the fabric of his clothing and, a couple of times, his saliva on my fingers.

And then, the kid lands a punch to my jaw. I see little black stars everywhere, and I can't hear anything. The world is quiet, deadly quiet. From what feels like a great distance, I feel a hand going through my pockets. I know it's happening, but there's nothing I can do because I feel as if I'm underwater. I raise my head a little, but it makes me dizzy. I slump back and black out.

TWO

When I open my eyes, I see a canvas of concerned faces looking down at me. One of them, an older African American guy with white hair, is staring into my eyes.

"You okay, kid?"

"What happened?" I ask.

"Looks like you were in a fight and the other guy took off. Hit you pretty bad. How are you feelin'?"

I try to sit up, but he puts his big palm on my chest and uses a small bit of force to keep me still. Someone else puts something soft under my head. I'm still woozy, and I can smell everything around me—the sweat from this Good Samaritan, a mixture of perfumes from the women in the crowd, and the trash baking in overstuffed garbage bins.

"Don't move," the guy says. "Help is on the way. We called, so someone should be here soon. Stay put."

A searing pain shoots through my head from behind my right ear. The fluorescent lights of the station are killing my eyes. I shut them tight.

"It's gonna be okay, just relax. The EMTs will be here

soon," someone says.

I feel helpless.

Then I remember something important. "Where's my guitar?"

The black guy sighs. "The guy you were fighting with took it. A couple of us ran after him, but he was too fast. Don't worry, though. We'll give the cops a good description."

"Shit."

"Yeah," he says. "This ain't your day, that's for sure."

I feel my pocket where the money was.

"Money?" I ask, my throat hoarse.

"Yeah, he probably got that, too, son. Don't sweat it. Just money, just a guitar. Nothin' all that important. You're alive, you ain't bleeding, and you're lucky he didn't have a knife or nothin'."

I play the day backward, trying to recall how I got here. Yoko's friendly face pops into my mind. What a crazy day. Just when I find a singing partner—and get a girl's number—my guitar gets stolen.

That's when the EMTs show up. They are very professional, strap me onto a backboard, and begin carrying me up the stairs. "Wait a minute," I say and lift myself a little so I can see the guy who was talking to me. "Thanks, man. I appreciate it."

"No worries, son. Hope they find your guitar."

The EMTs keep going, taking me outside to a waiting ambulance. Along the way, I'm conscious enough to see people pointing their phones at me and taking photos. I'm gonna wind up on someone's Instagram feed for sure. They tell me they're driving just a few blocks to Roosevelt Hospital, where I get asked tons of questions, some of them by cops who suddenly show up and want a description of Giant Annoying Kid. I give it to them and describe my guitar, and they take off like Batman and Robin. I only hope they're half as effective.

A nurse appears with more questions, and when I give my date of birth she asks for my parents' phone number.

"My mom's out of town, and I'm staying with my grandfather."

"What's his phone number?"

I rattle it off, impressed that I even remember it since almost every time I call him I'm just pressing a photo of his face on my smartphone.

"We'll get in touch with him," the nurse says.

My head is throbbing, the pain knifelike, and I am dreading my granddads getting here. I know they are going to bug out when they hear about the fight. I'm only hoping I can talk them out of calling my mother, who will shut down all subway performances. Not that it really matters since I don't have a guitar right now and have no reasonable expectation of getting mine back. I doubt it's a high priority for the NYPD, even though it's a very big deal for me.

That Martin acoustic is the first and only guitar I've ever owned and I love it, even though it reminds me of my parents' divorce. My mother bought it for me not long after my dad left us for some woman named Judy he met at a Yankees game. It always burned my father that Mom thought baseball was stupid and wouldn't go to games with him. The games were expensive, and he could barely afford one ticket on his barista salary, so he began buying the cheapest bleacher seats, and that's where he met Judy. I don't think Mom ever forgave herself for that, although now—no surprise—she hates baseball even more.

After Dad left Mom and me for Judy, I became angrier and angrier until I found myself starting fights and shoplifting. It's not that I wanted to do those things; it was like I couldn't help myself. At thirteen years old, I was a pint-sized terror. I'd go into Starbucks and see how unprotected all the mugs and tea bags in the front of the store were and would stuff them into my backpack. Then I'd sell them for a couple of bucks each to kids who needed to buy birthday presents for their parents. It was a good business until I got caught. A Starbucks employee, an older guy, called me out for stealing and grabbed my arm. I kicked him in the shins. He dropped the stolen mug, and it shattered. A much younger and stronger barista came over and grabbed me and held me until the police were called. If you're thinking that it's all very Freudian that I was stealing from a coffee shop and my absent father was a barista, I applaud you. Congrats, you could be a shrink—the next stop on my wayward train. The store manager agreed not to press charges if I got some "help."

And so began "Saturdays with Terry." I thought of it as a very bad reality show where this bratty thirteen-year-old spent every Saturday from 1:30 to 2:20 in the shrink's office on the Upper West Side. My mom escorted me there and back and waited outside Terry's office during every session. I refused to talk to her before or after the appointment, which for a talker like my mom was the ultimate punishment. As for Terry, I thought he was a cool guy, but I was so angry about being there that I refused to talk to him, too.

After our introductory session, Terry turned the tables on me. He would not talk until I did, so we spent entire fifty-minute sessions with neither of us saying a word. I started to feel bad about my mother spending her hard-earned money on this, but I was stubborn. And then one day, while I was staring out the window feeling sorry for myself, I happened to notice a guitar leaning against the wall behind Terry's chair.

"You play?" I asked, pointing to the guitar.

"Yes. Do you?"

"Nah."

"Well, let me show you something."

He played "Fire and Rain" by James Taylor. I had heard the song hundreds of times because my mother thought James Taylor was the sexiest man alive. I had seen pictures of him when he was young, around the time he wrote "Sweet Baby James," so I could understand that, but she even liked him as an old bald guy. *That* was weird.

When Terry finished, he handed me the guitar. Incredibly, we were both lefties, which was a minor miracle. If he had been a righty, I don't think I'd be playing guitar today. "It's an easy song to play," Terry said. "Here, put your fingers like this . . ."

He began showing me the chords I needed to know. After that day, our sessions turned into guitar lessons. He even brought in an extra guitar so we could play together. Along the way, he asked personal questions and I answered them, a small price for learning how to play.

"You're getting better," he said after about a month. "Imagine what you can do if you take some lessons and buy a guitar."

What I didn't tell Terry, although I'm certain he figured it out on his own, is that I was feeling less angry than I had been since Dad left. I had even stopped shoplifting and being resentful toward adults.

One day, Terry left me practicing in his office and walked out to get my mother in the waiting room. He told her he had diagnosed me with oppositional defiant disorder or ODD. I listened to him describe it. He was more or less telling her what she already knew: I was a pain in the ass. I enjoyed playing that role, though

I didn't know why. I thought maybe Terry was right, maybe there was something wrong with me, and he hit the nail on the head. I have ODD. I am ODD.

"So what do we do?" Mom asked.

"Well," Terry said. "I think we have a very easy fix here—guitar lessons."

"Really?" Mom sounded surprised.

"Yes. Lenny enjoys playing guitar, and he'll only improve with lessons and his own guitar."

I hated to admit it then, but everything Terry said that day was absolutely right. I loved guitar, and if that was the way to keep me out of trouble, Mom was all for it. She took me to the big Sam Ash store on West Thirty-Fourth Street and, with the help of a good-natured salesman and a few other guitar players who were interested in getting a kid a good first guitar, I settled on a Martin acoustic. It felt great in my hands, and it was mine for $350.

Now it's gone and I feel my anger rising from deep inside. All because of stupid Giant Annoying Kid! He didn't even want the guitar; he only wanted to get revenge. I force myself to take some of the three-part breaths that Terry taught me. I have to stay calm if I want to convince the granddads not to tell my mother.

While I'm practicing the spiel I'm going to give Grandpa, a male nurse shows up next to my bed. "Off to take a CT scan, buddy. The doctor wants to peek inside your skull and see what your brain is made of. How are you feeling?"

"Does it mean anything that my head is throbbing?"

"Probably, unless it's always throbbing. We'll check you out."

All I can see are the fluorescent lights on the ceiling as the nurse pushes me down a bunch of corridors, into an elevator, and down more corridors.

"We've arrived," he says.

The CT machine looks like a big white donut and I'm the one going through the hole on a narrow bed. "Just hold still so the radiologist can get some good pictures," the nurse says as he gets me settled on the bed. "I'll be right through the window waiting for you." He leaves the room, and the bed slides through the hole. I keep my eyes closed the whole time and do my breathing exercises. After about fifteen minutes, the CT scan is done, and the nurse brings me back to the ER, where the first thing I hear are the sounds of the Joes' voices.

"Hey, guys, I'm over here!" I yell.

They're at my side immediately. Grandpa has tears in his eyes while Joe is, as always, calmer and ready to take control of the situation. Joe has been a teamster his whole life and defies the stereotype of the elderly gay gentleman. He's big, tough, and nobody's fool, and he looks every bit like the union shop steward he is.

"What in the world happened?" Joe asks.

I run through the short version.

"I told you to take something for protection, didn't I?" Joe says. He owns a vintage blackjack that he has begged me to carry on more than one occasion. That or his old set of brass knuckles. In Joe's New York, you always need to be prepared for physical combat.

Grandpa, a lighting tech for Broadway shows, wouldn't hear of it. "Lenny is not going to need those things," he told Joe at the time. "You've been down on the docks too long. New York is a lot more civilized than it used to be."

So much for that theory.

"Looks like I was right," Joe says now, lording it over his partner.

Grandpa puts up his hand. "We can fight later. Lenny, how are you feeling? That's all I want to know."

23

I open my mouth to talk about my aching head when a doctor appears. "Lester Funk?" he asks me.

"Lenny, not Lester."

"Lenny, I hear you got into a fight, and yes, I know, I should have seen the other guy, right?"

"Well, I don't know about that, but I did get in a few punches."

"Attaboy," says Joe. "You gotta hit them back twice as hard."

The doctor shines a bright light into my eyes and tells me to follow his finger with my gaze. "You can sit up now."

I do as he directs.

"How do you feel?" he asks.

"My head hurts."

"Any dizziness?"

"No."

"Nausea?"

"Nope."

"Well, I don't see anything in the CT scan to be concerned about. There's no bleeding in the brain or anything like that. Every brain is unique, though, and yours is a little different than others I've seen but it's nothing to worry about. Most likely you just have a mild concussion, which happens when you get punched in the head and fall down."

"Right," I say. Just what I need, a doctor who's a comedian.

"What should he do?" Grandpa asks.

"Nothing much. Take a pain reliever, over the counter. Aleve is good. Rest up tonight, and if you feel okay in the morning, go about your business. If the pain gets worse, give me a call, but I don't think that's going to happen."

"I can go home?" I confirm.

"You can go home."

"I don't want you playing in the subway anymore," Grandpa says, as soon as the doctor leaves.

"At least not without my brass knuckles," Joe says.

"Joe," Grandpa says sternly.

I put up my hand. "Don't worry about it. The kid I was fighting took my guitar. I can't play in the subway without a guitar."

"Oh no," Grandpa says.

"Yeah, it sucks . . . Let's just get out of here."

As soon as we're alone in the reception area, I turn to Grandpa. "Please tell me you haven't called Mom."

"Not yet."

"Please don't."

"That's what I told him," Joe says. "She's got enough on her plate. You're fine, so let's move on. We'll tell her when we see her."

"Thanks, Joe."

Grandpa looks at me. "Okay," he agrees. "We'll keep it to ourselves. *For now.* Come on. Let's go home."

Donovan Day

◀◀ **THREE** ▶▶

I t's after midnight when the cab drops us off at the Joes' apartment. Commerce Street is treelined and dark in that romantic sort of way. As if on cue, a couple strolls by arm in arm. It's a warm summer evening, but I almost expect to see mist rising from the sidewalk to be captured in the reflection of the vintage streetlights. Brownstones and row houses line both sides of the street except for a lone apartment building at the corner where Joe scored a rent-controlled apartment back in the 1970s. The quiet surrounds us and provides me with a sense of peace that calms my thoughts about my stolen guitar. Maybe it's the pleasure of the familiar or maybe it's the painkillers, but I am feeling better.

The Joes' apartment is on the ground floor. After we settle in, they make tea while I take a quick shower. By the time I join them around the kitchen table, I almost feel normal. Grandpa hands me a cup of chamomile tea. "I brought you something that might help."

I'm thinking he means the tea, but he opens his other hand to reveal a small blue iPod. "This goes back a few years," he says. "Before everybody started putting all their songs on their phones, but it was pretty cool when it came out."

"An iPod Nano?"

"Yep, but this one is special," he says. "I personally loaded it with all my favorite songs. All classic rock and folk, all the time. I know you're a fan so now you have them all in one place."

I take the iPod from him. "Thanks, Grandpa."

"Sure. I thought maybe you'd enjoy listening since you can't play right now. But give your head a break and stick to something on the folky side for now."

"Yeah, skip the heavy metal," Joe jokes.

"Thanks," I say. "Well, it's been a long day. I'm gonna turn in."

The Joes wish me good night and I head to bed.

In the spare bedroom, which is my bedroom while my mother is out of town, I spin the little dial on the Nano and look over its thousands of songs. No one my age uses these anymore now that Spotify and Pandora have taken over the music industry. I know Grandpa purchased these songs through iTunes or transferred them painstakingly from his CD collection. He's not kidding when he said he loaded it with classics. These are not *some* classics, these are virtually *all* the classics. I put in my earbuds, make sure the volume is turned down low, and opt for James Taylor's "You Can Close Your Eyes" from when he was young and his hair was long. Back then he was considered the nation's folksinger and even wound up on the cover of *TIME Magazine*.

Well the sun is surely sinking down, but the moon is slowly rising.

James Taylor's beautiful, clear voice is just the thing. I concentrate on his guitar picking and the sound of his fingers sliding up and down the frets. Wow, the sound on this iPod is way better than my smartphone. It's almost like he's playing in my bedroom. I'm lost in the song when I smell something burning. I open my eyes to make sure everything is okay in the apartment, except I'm not in the apartment anymore.

I squint at the scene in front of me, confused. I'm in front of a campfire. It's so close I can feel the heat on my face. I watch the flames move back and forth, carried by a slight wind. I close my eyes. It's gotta have something to do with hitting my head.

James Taylor's voice is magic, but I can't shake the smell of the campfire. I move one of my hands down next to me to feel for the iPod, but instead I feel dirt. I open my eyes again. It's the same campfire scene, so this time I look around. Not twenty feet in front of me is a very young James Taylor singing and playing guitar. His eyes are closed in concentration. There are a dozen other people sitting in a circle, including a woman next to James who looks exactly like . . . Carly Simon? What is going on?

Carly is a gorgeous woman and always showed off her body in all its glory on album cover after album cover. She also happens to be as talented, if not more so, than James and matched him hit song for hit song back in the seventies. The only reason I know any of this is because my mother was always insanely jealous of Carly. The couple was a bit of an obsession for her.

If I am having a hallucination brought on by the concussion, it's pretty intense. It feels as if I am sitting with them on a crisp fall evening. There is even a hint of the sea in the air, bringing to mind Martha's Vineyard, where James and Carly raised their family.

The doctor didn't mention that anything like this might happen. I put my hands over my eyes, but I don't really want everyone to disappear. I want to be part of

James and Carly's inner circle, and if this is all a dream or a hallucination, it's a damned good one.

The next time I open my eyes, everyone is still there, but now they're all looking at me.

"Hey, man, who is this guy?"

What? That's James Taylor talking to me! He's looking right at me!

I've never had a dream like this before. It's so vivid.

The guy next to J.T. says, "I don't who he is, James. He wandered in here, I guess."

"I heard the music," I say. "Is it okay to stay?"

James doesn't answer, but he does give an imperceptible nod that I take to mean I can stay. I'm not going anywhere unless they throw me out, and I wouldn't know where to go even if they did.

Now Carly is whispering in his ear, and I'm worried they're going to kick me out, but then I hear her. "I think we should release a duet, James," she says.

I remember their duet, a song called "Mockingbird." These must be the years when they were married to each other, the happy phase before it all fell apart and Carly married someone in his band, the drummer or guitar player, I can't remember which. Mom would know. The thought of my mom makes me sad because she's so far away. And if I'm really back in the 1970s, she hasn't even been born yet. There are so many wild thoughts going through my head that I can't think straight.

I lean back and look up at the stars. James and Carly are lost in their own conversation and the others are quiet, staring into the flames. I close and then open my eyes again, waiting for the whole scene to vanish, but it never does. In some ways, it's completely ordinary: a group of friends sitting around a campfire playing music on a beautiful summer night. Happens all the time. But the presence of a young James Taylor and Carly Simon shake things up in a very big way. This could not be happening in 2015. The couple broke up somewhere in the late seventies or early eighties, I think. It doesn't make any sense. I blink my eyes a couple more times to see if the whole scene will just go *poof*!

"Hey, what are you doing?" It's a girl, a teenager, who has come to sit next to me.

"Nothing," I say. "Just chillin'."

"Why are you blinking so much?"

"Blinking? I guess because I can't believe I'm here."

"I know what you mean," she says.

"You do?"

"Sure. I was in Manhattan last night with my parents, and today I'm sitting here with James Taylor and Carly Simon at their place on the Vineyard. It's a trip man, like time travel almost," she says.

I laugh. "Yeah, I see what you mean."

And the truth is I do, much more than she'll ever know.

"I'm Daisy," she says, sticking out her hand.

"Lenny."

She looks to be about my age. She has those classic California girl looks like Christie Brinkley—long blond hair, freckles, blue eyes, and a smile as wide as the ocean. I must be dreaming because only a guy could dream up a girl who looks like Daisy. But she seems so damned real.

"How do you know James?"

"I don't, except for his music. I just kind of woke up here."

She thinks about that for a couple of seconds. "I dig it. Far out."

I guess people really did talk this way back in the seventies. "How about you?" I ask. "How do you know

James?"

"Carly's dad is a family friend. She used to babysit me before she became *Carly Simon*, y'know?"

"Really? Was she good at it? Babysitting, I mean."

"That's a funny question. I don't know. I was a baby." She laughs.

A thought occurs to me. "Are you stoned?"

She giggles. "Yeah, aren't you?"

"I must be," I answer, and I mean it, though I don't know how I *could* be. Maybe this is what it feels like.

Daisy seems antsy, like she can't sit still. "Wanna go for a walk?"

"Sure."

She takes my hand and guides me away from the little circle. It's dark away from the campfire, but Daisy seems to know where she's going. She takes me to the edge of the water and kicks off her shoes. I do the same and we walk in the low surf.

"I love the feeling of the water on my toes," she says.

"Me too," I say with a laugh.

"There are so many stars out here. You can't see anything like this in the city."

"Tell me about it," I say.

Just then, we hear laughter from the direction of the campfire. "Maybe we should go back," Daisy says. "Do you want to?"

"No, not really," I laugh again.

As cool as it is to see James and Carly, I can't take my eyes off Daisy, and I think maybe something might happen. There's magic in the air. I can feel it. Daisy is giving me a funny little look. Everything is still around us except for the gentle lapping of the waves. I dig my toes into the sand and surf and reach for her. I put one hand on her waist, and I'm overwhelmed by how good she feels. She smiles, which I take as a go-ahead, and I lean in for a kiss. Our lips touch, and it's perfect. We fall into each other's arms and kiss for what seems like a very long time. This better not be a dream.

At some point, Daisy pulls away. "Lenny, I have to get back. I don't want Carly to come looking for me. She'll never let me visit again if I don't listen to her. She's way more strict than she lets on, at least when it comes to me."

I'm breathless. It's the last thing I want to do, but I can't disagree without sounding like a jerk. "Okay. Let's go back."

We walk hand in hand through the dark, our fingers intertwined, until we get to the campfire. Everyone is gone except for a guy putting out the fire.

"Carly was asking about you. You better let her know you're back."

"Okay. Come with me, Lenny."

I follow her through the house until she stops and knocks at a door. Carly answers in a T-shirt and underwear. "Just wanted you to know I'm back," Daisy tells her. "I'm okay."

Carly gives us one of those smiles she's so famous for, her lips sexy as hell. "Thanks for letting me know." Then she looks at me. "What did you say your name is?"

"Lenny."

"Lenny what?"

"Lenny Funk."

"And where do you live, Lenny Funk?"

Why does Carly Simon care where I live?

"Um, 55 Commerce Street in the West Village."

"Okay, Lenny Funk of 55 Commerce Street in the West Village. You better be nice to my girl Daisy here or I'm going to come looking for you."

"Um, yeah, okay."

"And Daisy, you be nice to Lenny, but not too nice. Do you understand?"

"Yes, ma'am."

"Do not call me *ma'am*! Now scoot. Good night."

Carly slams the door behind her.

"That was weird," I say to Daisy.

"She's protective because she knows my parents, but she's cool. Don't worry, she won't do anything weird. Come."

She leads me to a bedroom lit by candles. "You can sleep here."

"What about you?"

"I'll be in my room. Take off your shirt and I'll give you a little massage, but that's all, okay? Lie facedown." I do, and she straddles my back. I feel her hands on my shoulders. "You're so tight. Let's see if I can help," she whispers. "This should mellow you out."

"I don't think I can feel any more mellow," I say.

I hear her laugh softly. Her hands are kneading my back for a while, and then she's gone and I'm alone in a strange bedroom in a house with James Taylor and Carly Simon. I don't have any idea what's happening to me, but I decide to go with it. It's not too hard, after all. I close my eyes. I'm so tired. Then it hits me.

What about my grandfather's iPod? Where did it go? I haven't seen it since I was in my own bedroom. I wonder if Grandpa's old iPod has anything to do with the trip I'm on. It's too coincidental. One minute I'm listening to James Taylor and the next he's in front of me. It has to be because I fell asleep with his music on. Maybe if I listen to something from 2015, I'll be back to where I once belonged? Who knows?

I feel in my pockets, and there it is. It's so thin, I didn't notice it at first. I don't remember even putting it in my pocket, but who knows?

34

I look through the iPod's music. I scroll and scroll and come to a song from Taylor Swift's *1989* album. I give a little chuckle. I can't believe Grandpa put TSwift on here. Or I guess maybe I'm just imagining he put it on here. I mean, this is a dream. I put the earbuds in, hit "play," and close my eyes to the sound of "Shake It Off."

Donovan Day

FOUR

unlight is streaming through the window as I crack open my eyes. It's that subconscious moment when you come out of sleep or a nap and you feel, for a second, like a baby being born. There's no other way to get this sensation. It exists for a half second and it's startling and delicious, maybe even a bit frightening, and then it's gone.

Thoughts of my dream come rushing in. I open my eyes and sit up. I'm back in the spare bedroom at the Joes' place. No more folk-singing celebrities, no more beautiful Daisy. The iPod is in my pocket and it's still playing "Shake It Off." That's weird . . .

My head is spinning. It didn't feel like any dream I'd ever had, and the odds of the same song being on the iPod when I woke up are ridiculously slim, but it had to be a dream, right?

I look at the ceiling and replay what I remember, which is *everything*. That kiss—that could *not* have been a dream. I linger over it about a thousand times before I force myself to get out of bed. I head into the bathroom and then trip over one of my sneakers. I pick it up to toss it out of the way, but I feel wet dirt inside the treads. I put the shoe to my nose—smoke, sea salt. The scene from the campfire comes roaring back. This has to have something to do with the concussion. That's a lot more likely than a magic iPod. My subconscious must have mixed everything together to create the most intense dream I've ever experienced. I probably stepped in some mud on the way home and didn't notice. There is no other reasonable explanation.

And another thing, my headache is gone.

I go down to breakfast. Only Grandpa is there. I know Joe is likely at the gym, where he spends a lot of time. Grandpa has his typical look of concern all over his face. "Hey, big guy. How are you feeling?"

"Fine."

There's no way I can really describe what I'm actually feeling. I still need to sort that out.

"I looked in on you this morning. You were really tossing and turning. You were talking in your sleep."

"What did I say?"

"Something about James Taylor."

"Really? I guess that makes sense because I was listening to 'Sweet Baby James' when I fell asleep." I hesitate. "Hey, thanks for that iPod. It has some great songs on it. How long have you had it?"

"I don't know, awhile. You like it?"

"Love it. The sound is great. You said you put those songs on there yourself?"

"Every last one. It's pretty old-school stuff with a few new tracks mixed in to keep me contemporary." He smiles. "What are you up to today?"

I have a pretty good idea, but I'm not going to tell him. "I'm not really sure."

"Don't do too much. You need to rest up and make sure you're one hundred percent."

"I will."

"Good. Let's see how you are in a couple of days. If you're good, your mother never has to know what happened, but if you're not, I'm gonna have to tell her."

"I feel good. I'm sure I'll be okay."

"I hope so, son. I gotta get to work. We have a matinee today, so I'm leaving early. There's stuff to eat in the fridge. Relax. Listen to some music."

"I will. I'm gonna check with the cops, too, just to see if there's anything new about my guitar."

Grandpa purses his lips. "Yeah, okay, but don't get your hopes up. We'll figure out something about your guitar. Maybe you can check on Craigslist and see if anyone is selling a used one that you like. We can check it out together. Do not go by yourself. Understand?"

"That's a great idea. I will. Thanks, Grandpa."

He gives me a kiss on the cheek and then leaves. The second he does, I fire up my laptop to check out used guitars online. A bunch look promising, and I send out a few e-mails to get more information as my mind wanders back to Daisy. Is there any chance she was real? I start googling James Taylor, Carly Simon, and Martha's Vineyard to see if there's any reference anywhere to someone named Daisy. I read more than I ever wanted to know about the Taylors' family life, like how many kids they had and their divorce, but there's not a single reference to anyone named Daisy in their inner circle.

I bite my lip. How can I find someone with only a first name? There's gotta be a way. I google "Daisy" and "Martha's Vineyard" and there are some hits, but most of them are about a convenience store on the island and the woman who runs it. I look at her photo, but she looks nothing like my Daisy.

But the photos give me another idea. I search for "Daisy" and "Martha's Vineyard" in Google Images. The first two pages are all about the owner of the convenience store and photos of daisies on the island, but on the third page I find a group shot from James Taylor's "compound family," as the article calls it. There are at least forty people in the wide shot and it's hard to see their individual faces, but there's a caption. And there, in the middle of all the other names, is a Daisy Dalton.

I feel a jolt of excitement—and a little bit of fear at what could've happened to me—and my fingers can barely keep up with what my brain wants to do next. I save the photo to my desktop and open it with the Picasa editor, then enlarge it as much as possible. I get close to the screen and examine the girl's face. It's her, I'm sure of it! That's my Daisy! The caption says the photo was taken in 1979, and Daisy looks exactly as I remember her. She's smiling in the photo, and I recall her looking at me like that just before our kiss. I can even feel her lips on mine. I've gone back and forth about whether it was real or not, but now I am convinced it happened. I have no idea how it's even possible, but I saw the face in this photo in front of me last night, and there's no way I could have conjured her up out of nowhere. She was there, I was there, it happened.

But where is she now? Thank God for Google. I plug in "Daisy Dalton" and hit RETURN. This is not what I want to see; most of the results have to do with Daisy Dalton the porn star. Not a chance. I keep searching and finally come upon a bunch of Facebook profiles of women with the same name. I go to Facebook and look for a Daisy Dalton in Massachusetts, and there she is—my Daisy, now in her midfifties. She's as beautiful as ever. Her looks have matured, her face is slightly heavier, and her hair is shorter. I hit the "About" and "Photos" icons to learn more, and luckily she's one of those people who doesn't care much about locking her information behind a secure wall. A cursory read of her page reveals that Daisy does a lot of yoga, makes jewelry, and has two children, a boy and a girl. Her son already graduated college and her daughter is going to New York University.

Daisy still lives on Martha's Vineyard, but her status update informs the world that she visits New York often to go to a yoga studio called Strala Yoga just a few blocks from NYU. And then comes the most amazing fact of all:

Daisy is taking an intensive yoga workshop at Strala this very week!

I jump up and down around the room. "Yes! Yes!"

It's an incredible coincidence. The universe is being very, very good to me. I sit down to look more when I notice a text on my phone.

Hey

Who's this?

Yoko Peng, your new singing partner

So that's her last name!

Hey. Great to hear from you, Ms. Peng. So you can't resist me, can you?

Um, I have a boyfriend, Lenny. Sorry But I do think you're a good guitarist.

Of course she has a boyfriend. All girls who look like that do. I'm not giving up that easily, but I do need to switch gears.

You'll never believe what happened after you left yesterday

What?

I got into a fight with that kid you chased away. He came back

No way

Yeah. Can I tell you about it in person? I have something else I need to tell you. It's about my guitar.

What? Just tell me!

The kid took it. No more guitar :(And I got a concussion

Might as well play the sympathy card.

Oh no!!! So sorry.

Yeah, it sucks. But something weird happened right after

What?

Long story. I'll tell you over coffee...

Okay. When and where?

I look up Strala Yoga online and see that there's an intensive workshop class that starts at two o'clock.

I just had an idea. You do yoga?

Yeah, why?

Wanna go to a class at two?

41

I thought you wanted to tell me some story
Yeah but this is part of it. You'll see.
Okay, I'll bring my mat. Where's the place?
Let's meet you at noon at Angel Coffee on Bleecker Street,
near Broadway. There's a yoga place nearby.
K. See you then
Later

. . .

I like Angel Coffee because it's a big enough place that you're not sitting two inches from the person next to you. You can actually have a private conversation, which is exactly what I need. It also happens to be around the corner from Strala Yoga. I wait outside the coffee shop for Yoko, who I spot from half a block away. She is wearing the Manhattan girl's yoga uniform—tight-fitting pants, a shirt from Lululemon, and flip-flops, and she had a yoga mat slung over her shoulder. I give her a little wave. When she reaches me, she leans in for a hug and an air kiss. So far, so good.

"So how are you feeling? You got a concussion?" she asks right away.

"Eh, I'm okay, thanks."

"What happened?"

"Let's order and then I'll tell you the whole story."

We both get iced nonfat lattes, and I pick out a quiet corner where there's no one within three tables of us.

"I can't believe he took your guitar," she says.

"I know. It totally sucks." Then I tell her about the hospital and the CT scan and all of that.

Her face runs the gamut of emotions, and she reaches out to hold my hand. "I'm going to give you back the money we got from singing," she says. "You need to buy a new guitar."

"Does that mean you're going to sing with me?"

She smiles. "Why do you think I wrote you this morning? I was thinking about it and I want to. But I guess it's on hold right now."

"I'm looking for a used one. I think my grandpa will lend me some money."

"Good Grandpa. And he didn't tell your mother? You are lucky."

"I know. But Yoko, there's something else I need to tell you."

"Okay."

This is the tricky part. I'd already decided I was going to tell her the whole story, the part about my grandpa's iPod and the dream and Daisy. I'm not sure how she's going to take it, and this may be a mistake, but I need to tell someone, and even though I barely know her, I feel like she'd understand. Or at least want to hear about how I met James Taylor, dream or not. I can't keep it inside. It will be better if I have a sounding board for the craziness so I don't go crazy myself. It's just too weird to keep to myself. And if I'm reading her right, she might just be up for an adventure. I take a deep breath and start.

Through every twist and turn, her eyes grow wider and wider, and she's squeezing my hand when I tell her how I found Daisy and she's in Manhattan and will be just around the corner at a yoga class in twenty minutes.

"Are you kidding me?" she asks.

"No. I swear everything I just told you is one-hundred-percent true. That's why I wanted to meet you here. Whether you come with me or not, I'm going up to talk to her."

"Let's go!" she says. "I'm in. I'm dying to see what happens."

We practically run out of the coffee shop.

Strala Yoga is around the corner on Broadway on the sixth floor of an office building sandwiched between a PetSmart and a Duane Reade drugstore. The guy in the lobby waves us in with a smile, and we take the elevator up with a group of girls in yoga clothes. We all get out on the sixth floor, and Yoko and I follow them down a long corridor. Yoko blends right in, and I've done my best. I've never taken a yoga class, but I'm wearing shorts and a T-shirt that I hope will make me unobtrusive. The part I haven't figured out is how I'm going to take an intensive class without breaking my ass.

We go into the studio where a group of athletic men and women are crowded around the owner, Tara Stiles. I've read about her online and know that she's a former model who created her own brand. The studio is beautiful, and the music pumping out of the speakers is happy and joyful.

A pretty woman sits behind the front desk. "Can I help you?" she asks.

"Yes," says Yoko, leading the way. "We'd like to take the intensive class. It's at two, right?"

"Right. Have you both done yoga before?"

"Sure," Yoko says. I hesitate, and the woman looks at me.

"Is that a 'no'?" she says with a smile.

"Right. No, I haven't," I say.

"Well, it might be challenging for you, even if you're in good shape. But you can go at your own pace. If there's something you can't do, don't force it. Remember, it's your yoga."

What the hell? "Okay, I'm in," I say.

I don't care about the yoga anyway. I'm just hoping Daisy is here somewhere. I rent a mat, pay for the class, and head into the studio where we place our mats at the back of the room. I look around, but I don't see anyone who could possibly be Daisy.

"You see her?" Yoko whispers.

"No."

"Maybe she's not here yet."

"Yeah, maybe."

Nearly all the people in the class are women and most are far too young to be Daisy. They all appear to be in great shape, too. I can see why some men take yoga. Every woman in here exudes inner beauty and looks incredibly happy. There is not a hint of anxiety in the air. I feel good already and I haven't even stretched.

"I need to hit the restroom," I say.

The restroom is down the hall, and as I'm walking toward it, the ladies' room door opens and out steps a willowy blond woman in her fifties. My stomach drops.

"Daisy?" I venture.

She stops and looks at me with a ready smile, but no recognition.

"It's me, Lenny. Remember Martha's Vineyard? James was singing at the campfire and you and I walked down to the water?"

She looks into my face and her expression does a one-eighty. Her mouth opens into a little *O*, and she puts her hands to her face. "Lenny? Is it really you?"

I pull her in for a hug. "Yes, Daisy, it's really me. I'm so happy you remember."

She pushes me away. "Remember? You've haunted my dreams for decades. But you look exactly the same! How is that possible? You haven't aged!"

A couple of women nearby are watching us.

"Can we go somewhere to talk?" I ask.

"Yes, yes! I've been looking for you forever, but I thought you'd be my age."

"I'll explain. Let's get out of here."

"Okay," she says.

"But I'm with someone. I'll get her. Wait here, okay?"

She nods and just stands there, clearly stunned.

I rush into the studio to get Yoko, who is sitting in a meditation pose with her legs crossed and eyes closed. "I found her. Let's get out of here." We grab our stuff and hurry out to the hall where Daisy is waiting

"Daisy, this is Yoko. Yoko, this is Daisy."

We follow Daisy downstairs. The woman at the front desk watches us, but she must know something serious is going on and doesn't interfere with our leaving.

"Let's go to my place" Yoko suggests when we get outside. "It's the perfect location to chat, you'll see."

Daisy and I shrug at each other, and the three of us hop in a cab.

Donovan Day

FIVE

The cab stops in the West Village just a few blocks from my grandfathers' apartment. Yoko didn't say much on the way over, and Daisy is still just staring at me. We all need to talk. Yoko insists on paying for the cab and leads us to an elegant brownstone.

"My grandfathers live a couple of blocks away, but their apartment is nothing like this," I say.

"Yeah, well, the story goes that my grandmother got lucky in real estate and bought this in the early eighties. I'll tell you more inside. Come on. My mother is probably home."

"What does your mom do?" Daisy asks.

Yoko smiles. "She writes crossword puzzles, if you can believe it. She's quite good at it, too."

"I didn't even know that was a job," I say.

"Shh, don't say that in front of her," Yoko says. "And don't ask her about it. She can talk about her job for hours, and it's not exciting, believe me."

Yoko leads the way and we find her mom in the kitchen, which looks like one you'd see on television. It's very modern and has pots and pans hanging all over the place. Yoko's mother is tall, like Yoko, and at the moment, she's putting carrots into a blender.

"Mom, these are my friends Lenny and Daisy."

She smiles. "Hi, there. It's nice to meet you both."

"You too! What are you making there?" Daisy asks.

"My lunch," Mrs. Peng says. "It's a protein shake. Would you like some?"

"Oh, no thank you," says Daisy. "But I do have those often where I live on Martha's Vineyard."

"I love Martha's Vineyard," Mrs. Peng says.

Yoko and I exchange looks as the two women chat about the island. I am desperate to get Daisy in a room where we can really talk, where maybe I can figure out what happened to me.

During a pause in the conversation, Yoko jumps in. "Well, Mom, I'm going to show them Grandma's memory room, okay?"

"Of course."

"What's a memory room?" I ask as we move out from the kitchen.

Yoko smiles. "You'll see."

As we move deeper and deeper into the house, it becomes more and more beautiful. The doors and windows are all finished with immaculately restored cherry wood. Giant bookcases are filled floor to ceiling. The house is dimly lit, and that only lends even more of an air of mystery to whatever Yoko wants to show us. Yoko leads us to a room on the parlor floor. The door is oversized with an ancient-looking skeleton key in the keyhole. She stops.

"I call this my grandmother's memory room. When she was alive, I was told it was just her office. She never called it a memory room, but you'll understand why I call it that when you see it. It's pretty much gone untouched since she died."

Yoko turns the key and pushes the giant door open. She turns on a dim light that casts a yellowish glow over everything. "Grandma did not like a lot of light."

The room smells musty and is packed with loads of stuff. It feels like it belonged to a hoarder who also happened to be a top-notch housekeeper. The walls are covered with photographs and posters. As I look closer, I see they all relate to the Beatles and other classic rock performers and groups from the sixties—the Hollies, Gerry and the Pacemakers, the Animals, the Who, Led Zeppelin, Donovan, and some British groups I've never heard of. In each photograph, the band members are posing with a young, hot Asian woman. Yoko and her grandmother are dead ringers for each other.

"Your grandmother knew all these people?" I ask.

Yoko smiles. "Yeah. She had a great big voice and met a lot of superstars back in the day. She did a lot of studio singing for them, even the Beatles."

"She must've had a lot of fun," Daisy comments.

"Yeah," Yoko says. "That's part of the reason why I'd love to talk to her. From what I've read in her journals, Grandma was pretty wild. I wish she hadn't died when I was so young."

The posters are from British concert venues I've never heard of in Manchester, Liverpool, and Brighton, and then some other small English cities.

"This is an incredible collection," Daisy says. "They're all original, aren't they?"

"Yep. Grandma knew most of the guys firsthand. She was a teenager at the time and got along with everyone. But she was closest to the Beatles, especially John. She was from Liverpool, just like they were."

Yoko points to a wall behind me where every poster advertises a Beatles show from the 1961 and 1962 tours. On almost every bill, the band is listed with many others, most of the time headlining but not always. There are a lot of guitars in the room, as well.

Yoko points out a few of them. "These belong to various artists, but these three right here belonged to John, Paul, and George. And these belonged to Pete Best," she says. She shows me a set of drumsticks belonging to the drummer who'd been kicked out of the Beatles just before they exploded into the international scene. Yoko sits down on a beanbag chair and motions for us to sit on the ones opposite her.

"Daisy—" Yoko pauses. "Lenny told me he met you back in 1978?"

"Yes," Daisy says. "I'll never forget that night. You disappeared the next morning and I asked everyone about you, but no one knew anything. It was like you were a ghost. Maybe you were a ghost. How come you haven't aged? I don't understand."

"I don't think Lenny gets it, either," Yoko said. "Do you, Lenny?"

"Nope."

Yoko digs in. "So Daisy clearly remembers you and you remember her and there's almost no way you two could have met in 1978 when Daisy was a teenager."

"Almost no way?" Daisy shakes her head. "It happened. I'm positive of that."

"Me too. Except . . ." I didn't know what Daisy was going to think of what I was about to say. It sounded nuts, even to me. "Except, Daisy, to me, we didn't meet in 1978. I wasn't even alive then. In my memory, we met last night."

"That's impossible," she says. "I was your age when we met and that was in 1978. I can prove it because it was when James and Carly were still together and they split in 1983. You remember them both at the campfire, don't you?"

"I do, but I remember it as though it happened last night. I met and kissed you last night. To me, it happened less than twenty-four hours ago," I say.

"Wow, I must be tripping," Daisy says.

"You're not tripping," Yoko says. "You remember meeting each other, but Lenny remembers it from last night and you remember it from 1978. The only way that's possible is if Lenny time-traveled."

I search her face for a sign that she's joking, but her expression is blank, lips pressed together. My stomach starts to twist.

Daisy laughs. "Time-traveled? Come on!"

"I'm serious," Yoko says. "I know how it sounds, but I think humans can go back in time and so did Jules Verne and any number of writers and scientists. Remember *A Christmas Carol* by Dickens and the Ghost of Christmas Past? And engineers, inventors, and crackpots have been trying to build time machines for more than a century. Don't you think it means something that so many people believe it's possible?" She looks at me and must notice I've gone pale because she gives me a small smile, and reaches out to squeeze my hand. "Well, I do. And I always wished I could do it. I told you how I never knew my grandmother because she died when I was four years old, but I've always felt weirdly close to her and wanted to get to know her. Part of it is this room. Whenever I come and sit in here, I feel like I'm transported back to the past, her past. I can almost see her interacting with the Beatles." She looks between me and Daisy. "Lenny and I met yesterday, too, you know, and I thought there was something special about him. I was drawn to him, and now I know why. It's not just because he loves the Beatles."

"Wow," Daisy and I say at the same time. It's hard to believe I could have time-traveled, but Yoko is right.

What else could've happened?

"I don't know how you did it, Lenny," Yoko says. "That's what we need to figure out and see if you can harness your power somehow. I think you'll be able to go back again. And maybe, just maybe, you'll be able to take me with you." She's grinning now, a hand on her hip.

"That's crazy," I say.

"Is it? Any crazier than what's going on with you two?" She points from me to Daisy.

"I need to think," I say.

"Me too," says Daisy

"Fine! Think. Look around, but let's try to figure this out," Yoko says.

I sit there, close my eyes, and go over what happened to me the day before. I know in my soul that what Yoko is saying is true somehow, but how could it be? How had I done it? And did I have control over it? Maybe it had to have something to do with the concussion. But it wasn't until I listened to that old iPod that I was able to go back . . . Then it hit me. Maybe the iPod operated like a weird, time-travel steering device. I *had* been listening to James Taylor when I woke up in front of the campfire where he was actually playing live . . . And I *was* listening to something contemporary when I woke back up in my bedroom . . .

Daisy interrupted my thoughts. "Wow," I hear her say. "Is this your grandmother?"

Yoko nods. "That's my favorite photo of Grandma."

I get up and see that Daisy is looking at a photo of Yoko's grandmother arm in arm with John Lennon.

"What's her name?" Daisy asks.

"Lily Chang."

"You look exactly like her in this photo. Exactly." Daisy shakes her head, an awed expression on her face.

"Yeah, I don't come across that many people who knew her way back when, but when I do, they always do a double take and say the same thing. I'm much taller than she is, like my mother. I must get that from my grandfather, whoever he is. It's the big family secret. She died without telling anyone anything about him. I wonder sometimes if maybe he's alive, and if he can tell me more about Grandma."

"What do you want to know?" I ask.

"Oh, everything! But there's one thing in particular. I want to know why she didn't record any solo albums. She had the talent. I've heard some demos. and she was great. She had a voice like Neko Case. And she left all these journals. There's no hint of who my grandfather is in them, but you know what *is* in them, besides a young girl's trials and tribulations?"

"What?" I ask. I have no idea what girls write about in their journals.

"Songs! Dozens of them. I sing them sometimes. They're good. I just don't get it. Why didn't she put out a record? It was so easy back then, and she had all the connections."

"What about your mom? Can't you ask her why?" I suggest.

"I have, but Mom claims not to know much. She says Grandma raised her to be Grandma's exact opposite, a perfect child. And it pretty much worked. I mean, Mom had one wild streak when she was around seventeen. She was in full rebellion, met my dad, got pregnant and had me. But the moment I was born, she turned boring. Ditto for Dad. He went to law school, became a lawyer, and now works for the New York City Police Department of all things. Believe me, every time I come in here, I wish Mom was more like Grandma."

"And you were four when your grandmother died?"

Daisy asks.

"Yeah."

"That's tough."

"It is, but as you can see, she left a lot of memories behind. Speaking of, I want to show you something very special." She crosses the room and picks up a blue guitar pick. "This belonged to John Lennon. It's from the his last recording session," Yoko says. "The night he died . . . Yoko Ono gave it to Grandma that same night, after John was killed."

"You never said anything about Yoko Ono. She knew her, too?" I say.

"Well, sure. If you knew John back in the day, you knew Yoko. She was glued to his side. Judging from Grandma's journals, they became good friends. They were both Asians, and there were not a lot them in London back then. Plus, they both loved John. After the Beatles broke up, John and Yoko moved to New York in the early seventies, and Grandma followed. They were all good friends and kind of moved into the Dakota together. It was Grandma who found the apartment for them. Eventually she became their assistant, and they got her an apartment in the Dakota, too."

"That is one wild story, Yoko," I say. "You should write a book or something."

"First things first . . . When are you going to take me back in time with you?"

"Yoko, come on. I don't even know what I did it the first time," I say.

"Think about it," Daisy says. "You must have some idea. If you did it once, you can do it again."

I want to blurt out what I've been turning over in my head. I want to tell them my theory about my grandfather's iPod. I want to tell them that I think I can do it again, but . . . I don't want to tell them anything yet, not until I'm sure. And I am certainly not going to tell them that I plan on testing out my theory tonight.

SIX

I leave Daisy and Yoko with a promise to let them know if anything strange happens. I needed to get away from them because it was getting too intense. I felt creepy talking to fifty-something Daisy about the night we made out, especially in front of Yoko. I needed to get away to clear my head.

After I have dinner and watch television with Grandpa and Joe, I say good night and go to my room. I haven't told them that my headaches have gotten worse. I hadn't felt them at all when I was with Daisy and Yoko, but now they're back with a vengeance. I'm not even in the mood to listen to any music, but I force myself. I have to test my theory. And I have a plan: I'm going to try to meet the Beatles and, if possible, find Yoko's grandmother. If she was with "the boys" as often as Yoko says, there's a good chance I'll find her. But that's a hell of a lot of ifs.

I spin the dial on the iPod until I find some early Beatles and cue up "There's a Place." I turn the lock on my door, lie down on my bed, and hit "play." John and Paul's harmony comes on strong . . .

...

I t's quiet when I open my eyes. I am sitting in a small living room that feels very stiff and proper. The furniture is old-fashioned, and the heavy drapes keep much of the sunlight from coming in. Wherever I am, it is not the recording studio or concert hall I'd imagined, and I wonder what this room has to do with the Beatles. But the magic seems to have worked again, because I'm definitely not in my bedroom.

I can hear voices coming from another room, and it sounds as though someone is on the telephone. Luckily, I dressed a little more era-appropriate this time. Instead of jeans, I'm wearing blue slacks and a black shirt. But when I look down, I'm mortified because I've forgotten to take off my sneakers, a dead giveaway that I am not from around here. I move my feet back under the chair and hope for the best.

The phone call is still going on, but I screw up my courage and walk toward the doorway to see who is in the other room. The closer I get, the more I can make out that the person speaking into the phone is a British male. His accent sounds distinctly more upper-class than Cockney. I've heard the Beatles speak many times, and I know it's not any of them. They had distinctive Liverpool accents, and they were proud of their roots and the fact that they'd made it without changing their working-class accents.

I peek around the doorway. The guy on the phone is turned to the side, so I can see his profile. Definitely not a Beatle. He has short hair, is wearing a well-tailored suit, and has a handkerchief in the breast pocket. At that moment, he turns in my direction, spots me, and holds up a finger. I take a step back.

It's Brian Epstein, the manager of the Beatles, the man who brought them from Liverpool to London to the world. I am in the inner sanctum. My theory has worked and I've traveled to the time I wanted to go to. Epstein had famously discovered the Beatles in 1962 and secured their first recording contract with Parlophone. I also know that Epstein died from a drug overdose in 1967, so I am somewhere between 1962 and 1967—the very height of Beatlemania. I hope Lily Chang, Yoko's grandmother, is nearby.

I listen more carefully and hear Epstein referring to "the boys," which is what he always called John, Paul, George, and Ringo. He's talking about an upcoming engagement, and I can tell the conversation was winding down. I turn and go back to the chair in the other room. Within minutes, Epstein joins me.

"So sorry," he says. "You're late. I was expecting you to come by a bit earlier, but that's fine. So . . . you're a reporter from an American newspaper?"

Okay, Brian, thank you for the hint. "Yes, Mr. Epstein. I'm sorry I'm late. My name is Lenny Funk, and I work for the *Daily News* in New York."

It's as good a story as any. Epstein loves getting publicity for his boys, and I know from my grandfathers that the *Daily News* had been the widest-circulating paper in the country back in the day. The Joes still read it, and a copy is always floating around their apartment.

"I see, and what are you drinking, Mr. Funk?"

"Um, just tea, thank you."

Score one for me. He's buying that story. "Lonnie," he calls into the other room, "fetch some tea and biscuits for both of us, won't you please?"

"Yes, sir, Mr. Epstein," says a black man who pops his head in.

Epstein shifts gears, a lot more interested than he was

a moment before. "And you want to do a feature on my boys?"

"Yes, I do, very much. That's exactly why I'm here, for a chat with your boys on their home turf."

"Lenny Funk," he says rolling my name over in his mouth. "Is that a Jewish name?"

"Yes, sir, I'm Jewish."

Epstein smiles. I remember that being Jewish was an albatross for him, but he apparently is happy to accommodate a member of the Tribe.

"May I ask your angle?"

"Angle, sir?"

"Well, yes. Surely you're not talking about writing a straight feature on the Beatles. That's been done a thousand times already. I thought you were suggesting something new for such a large readership."

I'm dancing as fast as I can, but I'll have to dance even faster if I am going to figure out a way to meet the Beatles. "Well, sir, I don't know if this has ever been done, but I'd love to see them in a recording session. What do you think the odds are of that happening?"

Epstein takes a long drag on his cigarette and gives it some thought. I flash back to some old photographs I've seen. They have captured him perfectly—the young gentleman, perhaps a decade older than the members of the Beatles, and always immaculately dressed.

"I'm afraid Paul and John would not like that, or George Martin for that matter," he says at last. "They're happy to do interviews, of course, but the studio is sacrosanct. I don't even turn up there much. They don't like anyone to be in there while they're creating the magic. I hope you understand."

"Of course."

"Do you have any other ideas we might explore? We certainly don't want you to go away empty-handed, not with all those readers in your back pocket."

A thought comes to me. "Well, what about a night on the town with the Beatles then? What if I went out with them when they let their hair down, so to speak? It would be the exact opposite of seeing them in the studio, or at work, if you will."

I was picking up his proper way of speaking. It's a habit of mine. I always unconsciously mimic others' speech patterns.

Epstein sips his tea and smiles. "That just might work, Mr. Funk."

"Please, call me Lenny."

"Very well, then, and you call me Brian."

We drink our tea. "When do you think I might meet the boys?"

"Oh, they'll be here any moment. We have a little business to discuss." A buzzer rings the very next second. "That's probably them now."

A wave of excitement shoots through me. Is it possible I am about to come face-to-face with the Beatles, my favorite band of all time? Lonnie goes to answer the door, and I hold my breath. Less than a minute later, John, Paul, George, and Ringo saunter in, all laughing and carrying on.

"Almost got me knickers, those girls did. Christ Almighty."

"It wasn't your knickers they were after, John," Ringo tells him. "They wanted a good deal more than that."

They hoot and holler and slap one another on the back. I feel like I am inside the film *A Hard Day's Night.* Their energy is incredible, and they are all very young and dressed in suits. These are the early Beatles, no doubt. Their hair is long, but there is not a hint of facial hair. I sit there with my mouth hanging open. Meeting James Taylor was nice, but these are the freakin' Beatles. I am tongue-tied, not knowing whether to introduce myself.

"And who's this, then?" asks Paul, reaching out a hand to me.

The other Beatles ignore me, but Paul is obviously curious. I grab his hand and look up at him, but I cannot speak. The young Paul—still a baby at not even twenty-five years old—is extremely handsome. It's all too clear why the Beatles were so big with the ladies. He holds my gaze intently, a pleasant smile on his famous face.

"My name is Lenny," I somehow push out. "Lenny Funk."

"Funk," spits out John "What kind of a funking name is that? You should change it, mate."

"Ah, come on, John, it's his name. He can't very well change it without insulting his parents. Isn't that right, Lenny?" Paul says.

"Well, I don't care what his name is. I want a drink," says Ringo, turning to Lonnie. "Scotch and Cokes all around, if you will?"

"I want a smoke," says John.

George has not said a word so far. He seems to be brooding as he looks out the window. "The bloody birds are gonna be the death of us, mates," he says.

"Yeah, well, you seem to like those birds just fine when it suits you. Don't bite the hand that feeds ya," John says.

They all crack up. I look over at Epstein, who is sponging up the atmosphere of his boys. There is something that looks like love in his eyes.

"What's on your mind, Brian?" Ringo asks. "And please don't tell me you've lined up more gigs. We just got back from the States last night. I need a vacation."

"Ed Sullivan?" I ask.

"Sure, we did the Sullivan show , and it was fine,"

Paul says. "But we had lots of gigs, too."

"God knows that Sullivan chap helped us immensely in the States," Epstein says.

"Yeah, and we made him a pile of money," John adds.

Right then, I know it must be 1964. like it was still the same year, and I know they appeared on *The Ed Sullivan Show* back in February 1964.

"We need to record the new album over the next couple of weeks, boys," Epstein tells them. "That way, we can get it out for the Christmas buying season here and in the States."

"No problem. We've got a bunch of new songs, haven't we, John?" Paul says.

John is pouting or thinking, it's hard to tell. He takes a long drag on his cigarette and doesn't answer.

"Excellent," Brian says.

"When do you need us in the studio?" asks George. "I was hoping to take a holiday with Pattie."

Brian opens his desk calendar. "George Martin had EMI hold Abbey Road Studios starting on Saturday."

"No holiday then, eh?" George complains. "Bollocks!"

"You can go in a week, George," Paul says. "You know the songs we've written. It's just a matter of playing them for Mr. Martin. You should be able to leave in a week."

"Excellent," Brian says again. "Then it's on. Cheers, boys."

They clink glasses, and Epstein looks over at me. "Lenny is a reporter from New York."

"Well, thanks for telling us so soon, Brian," George says bitterly.

"No harm done," I say. "Let's just consider everything so far off the record. You didn't know who I was so I won't use anything I just saw or heard. Deal?"

"Be still my heart, a reporter with a conscience," John

says.

Ringo laughs. "I like him already."

"Thank you, sir," George says, slapping me on the back.

"Good, good," Epstein says. "Maybe you'll be willing to help Lenny with his assignment. He wants to go out on the town with you boys. See how you unwind and all that."

"You'll never keep up, Lenny," says Ringo, then on his second Scotch and Coke.

"Try me," I answer. Their own cockiness is feeding mine.

"Well, let's go then. Off to the Ad Lib, eh?" suggests Ringo.

"Can't go I'm afraid, lads," Paul says. "I'm off to see Jane and the folks, you know."

"Jesus, you're more married than I am," John says. They begin play fighting with one another as Lonnie opens the door. I follow as they all scamper downstairs to a waiting car.

Brian's chauffeur wants to drive us, but Ringo will have none of it. "Just got me license. I'm taking the Aston Martin," he tells John and George. "You guys take the Bentley. I'll drive Lenny."

I'm not going to argue, that's for sure, and we split up. Even in the short time I've seen him, I can feel Ringo's good-natured charisma coming off him in waves. He starts the car and adjusts his rings.

"Ever been to the Ad Lib?" he asks.

"No, what's it like?"

"You'll see soon enough," he says, a gleam in his eye. "Watch this."

By now, the girls at the far end of the cobblestone street are in a tizzy because they know the Beatles are on the move. Ringo guns the engine and heads smack toward the iron gate at the end of the lane. It's already swung open for the Bentley carrying John and George, and dozens of young girls are crowded on either side, almost blocking the road.

Ringo doesn't let up on the gas for a second as he heads toward them. I gasp and hold onto the dashboard, noticing—not for the first time—that the car has no seat belts. I am sure we are about to kill someone when, miraculously, the girls back off.

I release the breath I didn't realize I was holding. "Wow, that was close."

"I know. Open the glove compartment and pull out the flask, will ya, mate?"

. . .

When we pull right up to the door of the Ad Lib, a flock of paparazzi standing outside begin firing their cameras in our direction. These are real old-timey flashbulbs. I can hear them pop and sizzle, and I smell the faint burning in the air.

Ringo throws his car keys and some money to a valet and turns to face the "snaps," as he calls them. "Hey, boys, this here's my friend Lenny. Smile, Lenny, will ya?"

"Where's Maureen?" asks one paparazzo.

"Taking a breather tonight, boys," Ringo says. "You know she can't keep up with me."

He is so chummy with them it's surprising. He knows a couple on a first-name basis and has real conversations with them, asking after their children and wives. I'm admiring his style when he has suddenly had enough and pulls me toward the entrance.

Inside the club, the air explodes with loud rock 'n' roll, and a cloud of cigarette smoke hangs over everything.

"Now that's music," Ringo says about the Everly Brothers song blaring down on the crowd.

The club is dark and filled with mod-looking girls who are wearing heavy eye makeup and extremely short skirts. There's a tiny dance floor jam-packed with London's swinging set. Ringo keeps stopping to say hello to people along the way until we reach the far corner where I spot John and George.

"Hey, Lenny," Ringo yells into my ear. "Meet Mick and Keith. They're with that blues band, the Rolling Stones."

"Hey, mate, good to meet you," Mick Jagger says, taking my hand. My heart basically stops beating.

Keith just nods. He's otherwise engaged with an incredibly hot girl on his lap. She can't be more than eighteen years old, but then again, Keith himself looks like a baby. The craggy face I know from 2015 is blemish- and wrinkle-free now. He is beaming, his hands on the girl's hips and his leg moving up and down in time to the music, literally bouncing her on his knee.

Keith is dressed in a white, billowy shirt with some frill on the collar and very long sleeves that just about cover his hands. He has on tight, blue leather pants and there's a matching leather jacket on the back of his chair. I watch him closely. He looks lean and mean, but every bit the dandy with his silk shirt open to his belly button.

I smile—it's all I can do in my awed state—and move on to the next table where Ringo joins John and George. There are, of course, beautiful women with them, but none of them looks like John's wife, Cynthia. It's clearly a boys' night out. George is engaged in head-to-head conversation with a gorgeous woman who has to be a model.

Ringo turns away from me and starts talking to all three of the other women at the table. John sits quietly. He seems distant, like he's thinking of something, but I hear him humming along to the music. The Beatles song "There's a Place" blasts through the speakers, and I can't help but grin. That's why I landed here. The iPod *is* a steering wheel, after all. I was right!

At that moment, Ringo goes off to dance with the women, leaving me with John, whose eyes are closed. I don't dare try to engage him in conversation. I know John doesn't suffer fools or newcomers gladly, and he has a scalding wit that keeps almost everyone at arm's length. But I am beyond happy to be here, whether he talks to me or not. I'm sitting at the Beatles' table in this hot club in Swinging London. It's a mind-blowing experience. No matter how many times I go over it in my head, it's unexplainable. Time travel has been written about countless times, but there are no first-person accounts. Is this what all those writers were hinting at? Did something like this happen to them?

I decide to stop thinking and soak in every morsel of what I'm experiencing. It dawns on me that maybe Yoko's grandmother is somewhere in the crowd. If she truly hung around the Beatles and all those groups, this would be her scene. I don't spot her, but I do pick out some very famous faces—young rock stars Eric Clapton and Rod Stewart, the singer and actress Judy Garland, and the film actor Anthony Quinn, who I only know because the Joes had me recently watch *Zorba the Greek*, one of their favorite classic films. And there, against the back wall, watching everything, is a very tall black guy playing air guitar—the Guitar God himself, Jimi Hendrix.

"I don't believe this," I say out loud.

"Don't believe what?" asks the famous voice to my left.

It's John, who is staring at me. Up close, I can see how thick his glasses are, and then I remember his poor eyesight.

"All these superstars."

He squints at me. "What did ya call 'em?"

"Superstars."

"That's a good word. Have you any paper or a pen, Mr. Reporter?"

I reach into my pockets. All I have is some cash, a MetroCard, and some old store receipts. One is from a frozen yogurt place in my neighborhood called All You Need is Yogurt.

I laugh and hand that receipt over with a pen.

"What's so funny?" John asks. He reads the receipt. "All You Need is Yogurt? What the hell is that?"

"Just a store near where I live."

"I mean *yogurt*. What's that?" Before I can answer, he's lost interest. "Oh never mind."

He begins to write. I try to read his upside down scratch, but all I can see is that it's either lyrics or poetry. I'm dying to know what it is, but I'm not about to interrupt the great John Lennon. Something in this room, this atmosphere, has given him an idea, and he's off and running.

"Quit staring at me with yer mouth open, ya boob," he barks.

I quickly turn away, glancing back at the room. There's plenty to see. Ringo is a terrific dancer and a magnet for good vibes. A dozen couples circle around him. George appears to be having a very serious conversation with that model. I look back at the Stones' table. Keith is heading for the door with his young girlfriend, while Mick is dancing near Ringo in his typically androgynous, hip-shaking way.

"Hey, John," a woman says. I didn't see her approach, but I turn toward the woman and try not to gasp. It's Lily Chang, bending over to give John a kiss. The resemblance between Lily and Yoko is uncanny; they may as well be twins. She has on a micromini that shows off the same long legs I'd seen Yoko displaying the first time we met. She also has the straight black hair and chocolate eyes that make her a dead ringer for her granddaughter. The only real difference is that she's not quite as tall.

"Lily, you are my sunshine, my only sunshine," John tells her.

His distant mood is suddenly gone, replaced by the lighthearted John. He pulls her onto his lap and tickles her. She squirms playfully, mock-trying to get away, but he won't let her and she clearly doesn't want to. "You're a bad boy, John."

"And that's why you love me, Miss Chang. Care to dance?"

He pulls her onto the dance floor, and they do the twist.

Just then, I hear a voice in my head say, *Get a photograph!*

Of course! I feel around in my pocket and slowly pull out my smartphone. John is deep into his twist, and no one is paying me any attention. I make sure the flash is off, adjust the settings for the low light, and then, as surreptitiously as I can, I set the zoom feature and fire off five rapid shots of John and Lily dancing. I check to see if they are coming out in this light and they are. Then I get bold and look around the room. I snap shots of Ringo dancing and George talking to the model.

At that moment, someone grabs the phone out of my hand. It's John, who's returned to the table without

Lily. "What's this, then?" he asks. "Are you some kind of spy?"

"Uh, it's just a phone," I say and realize that I've dug the hole even deeper.

"A phone?" he says. "Mate, I don't know what this is, but I know it's not a phone." He turns it over, having no idea how to turn it on or what to do with it. Then he looks at me with a dead-serious gaze. "Tell me what this is, and don't lie to me."

I panic. "It's a phone. Look, John, I don't know how to say this, but . . ."

"Yes? But?"

"Just . . . I'm not a reporter and I'm not from here. I mean, not from London in 1964. I'm from the future and so is my phone."

He laughs. "Are you a lunatic, man, or are you tripping? Took a couple of hits of the good stuff before coming out tonight, did ya?"

"No, John. I swear." I'm talking very fast now. "I'm from the year 2015. This is a phone and a camera and a bunch of other things. Here, let me show you."

I pull up the photos I've taken of Ringo and George but not the ones of him and Lily.

"Lenny, I don't know who the hell you are or what this gizmo is, but you'd better start telling me the truth. Just give us some truth, man."

"John, I told you. I'm from the future."

"And I'm a flaming pie salesman! Bollocks! I'm keeping this thing until you tell me the truth. Maybe Eppy will know what it is."

I shake my head. "He won't know. I told you, it's from the year 2015, I swear."

"You're daft, but okay, I'll play along. In the year 2015, they have phones like this?"

"Yes."

"Okay, then, show me how it works. Call someone."

I hesitate. "I can't because there is no phone system that exists now like the one you need to use this phone. It's what we call wireless. It uses satellites, not phone lines. That's why it's not connected to anything."

"You're out of yer bloody mind, ain't cha? Just escaped from the nuthouse?" he asks.

His reaction, I realize, is perfectly normal, but for some reason, I want to convince him. I look down at the phone. "Here's a list of my phone contacts. The people I call all the time. You can see their phone numbers and photos. It's just that I can't reach them now without the wireless network that exists in 2015."

"So it's a phone and a camera, according to you. What else can the thing do?"

I snap my fingers. This is an opportunity to show him some games I've loaded, and even some books I've read. He slowly comes around and is impressed. Is that what I was really after, to impress the great John Lennon? I keep looking around to make sure no one else is coming, especially George, who is very skeptical about pretty much everything. Ringo would probably just laugh it off.

"Uh, how about we take a selfie?"

"What in God's name is a selfie?"

"It's a photo of us together that we take ourselves."

He crosses his arms. "Show me."

I toy with the settings a moment, reach out my arm, and move my head closer to John's. "Okay, smile."

Incredibly, he does, looking at our image on the screen as if mesmerized. I take the photo and show it to him—me and John Lennon, side by side. I am ecstatic. This is real proof no one can deny.

John looks at the photo, turns the phone over and over in his hand, and then gives it back to me. "Tell me more about the future. What else do you have in 2015 that we don't have now?"

"You believe me?"

"I don't know what to believe, but tell me more. What do you have there that we don't have here?"

I tell him about computers and try to explain the Internet.

"What about us?"

"The Beatles, you mean?"

"Yeah, does our music still get played in 2015?"

"John, you guys are the most popular music group of all time. Everyone loves your music, even in my day."

He smiles proudly. "I don't know if you're lying to me or if you're a lunatic, but you are different, I'll say that much. This thing, this phone or camera or whatever it is? If you invented this thing, you need to come work for us. Brian can set you up in his office."

"Work for you?"

"Yes. You say you know all about what music will become. You can give us a head start. Tell us what we need to know."

"What do you mean?"

"I mean, I keep hearing different sounds in my head, but I don't know how to make them happen in the studio. I have to explain every bloody thing to Mr. George Martin, who gives me blank stares like I'm out of me bloody mind. I was just thinking of a song based on a book I'm reading called *The Tibetan Book of the Dead*. Look, I wrote down these lyrics on your receipt: 'Turn off your mind, relax, and float downstream . . .'"

John was composing the beginning of "Tomorrow Never Knows" while sitting next to me. On my freakin' yogurt receipt!

"What's that called?" I ask, even though I know.

"I don't know yet, but I will. I always do."

"Great start," I say.

"Yeah, but I keep hearing something in my head, the way my voice is supposed to sound, and it's not like my voice sounds now. I want it to sound like, I don't know, like maybe the Dalai Lama shouting from a mountaintop. Do you understand? Can you help?"

"Well, I don't know much about recording, but you need a different microphone than the one you're using. Either that or you need to run your voice through a different system. Like instead of a voice mic, maybe one that you usually use for the instruments."

I didn't tell John that I'd just finished reading about how he'd recorded the song in a book by the Beatles' sound engineer and the advice I just gave him is exactly what sound engineer Geoff Emerick is going to suggest in a year or so.

"That's bloody genius!"

I shake my head. "Nah, you guys are the geniuses. Just keep making music together as long as you can and everything will be all right. That's all the advice I can give you."

"You've gotta come work for us. You've gotta tell Paul some of your ideas."

I don't know what to say, so I shake my head. "I'd love to, but I gotta go."

I have no idea what the correlation between time here and back home is, but something tells me I shouldn't stay too long. I don't want to get stuck. And now that I have these photos, I am bursting to show them to Yoko and Daisy. As fascinating as it would be to stay, I don't belong here.

John gets a serious look on his face. "You're telling me the truth about you being from the future, right?"

"Yes."

He handed the phone back. "So, what else? Other

children after Julian?"

"Yes."

"With Cynthia?"

I hesitate, and he nods.

I vow not to say a thing about Yoko Ono, even though, like a lot of Beatles fans, I wish John had never met her. The Beatles might have collapsed under their own weight anyway, but as far as I was concerned, Yoko was the instigator.

"I'm gonna leave Cynthia, you don't have to tell me that."

"Why do you say that?"

"She's the love of me life, but she's a northern girl and things are happening fast. I need someone who can challenge me more, a female version of Paul, if you want to know the truth."

He smiles. He hasn't met Yoko just yet, but she would be his eternal challenge, his arty genius. "Tell me about the woman I wind up with. Give us a hint, will ya?"

"I can't. It's not my place."

"Come on, man. I took that selfie with ya, didn't I?"

"She's different, and she will challenge you."

"What else?"

"Nothing. Let life happen, okay?"

But I've clearly opened a can of worms. Now John wants to know everything. "Listen, mate, I want the truth. What happens to all this Beatle stuff? What happens to me? To Paul and the rest? I wanna know."

I blurted out, "John, I can't—"

"Can't what?"

"I can't affect the future. And I'm afraid that will happen if I tell you too much."

"Bollocks to that! You're here for a reason."

"John, I can't. You're just gonna have to live it, man. I gotta go."

I get up to leave, but John grabs my wrist and has me

in an iron grip. I can't break free, but then I remember that John is as nearsighted as they come, blind as a bat without his famous specs. I reach out with my other hand and pluck those glasses right off his face.

"Hey!"

He releases my wrist. I put the glasses down on the far end of the table and pat him on the shoulder. "I have to go. Maybe we'll meet again."

John begins screaming for help, for someone to stop me, but the music is blaring and I am moving too fast. I dart around the tables and head for the door. That's when George leaps out of the shadows and gets me in a bear hug from behind. George is thin, and my instincts take over. It pains me to do it, but I kick backward and let George have it hard in the shin. He drops his hold, and I fly out of the Ad Lib and into the night.

I don't know where I'm running, but I keep going. I can hear the paparazzi screaming at me and flashbulbs popping as I run. After a few blocks, I came to a quiet alleyway and stop to catch my breath. It all feels so real that it must actually be happening. Who knew the secret to time travel was an old magic iPod? Very weird, but there's no denying what's happening.

I keep walking until I find a small neighborhood park and sit on a bench to collect my thoughts. There's no one around. I don't know if it's going to work again, but I'm going to try to get back the only way I know how, the way I did it the first time. Before I left on this trip, I loaded some new songs from the current year onto the iPod. I find the latest from Bruno Mars, put in my earbuds, and close my eyes. I say a silent prayer just in case.

Donovan Day

SEVEN

Lenny. Lenny, wake up."

My headache is back with a vengeance and so are my grandfathers.

"Lenny, you were talking in your sleep again," I hear Grandpa say.

I realize I'm back. Like last time, I have no memory of actually *traveling* anywhere. I'm back and that's it. One minute I was in a London alleyway, now I'm back in my bed. Crazy. But I can't say any of *that* to the Joes. "Sorry. What's happening? Please don't yell. My head is killing me."

Both Joes look at me with that concerned-parent look on their faces. They exchange a glance "Why didn't you tell us your head was still hurting you?" Joe says, probably expressing what both of them are thinking. "This could be serious, Lenny."

I hold up a hand. "Shh."

"Okay, we'll be quiet, but you're getting another checkup today," Grandpa says. "I have a friend who's a doctor. He's one of the best, and you can't get out of it."

I have no choice but to go along. "Fine," I say.

"Fine," he says, and that is that.

He gets on the phone and returns a few minutes later. "You're going for an MRI later this afternoon. They're going to look deeper into your brain to make sure everything is working properly."

"I already had one of those."

"No, not one of these," Grandpa says. "You had a CT. This time, it's gonna be an MRI. It's a different kind of scan. And this guy is one of the best, so if something's going on, he'll find it."

"How do you know him?"

They both smile, but Grandpa is the one who answers. "He introduced me and Joe at an AIDS benefit. He's done a lot for the gay community. Even helped to develop the cocktail that keeps HIV at bay."

"Okay, what's his name?"

"His name is Jonah Robert. He's an immunologist and neurologist. I told him you'd be there at two. I'll text you his address."

"You want me to go see Dr. Robert?"

"Yes," says Joe.

Only the most die hard Beatles fan would get the reference, so I'm not surprised he misses it. "Dr. Robert" is a song by John Lennon about an infamous New York doctor who hooked his patients up with LSD and whatever drugs they asked for. I'm guessing this guy is different.

"Okay," I said, even though I'm a little worried.

I don't like people looking inside my head. Ever since middle school, when I was angry at the world, I worried something might be physically wrong with me. They haven't found anything yet, but they keep checking. What if this guy finds a brain tumor? What if they insist I take drugs that prevent my new time-traveling hobby? I don't want my brain "fixed" if that's the case, but the decision is out of my hands. Once the Joes make up their minds, it is better to go with the flow. There is no getting out of it. If this doctor does find something, I'll deal with it later.

Soon they have both gone to work and the apartment is blissfully empty. I look at my phone. There are five texts from Yoko.

Well?
Anything happen last night?
Call me please
Please?
Call me!

Yoko. I haven't thought of her for hours, but now our last conversation comes rushing back. I feel a pit open up in my stomach. Why does she have to have a boyfriend? It changes everything. But she won't be able to resist me once I show her these photos.

I dial her number, and she picks up on the first ring.
"Well?"

"Good morning to you, too."

"Lenny, tell me. Did anything happen last night?"
"What makes you ask that?"

"Women's intuition. After you left, Daisy and I talked, and we both know you had something on your mind but didn't want to tell us. We all but saw the light bulb go off over your head. So?"

"Sure your boyfriend won't be jealous if we're talking?" I ask, trying to sound like I'm just teasing. We haven't talked about her boyfriend before, not really. Just that he exists.

"You are such a baby," she says.

"Yeah, I know. A baby who just happened to meet the Beatles last night."

Yoko screams. "What? You did not!"
"I did."

77

"Don't play games, Lenny."

"No games. It's true. I kind of had a breakthrough."

"Tell me everything."

"What's to tell? I was visiting with Brian Epstein when they all walked in."

"They?"

"The Beatles. They were hyped up. We all went to a club. Wait, not Paul because he was going on a date with Jane Asher, but the rest of us went. Ringo drove me in his Aston Martin, but we all met at the club, the Ad Lib. Have you ever heard of it? John and I kind of got into a fight and I took his glasses. I gave them back, though. Then George tried to get tough with me, too, so I kicked him and ran off. But not before I got some photos."

"You got photos," she says. She might as well be saying *Yeah, right* for how incredulous she sounds.

"Yes, I took some photos."

"And what do they show?"

"Only John dancing the night away with your grandmother."

"Lenny, stop."

"What?"

"That's not funny," Yoko says. "Don't joke around about my grandmother."

"I'm not joking. She and John were dancing, and I took some photos with my smartphone."

Yoko doesn't say anything.

"Hello?" I say.

"Lenny, if you're lying to me, I'm never going to talk to you again."

"I'm not lying. Wait, hang on, let me check something."

I take out my phone and scroll through the photos. They've survived the trip back, thank God.

"Yeah, they're here," I tell Yoko.

"I'm coming over right now. What's your address?"

Minutes later, there's a knock on my door. Yoko is there with wet hair and a very tight T-shirt with skinny black jeans. Her bra is barely holding her in.

"You're killing me," I say as I show her to the sofa.

"What?"

"Do you have to be so sexy?"

"Don't be silly," she says, brushing my pseudo-compliment off. I'm sure she hears it all the time. "Let me see the photos."

"Wait, let me find them."

She sits close to me on the sofa while I search through my icons. Our thighs are touching, and the intimacy of the moment is driving me a little insane. I'm having trouble focusing on the photos.

"Come on, come on," she pleads.

"Okay, here they are."

I show her the three I took of John dancing with Lily. Yoko starts crying and gives me a big hug. "Oh my God, Lenny! Lenny! You did it!"

I'm as excited now as she is. "I knew it was her because she looks just like you."

"Lenny, you are the best!" she says, and then she leans in to kiss me on the lips.

I kiss her back, but when I part my lips a tiny bit, she pulls back. "No, no, we can't." She pauses. "Uh, show me more?"

I want to kiss her again, to persuade her to get rid of that boyfriend of hers and give me a chance. But she said no, and I have to respect that. So I show her the selfie of me and John.

"You've got to be kidding! How does it work?"

I tell her my theory about the iPod. "That's all I've figured out so far. I don't really know *how* it works, and I'm not sure I ever will, but these photos are the proof I needed to convince myself the whole thing isn't some crazy hallucination."

"And you swear these are not photoshopped?"

"Come on, Yoko, I'm not that good. They're real."

"So it's as simple as cuing up a song on the iPod?"

"Sort of. I think so, that is. At least so far."

She meets my eyes, her gaze serious. "Lenny, I want to go with you."

"What do you mean, go with me?"

"I want to go back in time with you."

"First of all, what makes you think I can take someone? And second of all, what about your boyfriend?"

I'm being relentless, I know, but she does something to me that I can't explain.

"Okay, I'm going to kill you. Stop talking about Dmitri like we're going to get married or something. He's a guy. Who cares? This is way more important."

"Dmitri?"

"Yeah, Dmitri."

"Nice name," I joke.

"Forget him. Let's talk about us. You and me going back in time to visit my grandmother. We'll figure out how to do it with me tagging along. Come on, it will be fun to have someone there who knows the whole story. Don't you want me to come?"

She puts her hand on top of mine and moves her face close, obviously flirting, but I have to admit . . . I could get used to this.

"I'll think about it," I promise. "Look, I have a doctor's appointment today. I gotta head out now."

"What kind of doctor?"

I laugh. "Nothing serious, just some guy who wants to look into my brain. My granddads are all worried about me."

"Meet me after the doctor today, then."

"Where?"

"Come to my place."

. . .

I meet Grandpa at Dr. Robert's office inside Mount Sinai Hospital at two o'clock sharp, and the good doctor ushers us in. He's one of those gregarious types who wants everyone to like him immediately. He smiles a lot and doesn't talk or look like any doctor I've ever met. He is wearing a Hawaiian shirt under his white hospital coat, and he is a big man, probably around six foot five with a large stomach.

"So this is your grandson," Dr. Robert says. "He doesn't look anything like you, which is lucky if you ask me." He winks at me.

Then the doctor turns more serious, asking me every detail about my fall on the subway platform. He looks in my eyes, feels my head, checks my motor reflexes, moves all my limbs this way and that, and then escorts me to the MRI machine. There are no surprises for me. It's more or less exactly like the CT scan I had.

After the MRI, Dr. Robert puts the pictures of my brain up on a screen where we can all see them. I have to admit, I am curious to see the inside of my skull, not that I can really tell if it is just like everyone else's or not. Dr. Robert looks and looks and looks, making grunts that sound neither negative nor positive. We meekly wait for his prognosis. It is nerve-racking the way Dr. Robert doesn't tip his hand one way or another. All he does is adjust his glasses and clear his throat. In the meantime, I look at all the stuff he has on his walls. That's when I spot a photo of a much younger Dr. Robert posing with John Lennon and Yoko Ono.

At that moment, he gets up to close his office door, clears his throat, and turns in my direction, almost as though he is reading my mind.

"I've never seen anything like this," he says.

"What is it?" Grandpa asks, his voice full of concern.

Dr. Robert puts up his hand. "I didn't say it's bad, just that I've never seen anything like it. Take a look here. This is the part of the brain that controls memory. Let me show you what a typical brain looks like so you can appreciate the difference."

He pulls up a so-called normal brain and points out one area that is rather small. "This is a brain scan that is very typical. You can see the area where our memories are located. See its size? Now look at yours."

"It's a lot bigger," I say.

"Precisely. It's huge, in fact. I suspect it is always like that, but the fall might have shaken something loose, made it more responsive, if you will. That could be what's giving you headaches. It looks inflamed. Have you been having any unusual memories or hallucinations, anything like that?"

"No," I lie.

"What about the headaches?" Grandpa asks the doctor.

"I don't know," Dr. Robert says. "The brain is a mystery in many ways. There's nothing obvious, like bleeding on the brain, so that's a relief. The only thing I see is this incredibly huge memory portion of his brain. I'm sure the headaches are related to the fall, but they should go away. I don't really want to prescribe anything, so just take Advil or Aleve, but Lenny, I definitely want to see you again next week and take another MRI to see if this area has stayed the same, grown larger, or shrunk. Set up an appointment at the front desk. And Lenny?"

"Yes?"

"Call me immediately if you have any weird dreams that you can't explain. I'm very interested. Like I said, I've never seen anything like this."

The way he is looking at me feels more like he's looking through me, like he has a sense of everything that's been happening to me. I know he doesn't believe me for a second when I said that nothing unusual is happening.

As we're leaving and my grandfather goes to make a call, Dr. Robert pulls me aside. "Are you sure nothing is going on that you want to tell me about?"

"No, nothing unusual."

"You know, Lenny, I work with people all day and look into their eyes when I give them good news and bad, and I can read faces."

"Okay."

"And your face is telling me something you're not," he says. "I would bet anything that there is something going on with you."

I don't say anything.

"You should be honest with me and your grandfather if you want the correct treatment. Do you understand what I'm saying? Don't worry if you think it's strange. You won't get in any trouble. Just be honest. You've got to confide in a grown-up about these things, trust me."

"Did you know John Lennon?" I ask, changing the subject.

"I did. I guess you saw that photo."

"When? How?"

"Ah, well, maybe I'll tell you sometime, when you're ready to be truthful about what's going on with you. Now we both have something the other person wants to hear, so when you're ready, call me day or night. We'll talk about you, we'll talk about me. Just give me some truth. Isn't that what John used to say?" He smiles.

"Yes, he did say that." I don't tell him that I heard John say it last night.

Dr. Robert hands me a card with his private cell phone number written on it and wishes us well.

Grandpa and I hail a cab and head back downtown.

"So what do you think of Dr. Robert?"

"Seems okay," I say.

"He's a great guy. He's very good with people. Kind of intuitive, if you ask me. I think he can see things in people that they can't see themselves."

That makes me nervous.

"I'll get off in the theater district," Grandpa tells me. "I gotta get back to work. Where are you going?"

"To see a friend of mine. Yoko. She lives almost around the corner from you."

He does a double take. "Your girlfriend's name is Yoko?"

"She is most definitely *not* my girlfriend. She's got a boyfriend named Dmitri."

"Tough break, kid."

"Tell me about it."

"You'll meet other girls. There're only a few million in this burg."

"Yep."

He gives the cabbie the theater address and the apartment address, then turns toward me again. "I have to admit, the name Yoko is unique," he says.

"Yeah, she says her grandmother was a close friend of John and Yoko's."

"Really? Wow. But that makes sense," he says. "I never met anyone with that name."

"I know, me neither. I met her in the subway. She

came over and started singing with me. We were gonna do it regularly, but now I gotta get a new guitar."

"Right. We've gotta work on that, don't we?"

"When?"

"Soon. Hang in there." He gets out of the cab and gives me some cash to pay the driver. "I'm glad nothing serious turned up. I'm relieved, and you should be, too."

"Oh, I am, believe me."

"Don't forget to call your mom," he says. "But don't tell her anything about the doctor. That's our secret, okay?"

"You got it."

. . .

I think about how I really do need to call my mom as I climb the front steps of Yoko's brownstone and ring the doorbell. Yoko answers and waves me in. Out of sight of her mother, Yoko gives me a very tight hug. "I've been looking at the photos all day. You've got to tell me more about what she was like."

"It's not like we talked for hours. She came over and pulled John onto the dance floor. It's not like we were formally introduced us. I didn't actually talk to her."

"What was she like?"

"Cute, like you," I say. "And she had great legs like you, too."

Yoko blushes.

"Did you just blush?" I tease.

"Shut up."

"So the photos don't lie. You could be her twin sister except she's shorter. That's the only difference."

I put my hand on the small of Yoko's back. Maybe,

just maybe, she's beginning to reconsider the whole boyfriend thing with me edging out Dmitri for the featured role. Maybe I do have a shot. I'm feeling pretty good about everything as we go into her grandmother's memory room when I see Daisy.

"Hello again, Lenny."

"Hi, Daisy."

"Yoko showed me those photos. Just incredible. And she told me how it works or how you think it works."

"What d'ya think? Make sense?"

Daisy laughs. "Nothing about you makes sense, Lenny, but I believe you if that's what you mean. I'm just like Yoko. I always thought there was something special about you. Can I see it? The iPod?"

I hand her the iPod, and she looks through the music. "Lot of great stuff in here," she says. "Your grandfather has great taste."

"Thanks," I say. "He's a little older than you."

She keeps spinning the little dial to look at all the artists. "The Doors," she says quietly, closing her eyes.

"One of your favorites?" I ask.

"A bit more than a favorite," she says. "I knew Jim Morrison. He was so beautiful but so messed up. I mean, we all were a little messed up on drugs back then, but he took it too far . . . obviously."

"When did you meet him?" Yoko asks.

"Around 1970, at the Whiskey in LA," she says. "That's where everyone met. We hit it off, and I became one of his groupies. There were always women around him. We were all so young, even him. I was sixteen, and I'd cook, make his bed, take care of things for him and Pam, his girlfriend."

She cues up "People Are Strange" and puts in the earbuds while Yoko and I watch. Just then, the doorbell rings. Yoko parts the front curtains and looks outside.

"Shit, it's Dmitri."

"Who's that?" Daisy asks.

"Her boyfriend," I say.

Yoko looks a little panicked. "What should I do?"

"Why not let him in?" Daisy asks.

"He'll be crazy jealous because Lenny is here. I'm not gonna answer the door," Yoko says, and then she goes to another room where I can hear her speaking to her mother, letting her know why she's not answering the door.

Yoko comes back in the room. "Let's hope he leaves," she says.

Then her phone rings. She doesn't answer. Next she starts getting texts. She reads one out loud to us.

"*I know you're in there. Why won't you let me in? Are you with another guy?*"

"Yes, tell him 'yes' and tell him to go away," Daisy says. "Believe me, Yoko, you have to get rid of men who are always jealous. They'll make your life miserable."

I nod. "I think you should listen to Daisy. Sounds like she knows what she's talking about."

Yoko sticks out her tongue. "Oh, you'd love that. Wait here."

The moment Yoko leaves the room, something in Daisy changes. She gets a look in her eye, a very determined look. "There's something I didn't tell you, Lenny."

"What's that?"

"I was in Paris with Jim Morrison the night he died."

"You were?"

"Yes. I should have stopped it. I watched Pam and those drug dealers give him all that shit and just stood back. I've always felt responsible for his death."

"It wasn't your fault. Let's face it: Morrison had a death wish. I saw that Oliver Stone flick."

"That was mostly bullshit. Jim was getting cleaned up," she says. "The group had just finished recording *L.A. Woman*, the biggest record of Morrison's career. You've heard those songs. Does that sound like he was drunk or high? I don't think so. It hadn't even been released when he died. He was about to get even bigger and maybe enjoy his success for a change, instead of giving in to his demons. The only thing he was abusing when he died was alcohol and food. He had stopped taking drugs. That's why he OD'd. He had been off the stuff and they gave him heroin, and he got weak."

I don't know what to say.

Daisy tunes the iPod to the song "L.A. Woman" and puts one earbud in my ear and one in hers. "Listen to this, Lenny. Really listen."

I do listen. "Great tune," I mumble.

And then Daisy grabs my hands. "I want you to take me back, Lenny. Take me back to the night Jim died. This time, things are going to be different."

Her voice is hypnotic and full of pain. I want to let go, but I just can't. Besides, I don't believe we're going anywhere. The other two times I traveled, it was at the end of the day, I was tired, and I woke up in the morning. Now I'm all hyped up and it's the afternoon, but why not try? Each time is an experiment. Can I take someone back with me? I doubt it, but why not find out? I grip Daisy's hands and close my eyes.

EIGHT

It's dark outside but very warm, a typical summer night. I watch a couple walk by arm in arm, stumbling a little from having one too many at dinner. The man says something to his date and laughs, but he's not speaking English. It sounds like French, a language I've wrestled with since sophomore year. I sit up a little straighter and see cobblestone streets and funny-looking cars. The low-rise buildings surrounding me look just like the Paris I know from my French textbooks.

This is getting ridiculous. I'm a time-traveling master! But I don't see Daisy anywhere. I'm not surprised. It was wishful thinking to imagine that the magic would work for two people. I'm still astounded that I can do it. It's impossible to take for granted, no matter how effortless it seems. For the millionth time that week, I question myself. How can I be time-traveling? Is it some mind trick my brain is playing on me? Am I going crazy?

But those photographs were real. I didn't imagine those photos. I took them in some club in the 1960s when John Lennon was still a Beatle. And still *alive*.

Without Daisy as my guide, I'm not really sure what I'm doing in Paris. She wanted to save Jim Morrison's life, but I don't know how to do that. I get up and start walking, trying to remember what little I know about Morrison. The Oliver Stone movie ended with the singer dying in his bathtub in 1971, but it's been long rumored that he actually overdosed on drugs. There was no police investigation into his death, even though he was one of the world's biggest rock stars. These days, TMZ would be all over it.

I keep walking and see a river that must be the Seine. Most of what I know about Paris comes from textbooks and the Woody Allen film *Midnight in Paris*, and judging from what's in front of me now, it's pretty damn accurate. I spot those little booths next to the Seine that sell books, photographs, and souvenirs, but all of them are closed. I pull my smartphone out of my pocket. I've changed time zones, as well as decades, but I know Paris is about six hours ahead of New York, which, judging from my phone, means it's around eleven p.m. I reach into my other pocket and feel around for the iPod, but it's not there. That's when I remember that Daisy was holding it, not me.

"Lenny. Hey, Lenny."

I spin around and see Daisy running toward me. My knees buckle, and I sit on the nearest bench. Incredible! She comes over to me, nearly out of breath from running. "Are you all right?" she asks. "You look pale."

"I can't believe you're here."

"There are no words. This is unreal! It's like we're on some kind of drug, but I've never felt more sober in my life. It's 1971, and we're in Paris."

"How do you know what year it is?"

"I found a newspaper. It's June 2, 1971, the night Jim Morrison died."

I feel faint. "Daisy, we're not supposed to be here, and I don't think we should try to change what happened. We don't know the consequences of altering history. Something bad could happen."

"Something bad already did happen," she says. "Jim Morrison freakin' dies tonight. That's about as bad as it gets."

"But other bad things could happen. We can't know."

"Lenny, this was probably the worse night of my life, and I'm gonna do everything I can to make sure Jim lives and doesn't take that shitty heroin. You can do what you want."

Daisy turns and starts walking away. "Wait, do you have the iPod?" I ask.

She thrusts it toward me. "Yes, here. I don't need it anymore. You got me to Paris. Thanks. Are you gonna help me save Morrison or not?"

Daisy's eyes are like pinwheels, spinning wildly. What can I say? I almost have to go, just to keep an eye on her. Besides, I'm curious to meet Morrison. "I'll go with you, but I can't promise anything."

She jumps up and down like, well, like a crazy woman. "Oh, Lenny! Thank you, thank you, thank you. Come on, we need to go."

We start walking. Daisy stops a man and speaks to him in French. He directs her to a nearby Metro stop. "Come on, we'll catch up to them at the club," she says. "Hurry, the Metro only runs until midnight."

"What time is it now?"

"Eleven thirty."

We have no French money, but Daisy is not deterred. She jumps the French Metro turnstile with surprising ease, and I follow. I don't have a choice. I don't want to lose her. I don't want to be adrift in Paris by myself with no money and no way to communicate, either. For better or worse, Daisy and I are now joined at the hip.

"Do you know where you're going?" I ask.

"I think so. We'll find out. Come on."

Her excitement is infectious. She is giddy as we hop on the train, talking a mile a minute about things she remembers from that night. It's a long ride, and by the time we arrive at our stop, it's nearly midnight. Daisy leads us through a maze of streets until we come to a club called the Rock 'n' Roll Circus. A crowd has gathered, and the bouncers are keeping them at bay.

"Now what?" I say.

"Now we wait. Jim and his girlfriend Pam will be here any minute."

I stop asking questions because I'm excited, too. I am about to meet the great Jim Morrison. I scan the sidewalk, searching every face for the so-called Lizard King. He was a charismatic as a human can be and the girls were wild for him. My friends and I love the Doors, but it's mostly because of Morrison's badass attitude. The songs themselves are all over the place— some shallow, some ponderous, and with more than a few masterpieces thrown in the mix.

I don't see anyone who looks even remotely like Morrison.

"Hey, Jim," I hear Daisy yell. "Over here!"

The guy she's yelling at looks like a mountain man, big and fat with a full beard. If Morrison is in there somewhere, I'd never have guessed it. He's standing with a woman who is no doubt Pam Courson, his longtime, drugged-out girlfriend.

Morrison stops and looks in Daisy's direction but clearly has no idea who she is. Then he smiles and walks over, but he winds up going right by us to hug an attractive teenaged girl standing nearby. I recognize that girl . . .

"Daisy-cakes," he says to her, flipping her over his shoulder and carrying her into the club.

Daisy and I can only stare at his back as the crowd swallows him up. "That was you! The teenaged you," I say.

Daisy's manic spunk has evaporated. "Oh my God, I can't believe it. I'm jealous of me."

Neither of us saw this coming. Of course Morrison wouldn't recognize this mature version of Daisy. He only knew Daisy as a teenager, and she happened to be standing right behind us. Now it makes perfect sense.

"Now what?" I say.

"We're getting in that club," Daisy says.

"But we don't have any money."

She looks around. "Follow me."

It turns out that Daisy knows the club well and directs us to a side entrance where the kitchen help come out to smoke cigarettes. She bums one off a woman and asks in French if she can use the restroom. We're in.

The Rock 'n' Roll Circus isn't too different from the Ad Lib where I'd gone with the three Beatles—loud, crowded, and smoky. Instead of beautiful English girls, this club is filled with stunning French women staring openly at Jim Morrison, who is holding court at the bar with a fifth of whiskey in one hand and Daisy in the other. They are having an animated conversation. His steady girlfriend Pam is next to them, looking bored out of her mind.

It takes awhile to break through the crowd, but Daisy and I manage to get close. At fifty-five years old, 2015 Daisy looks out of place, but not me.

As I approach Jim, Pam looks at me. "Who are you?"

"Lenny. What's your name?"

"Pam. Is this your mother?" she says, motioning in Daisy's direction.

"I'm Daisy."

"Daisy?" Pam says. "That's weird. Two Daisys in one bar? Maybe you can start a daisy chain!" She howls with laughter at her own joke.

"Well, as a matter of fact . . ." Daisy starts, but I turn to her.

"Be cool," I whisper. "She doesn't need the truth."

"Hey, Jim," Pam says. "This chick's name is Daisy, too. They look alike, don't they?"

Morrison and the young Daisy both look over. "Shit," he says. "You could be Daisy's mother, you know that?"

Even Daisy sees the resemblance. "Wow, kind of trippy."

For the first time, Morrison notices me and sticks out his hand. "Who are you, kid?"

"Lenny. Good to meet you."

"Hey, Lenny, what's your game?" Morrison asks. "Why are you an American in Paris?"

"I'm a musician. I play a little guitar and am just hunting around for a gig."

"That's cool, man."

Morrison takes a gulp of whiskey and pours what's left of the bottle down young Daisy's throat. She gives him a big, wet kiss, which makes Pam stomp off to the back of the bar. Then the singer leans against the wall, pulls out a small notebook, and ignores us. He begins writing as the bartender puts a fresh bottle in front of him. No one speaks to him, and I'm pretty sure that's the way he wants it.

Young Daisy looks right through me; we won't meet until years from now. Instead, she focuses all her attention on 2015 Daisy. "Where are you from?"

And so begins the weirdest conversation I have ever heard. Two people, who are actually the same person, chatting about each other's backgrounds that, go figure, are full of similarities. I shake my head. Now I understand why people drink. I'm sorely tempted but hold off. I've had exactly two beers in my life, and I have never tasted hard liquor. Something tells me that a night as weird as this one is not a good time to start.

I keep an eye on Pam, who is talking to two stoner-looking dudes in the back of the club. I can't tell if they are French or American, but Pam is pointing at us and all three of them are looking in our direction. It's obvious she's complaining big-time about young Daisy, and I'm sure she's suggesting new and exciting ways to make her disappear. Meanwhile, the two Daisies are chattering away like old friends.

Finally, Pam returns and begins whispering in Morrison's ear, making him laugh. He puts away the notebook, and Pam signals to the French guys. They walk over to where we're standing with expressions that are somewhere between dead serious and dead. Pam introduces them, and I'm so close that I can hear her talking to Morrison. "They have some good shit for you."

"Oh yeah?" he says playfully. "Whatcha got? Horse?"

Morrison lets out a giant laugh and throws his head back, mimicking the whinny of a horse. "Forget that shit, man. I got this," he says, holding up his bottle.

"Aw, Jim, come on, honey, I need some. Come to the bathroom with me," says Pam.

"Jim says he doesn't need it," 2015 Daisy tells her. "Why don't you leave him alone, Pam?"

"No one asked you, Mom!" Pam shouts.

That does it. 2015 Daisy shoves Pam, and soon they are fighting, pulling at each other's hair and clothing. Morrison doesn't move a muscle to break it up. Neither does young Daisy, who stands there laughing. Meanwhile, one of the French guys keeps nudging

Morrison toward the bathroom. I know I shouldn't get involved but I don't like this guy, so I stick out a foot. He loses his balance and goes flying.

Morrison laughs at him, and I take that opportunity to grab his arm. "Let's split, man."

I don't know why, but Morrison listens to me, and I'm able to pull him toward the door. I turn around once to see 2015 Daisy breaking away from Pam while a bouncer steps in front of the French guys and stops them from following us. I move Morrison along. Outside, 2015 Daisy catches up to us. She spots a waiting limo and piles us all in, barking something in French to the driver. We take off just as an angry Pam explodes out of the club and chases us down the street.

"Keep going," Daisy yells in English.

"Where are we going?" Morrison asks, still clutching his whiskey bottle.

"I don't know," Daisy says.

"Take us to Pére Lachaise," I shout at the driver. It's a huge cemetery for the rich and famous, and I only know of its existence because it's where Morrison was buried after his death. Thousands of rock fans have made pilgrimages to his grave since 1971. Suggesting we go there, of all places, is a twisted idea, but it's somehow fitting.

"Yeah, man," Morrison says. "Take us to that cemetery. It's spooky at night. Good idea."

Morrison begins mumbling some poetry as the driver races through the empty streets. It's just me, Daisy, and Morrison. Everyone else is back at the club or somewhere out on the street, and I'm confident they have no idea where we're heading.

"Brilliant," Daisy whispers to me. "Anything to keep him from going back to the club. That's the danger zone. Pam will never look for him in the cemetery."

The gates to the cemetery are blessedly open, and we sail in. The driver stops and says something to Daisy. She replies in French and then turns to me. "This is where we get out."

Morrison leads the way, holding on to Daisy for balance. A full moon lights up the headstones, making them very easy to read. "I need to find Molière," Morrison says. "Or Voltaire. At the very least Voltaire!"

And so we look. It's not easy. This is one very dense cemetery, and we stumble from headstone to headstone, reading names out loud as we go.

"This is so trippy, Lenny," Daisy says. "No one would ever believe this. Is Molière even buried here?"

"I have no idea," I say.

Morrison is in fine form, bellowing out poetry between long pulls from his whiskey bottle. As the night wears on, I become more and more positive that he will not die on this night, that somehow we've done the impossible. I have no idea what might happen instead, but we've saved a man's life, a man who is a hero to many. Maybe he'll go on to write a bunch more hit songs or maybe he'll die from an overdose on some other night. Regardless, we've changed Morrison's future and altered the lives of many others. It's a scary thought, but there's no turning back now.

We walk and walk until Morrison literally falls down on Molière's headstone. It's very worn, but he's found it, and he sits at its base, still quoting his own poetry.

"You found it, Jim. You found it," Daisy says.

Morrison looks exhausted. He takes one last pull on his bottle and tosses it backward, where it shatters. Then he closes his eyes and falls asleep.

"Well?" I say to Daisy.

She gives me a high five. "We did it."

"I'm beat."

"Me too," she says. "But we need to stay with him for a bit. He died around two a.m., so I want to wait."

I nod. "Okay."

Somehow, I manage to keep my eyes open until dawn, but I'm the only one. I shake Morrison and Daisy, and we mange to find Morrison a cab so he can get home.

I turn to Daisy. "We need to get back."

"Yes."

I pick out an Ed Sheeran song and hand Daisy an earbud. The adrenalin of the adventure has worn off, and the soft glow of dawn is in the air. Daisy snuggles into my shoulder.

"Close your eyes and pray," I whisper.

NINE

When I open my eyes, I am back in Yoko's house, Daisy sleeping at my side. We're in Yoko's grandmother's memory room. The light is peeking through the heavy curtains. I guess it's morning, and, if that's true, I'd better get home in a hurry so I can sneak in before the Joes wake up. If they catch me, they'll be upset that I broke my curfew, but I can handle them. It's Yoko I'm worried about. She's going to be plenty pissed that we time-traveled without her.

Daisy stirs next to me. "Oh, Lenny, are we back?"

"Yes."

She stretches. "Absolutely mind-blowing. You didn't slip me some kind of hallucinogen? That was real?"

"One-hundred-percent real."

"I feel fantastic! It was so great to see Jim again, even though he had no idea who I was. Thank you," she says.

"Don't mention it. And I mean really, don't mention it to Yoko. She's not going to take it well." I get up. "I need to get home."

Of course, that's the precise moment when the door cracks open and Yoko walks in. She stiffens the second she spots Daisy lying next to me. "Well, well, don't you two look cozy," she says.

"Hi."

Yoko is wearing a long T-shirt and looks adorable, but her eyes are flashing red. "I am so mad at you, Lenny. Where were you? You disappeared last night. Where did you go?"

I never really thought about it but now I know that the time travel is not just taking place in our minds; our bodies go along for the ride which explains why Yoko could no longer find us. But I'm not about to go into that kind of detail right now. I can't think of what to say.

"I wish you could have been there," Daisy says.

"Where?" Yoko demands.

"Paris. We went to see Jim Morrison. God, I've missed him so much."

I can nearly see steam coming out of Yoko's ears. "What? Lenny, I thought you couldn't possibly take someone back in time with you! But somehow you took Daisy, not just back in time but all the way to Paris to see Jim Morrison?"

I'm almost stuttering to get my side of the story out quickly. "I didn't mean for it to happen, and I *was* telling the truth. I didn't know if it would work."

"It was my idea, Yoko," Daisy says. "Don't worry. You'll get your turn."

"My turn? It was my idea!" she yells.

I try to shush her. "You're going to wake up your parents."

But there's no stopping Yoko. She is livid. "I can't believe you two. And you, Lenny, you are such a liar," she says.

"It just happened."

Yoko mimics me and not in a nice way. "Oh, it just

happened, did it? The second I leave the room to talk to stupid Dmitri, you two take it upon yourselves to time-travel without me. Why couldn't you wait?"

"We didn't know what was going on with you and Dmitri," I say.

"Forget Dmitri. You'll be thrilled to know I had a big fight with him, and we broke up."

"I'm sorry," I say.

"Oh, shut up. Now I know you're lying."

I can't help but smile. "Okay, I'm not sorry. Not about that part."

She actually stomps her foot. I've never seen anything so cute, but I know to keep my mouth shut.

"I hate you. I suppose you think now I'm going to throw myself at you, but I'm not. Get out of my house—now! And take your cougar momma with you."

"Yoko, come on, " I try to reason with her.

"No. I want you to leave before my parents come down."

I brush myself off and give Daisy a helping hand to stand up. "Okay, we're leaving," I say. "Maybe we'll talk when you calm down."

"I am not going to calm down. I thought you were different, Lenny. That's what hurts so much. You're just another guy." She pronounces the word *guy* like it's the worst curse imaginable. I attempt to say something, but she puts her hand in my face.

"Okay, okay," I say, and we leave.

"Don't worry, Lenny," says Daisy. "She'll come around. You've got to give her a couple of days to calm down."

I should go straight home, but Daisy convinces me to have breakfast. "We need to process what happened last night," she says, and I know she's right. There are so many thoughts and scenes going through my head that

I feel like I'm going crazy. We also don't even know what happened to Morrison now that we saved his life.

It's only seven as we settle into the Cornelia Street Café just a few blocks from the Joes'. It's one of their favorite places. I text them the moment we settle into a booth to let them know I'm alive.

Grandpa texts back immediately.

Okay. Call your mother this morning. She wants to know how you're doing.

I put the phone down and look across the table at Daisy.

"It was kind of funny being called a 'cougar momma,'" she says.

"Yeah."

"So, about last night . . ." Daisy says.

"I know. Wow."

"Crazy, crazy," Daisy says. "Seeing Jim again, that was pure magic! There are so many little things you forget about a person, even someone like him. Thank you for that, Lenny. It was . . . just . . . I don't even know."

I nod. "Now, before we look, what do you think happened after we left him there?"

"Oh my God, I almost forgot about that! He could be alive, right?" She looks at her smartphone, but I put my hand over it.

"What do you think happened?"

Daisy thinks for a second and then returns to her phone to google Morrison. "I have to know."

I look him up on my phone at the same time. Immediately, I see from his Wikipedia entry that he's still alive. Daisy puts her hand over mine. "He's still alive!" she says.

I read on. It turns out that Morrison and the Doors went on to make several more albums to the usual mixed reviews. One in particular was called *Paris* and had a song on it called "Daisy." The group stayed together for twenty more years, even through Morrison's solo records and outside projects, like his books of poetry. Then, in the early nineties, he dropped out of sight, and when he resurfaced, he was drug free and was living in the Arizona desert as a shaman. The articles all say that's where he is now, running his own wellness clinic fifty miles outside Phoenix, where he helps people kick drugs and find God the natural way.

"Are you reading what I'm reading, Daisy?"

"Amazing. I'm so happy for him."

She looks at me. "I'm going to Arizona. I have to see him."

The articles say he never married, but he has a dozen children by at least six different women, all of whom he considers his wives.

"You saw this about his wives and children?" I ask.

"Yeah, who cares? I don't want to have his baby. I just want to be near him. This is a miracle, Lenny."

I nearly drink my entire cup of coffee at once. "It really is a miracle. I guess the past can be changed."

"Absolutely."

I think about that for a moment. "Of course, we don't know what else we did by keeping Morrison alive that night."

"What do you mean?" Daisy asks.

"Think about it. He's famous, so we know what happened to *him*, but what about all the other lives that were changed because he lived?"

"Well, the Doors stayed together but don't tour anymore. And they're all alive," she says.

"Yeah, but what about somebody like Pam, Morrison's girlfriend?"

We dive back into our smartphones to look her

up. The story is not quite as happy. It turns out that Morrison's gal pal Pam died of a drug overdose in 1975.

"But that's what always happened," Daisy says. "Pam was a mess, God rest her soul. Even in the past that existed before we saved Jim, Pam died of drugs a few years later. We didn't have anything to do with that."

. . .

After breakfast, Daisy walks me home. "When are you going to leave for Arizona?" I ask.

"As soon as I can."

We're outside my grandfathers' apartment building. "Well, this is where I live."

"Lenny, I can't thank you enough," she says. We hug, and my grandfather picks that moment to open the front door.

"Hi, Lenny. You didn't tell me you had company last night," he says when he sees Daisy.

"Hi, there," she says brightly. "I'm Daisy. Lenny has told me all about you. He's a great kid."

"Oh? Lenny never told me much about you . . . Daisy did you say your name was? How long have you two known each other?"

Daisy and I exchange a look and burst out laughing. "That's a tough question, Grandpa."

"It feels like forever, but it's only been a few days," she says before changing the subject. "Lenny showed me the iPod you gave him. Great tunes. We were listening to it last night and kind of lost track of time."

I can tell Grandpa is flattered. "I'll give him a break this time," he says and then turns to me. "You need to call your mother, Lenny. She wants to hear from you."

"I will right now, Grandpa. I gotta go, Daisy. Good luck in Arizona."

Daisy gives me a big hug and a kiss. "I'll never forget you, Lenny," she says. Then she walks away.

Grandpa and I watch her go. "Lenny, it's none of my business," he says once she's gone, "but isn't she a little old for you?"

"It's not like that, Grandpa. She's just a friend."

"Okay. I mean, she seems like a nice woman, but she's your mother's age."

I laugh. "Speaking of mom, I'll call her now."

"Okay, I'm off to work. See you for dinner?"

"Yeah, I should be home. If not, I'll text you."

. . .

I grab a cup of coffee, settle in, and dial my mom's cell. She picks up on the second ring, sounding very upbeat. "Lenny, my son and only, I've missed you!"

"Hi, Mom. How's it going out there with Caroline?" That's Mom's sick cousin.

"Better. Some days better than others, but I think she'll be good to stay on her own in a week or so."

"Are you having any fun?" I ask.

"Some. I have been able to take yoga classes almost every day. There's a studio five minutes away."

"That sounds good," I tell her. My mother happens to be in fantastic physical condition and can do yoga poses I can only dream about. It hasn't helped in the romance department, though. Guys just don't seem to ask her out, and I'm not sure why.

"How's your summer going?" she asks.

"Pretty good."

"Been playing guitar?"

For her, the guitar is my life preserver, the thing that got me out of my rebellious years, so she wants to make sure I stick with it. "Yeah, some. I met a girl who wants to sing with me."

Mom loves any kind of news about a romantic interest of mine. "Really? Do tell. What's her name?"

"Yoko. She's Asian."

"Yoko. Wow, I never heard of anyone with that name except—"

"Yeah, I know," I cut her off, wincing at how often Yoko must hear that over and over. "I think she's sick of hearing that from people, but her grandmother knew the Beatles and was friends with John and Yoko, so it makes sense."

I skip the part where Yoko told me she never wants to see my face again. Might as well keep things positive. "Wow, that's interesting," Mom says. "Have you met her grandmother?"

"No," I lie. "She died when Yoko was young, but she left behind a lot of memorabilia from the old days. Her grandmother grew up in Liverpool and used to hang with the Beatles and a bunch of the other big British groups. She had a great voice and sang on a bunch of albums."

"What's her name? Was she well known?"

"Lily Chang. She never made a record on her own so I doubt you've heard of her."

"Yeah, it doesn't ring any bells, but wow . . . How's the granddaughter? Girlfriend material?"

"Definitely girlfriend material, but she hasn't fallen for my obvious charm. Not yet anyway."

"But you said she's singing with you?"

"Yeah, but we had a fight. She's kind of pissed at me right now."

"So give her time. She won't be able to resist you once she gets to know you. What was the fight about?"

"She thinks I went back on my word."

"Did you?"

"Not intentionally."

"Hmm. Maybe you should apologize."

"I did, but she's angry."

"Buy her flowers or do something special for her. She'll come around."

"You think?"

"A woman needs to know you care, Lenny. Show her. And ramp it up beyond just a straight apology. Actions speak louder than words, right?"

"Yeah, I guess you're right. I'll do something."

"Good. I'd love to meet her when I get back."

"Hopefully you will, Mom. Thanks for the advice."

I hear her getting distracted by something happening on her end. "Lenny," she says, "I need to get going, but good luck with Yoko, and let me know if you want me to call as a character reference."

I laugh. "I'm sure that will convince her, Mom."

"Bye, Lenny. Love you, darling."

"I love you, Mom."

I log on to Facebook and go straight to Yoko's page. Everything's been happening so fast that I haven't looked her up until now. She's one of those people who half blocks her page from the public. I can see photos of her with Dmitri and other friends, but her actual friend list is behind the privacy wall. I flip through the photos and wonder if they really broke up.

I check her relationship status: It's COMPLICATED.

Then I check his: SINGLE.

Bingo! *That* is good news.

I go back to her page and scan her high school and interests, pages that she likes, and then it smacks me in the face. Tomorrow is her seventeenth birthday! Mom is right. I think Yoko would appreciate a present, and I'm going to give her exactly what she wants . . . if she'll talk to me, that is.

Donovan Day

TEN

The next day I walk over to Yoko's house after dinner. I'm hoping she's home and has not fallen back into the arms of what's his name. On the other hand, she could be out to dinner with her folks, but I have to take a chance. She's not answering my texts or taking my phone calls. A face-to-face meeting is all I have left—that and my birthday gift.

I ring the bell, and Yoko answers. She starts to close the door the instant she sees me.

"Wait a minute, Yoko, please. I have something for you . . . for your birthday."

She relents and opens the door a crack. "How did you know it was my birthday?"

"There's this thing called Facebook."

"But we're not Facebook friends."

I have to tread carefully. Yoko, for once, does not look fantastic. Her skin is blotchy and her eyes red. She's clearly been crying. Her hair is pulled back, and she's wearing sweats. I'm thinking this birthday is not going as she'd planned.

"True, but I could still see it was your birthday."

She stands there, holding the door open about three inches. "So what do you want?"

"Can I come in? I have a gift, but I don't want to give it to you out here."

"Where is it?"

I pull out my iPod. "It's in here."

She raises one eyebrow, opens the door, and lets me in. Then she turns and walks away. That's when I see Yoko's parents, Mr. and Mrs. Peng. I can't follow Yoko without saying hello to her mother and introducing myself to her father.

"Hello, Mrs. Peng, Mr. Peng. My name is Lenny Funk."

We shake hands. "Good to meet you, Lenny."

I don't really know what else to say so I just jump in. "Well, I'm here to wish Yoko a happy birthday."

"That's nice of you," says Mrs. Peng. "She could use some cheering up. She's been moping about all day."

"Lenny!" Yoko calls from the other room.

"Would you like a piece of birthday cake, Lenny?" Mrs. Peng asks.

"Um, I'd better not, but thank you."

Yoko comes over to pull me away. "Mom, Lenny and I are going to Grandma's room if that's okay."

"That's all right, yes, but please leave the door open."

"Yes, Mom," she yells in a singsong voice as she leads me to the memory room.

Yoko leaves the door open a crack, and then casually sits down and begins sobbing softly. It's tough to watch, and I'm not sure what I'm supposed to do.

"This is the worst birthday ever, Lenny. I broke up with Dmitri, none of my friends are around, and life just sucks." She pulls a tissue out of a box and starts blowing her nose.

I take a deep breath. "Maybe I can help."

"Anything is better than this."

"I think we should try it."

She stops crying. I'm certain she knows what I'm about to say, but she tilts her head. "Try what?"

"I think we should try going back in time, both of us. It worked with Daisy so I think it will work with you, too, but we won't know until we try. So . . . ?"

Well, that's it. Yoko jumps into my lap and wraps her arms around me. "I was hoping that's what you were gonna say."

And then she kisses me. It's not quite as wonderful as I'd hoped because I feel like I'm taking advantage or something. But all my nerve endings still light up, and I kiss her back before she can have a change of heart.

It's over almost as quickly as it began.

"I'm so excited. What do we do?" she asks.

I've given this some thought. "We need to find a time or place when we think your grandmother will be with the Beatles. When I went back with Daisy, she knew Jim Morrison was going to be at a certain club at a certain time. So we need something like that. Ideas?"

"Not off the top of my head, but there must be something here that can help us," she says, looking around the room.

Over the next half hour, we look at every photograph hanging on the wall, and every record sleeve where Lily Chang has a credit. She sang backup with a lot of bands, including the Beatles, but the band did not credit her on any of the albums. Lily was their friend and maybe she didn't ask for any credit, but it's a dead end.

"Where's that photo of John and your grandmother?" I ask.

Yoko pulls her favorite photo of John and Lily off the wall, the one where Lily looks like her twin. "Here it is."

"Any idea when this was taken?"

We look on the back, but there's no inscription. "Nope. I know it's the mid-sixties, but that's not gonna help us," Lily says.

I shake my head. "We need to be more precise," I say. "Anything in her journals?"

"Not that I remember, but let me scan them quickly."

Lily takes out the journals and flips through them while I walk around, scanning the room. There is a VHS collection of some of the Beatles' promotional films, like *Revolution*, *Hello, Goodbye* and *Get Back*. They were the first music videos, really. The Beatles made them for their fans because they had stopped touring. I look at each one, and something on the back of the VHS box for *Hello, Goodbye* catches my eye. I only saw copies of the film once or twice on YouTube, but there, on the back of the box, the Beatles are dancing around with a bunch of girls in Hawaiian grass skirts. I hold up the box. Unless I'm crazy, one of the dancers looks Asian. In fact, she looks like Lily Chang.

"Yoko!"

"Did you find something?"

"Maybe. Look at this. See this girl right here?"

Yoko's reaction tells me all I need to know. "Oh my God. You think it's my grandmother?"

"You tell me," I say.

"I don't know."

"Let's watch it."

We search for the video on YouTube until we find one with good quality. Toward the end of the song, the Beatles change out of their gaudy Sgt. Pepper costumes and come out in street clothes. That's when the girls join them for a silly dance routine. John, in particular, really gets into it with them. "That's Grandma!" Lily shouts.

For the second time today, Yoko kisses me. "I'm so excited! Take me back, Lenny. Take me back."

I nod. "Are you ready?"

"I am up for anything tonight, Lenny."

I try not to think too hard about that statement. "Okay, let's do it," I say.

"Right now?"

"It's your birthday, so why not?"

"What about my parents?"

"I don't know. Tell them we're going out for a while, tell them anything. Or I mean, we can always do it ano—"

"No!" she interrupts, and I can't help but smile. "Don't move."

"Wait," I say. "You can't go in those sweats. Better put on something that fits in with the times."

"Good idea. What about you?"

I've already thought of this, and my clothes are generic. "This will do."

"Be right back."

She returns dressed in a miniskirt and blouse that could very well be from the mid-sixties. "Nice," I tell her. "What about your parents?"

"I told them we're going to listen to some records and maybe go to your house. That way if we're not here, they won't panic."

She closes the door all the way. "Let's go."

I cue up "Hello, Goodbye" on the iPod, we split the earbuds, and close our eyes. "Now give me your hands," I say, and she intertwines her fingers with mine.

Donovan Day

◀◀ ◀ ELEVEN ▶ ▶▶

The trip back always seems to be the same. In the split second before I open my eyes, it's like time is a record needle skipping over a scratch, and there's a slight variation in the atmosphere that dissipates as quickly as I become aware of it. The first thing I hear is someone testing a sound system, repeating "Check, check" over and over.

I look in that direction. Yoko is sitting next to me in the balcony of an ornately decorated theater. The place is mostly empty. There are only a dozen or so people sitting in the first couple of rows of the orchestra section, and they appear to be part of the production crew. No Beatles are in sight, but there are technicians on stage tuning up instruments and a cheesy backdrop that looks psychedelic, very much from the sixties. Clearly, the techs are preparing for someone to come on stage and sing.

Yoko is still a little out of it, but she jumps when wicked feedback blasts out of an amp. "We're here," I whisper.

"The drum kit doesn't have any band name on it,"

she says. "That's not a good sign."

Both of us are used to the distinctive logo of the band's name on the bass drum. But before we can speculate on what that means, we see the techs walk offstage.

"Okay, play it," someone says.

Paul McCartney's voice booms over the sound system, singing "Hello, Goodbye."

Yoko digs her nails into my arm.

Then, just as we hoped, John, Paul, George, and Ringo come out. They're dressed in those famous Sgt. Pepper costumes, and George is wearing a three-cornered hat. I read somewhere that John hated this song and wanted them to film "I am the Walrus," instead, which he considered to be superior. Paul won out with the film, but history proved John right.

Yoko and I lean forward as the house lights darken and the Beatles pick up their instruments and Ringo sits behind his drum kit. I can feel Yoko nearly vibrating with excitement. There's some conversation onstage that drifts up to the balcony.

We can hear Paul's distinctive voice as he talks to a cameraman. "Okay, the first shot should be wide and establishing, and then we'll do the bits." Clearly, he is acting as the director, which isn't surprising given the way Paul more or less took over management of the Beatles after Brian Epstein died of a drug overdose.

"Okay, we'll open wide and stay on that," the cameraman says, repeating Paul's directions back to him.

"Curtain coming down!" someone else yells.

The curtain comes down, and then, within minutes, it starts to go up as the music starts, and the Beatles begin lip-synching the words to the song, mock playing their instruments since everything is prerecorded. It's not their finest moment, but it's still the Beatles in the prime of their music-making career. They move around the stage as the music plays, not looking all that enthusiastic. Ringo in particular looks like he's had a very hard day's night, while John looks blow-dried and fake. It's obvious a stylist has done up his hair with loads of hair spray.

After one take, George says, "Can I go home now?"

Paul fake punches him in the arm and orders the camera to be trained on George. Paul gives him some instruction, telling him to move quickly to the side so the camera can pick up Ringo playing the drums behind him. John and Paul also stand to the side.

When it's finished, Paul says, "Okay, now it's my turn."

"Does that mean I can go home now?" John jokes.

"No, we need all of you lot on your feet because the camera might catch you in the background of a shot," Paul says.

The song plays again, this time the camera was trained on Paul, who monkeys around making goo-goo eyes for the camera. There are no monitors hanging over the stage as there would be now, but both Yoko and I know the clip well enough to see what's happening close-up. As always, Paul is the ultimate showman, but even he looks a bit stiff prancing for the camera.

There are endless takes, and an hour passes before the band gets to the end of the song, the fun part where they cut loose and dance around. It's a free-for-all as the dancers in grass skirts come out of the wings doing the hula and the twist. It's the happiest the Beatles have seemed all day as they dance and mug for the camera. Yoko squeezes my arm tighter and tighter.

"That's her," she says. "Over there on the far left. That's my grandmother!"

I shake my head. It's too much to process in a logical

way. At least three of the people on stage—Lily, George, and John—are dead in 2015, but here they are as alive as ever. There's no way to make sense of it.

The dancing goes on and on, and then, just like that, it's over. The music stops and the house lights come up.

"I'm going down there," Yoko says.

"Okay, but let's be careful."

We stand up and hear footsteps behind us. "Who are you, then?" comes a voice. We spin around just in time to see two burly guys walking down our row from opposite directions. "Have you been here the whole time?" one of them asks.

"Yes."

"That's not allowed, you know. Are you from the tabs?"

"No," Yoko says, "just fans."

"Americans, eh? Well, fans or not, you can't be here spying on the Beatles. Let's go, you're out of here. You should be thankful I don't call the bobby."

Yoko and I make eye contact. We've come so far and are so very close that to get kicked out now seems like a very cruel joke. We walk between the bouncers meekly, and they lead us downstairs. I'm thinking about what to do next, but there doesn't seem to be time to do much. If we don't do something, we're going to be out on the street pronto. I'm desperate and notice that the security guards are not really holding me. They're just walking next to us. Without a word to Yoko, I take off in the opposite direction of the stage. The guards are caught unaware. They both chase me, leaving Yoko alone.

I begin running all over the theater, up and down rows. The stagehands see what's going on and began to cheer me on, laughing at the two security guys. I know I might catch a beating when they grab me, but I keep going. I cut back and forth, here and there, and elude them over and over, until finally they cut off my escape to the back of the theater. I head back toward the stage and dart up a little staircase, somewhere behind the scenes, when I run right into John Lennon. It's too late to pull up short and I slam into him, both of us tumbling to the ground.

"Bollocks," he says.

As we untangle ourselves, I see Paul standing over us, trying to lend John a hand. "What the hell, mate?" Paul says. "What's going on?"

The security guys catch up and grab me roughly by the arms as John gets closer and stares through his granny glasses. He looks at me carefully. "Where do I know you from?" he asks, much to my surprise.

"I'm just a fan, Mr. Lennon."

It never occurred to me that John would remember me from our encounter at the Ad Lib. Actually, he doesn't quite remember, but he knows we've crossed paths somewhere. "You're lying," he says to me, and then turns to Paul. "He's lying."

John keeps looking at me, trying to place me. I met Paul, as well, back in Brian Epstein's apartment, and he suddenly snaps his fingers and says, "You're the reporter we met at Eppy's house, God rest his soul."

"Yes, that's it! The guy with the crazy phone," John says.

"We're sorry, John," one of the security guards interrupts. "We caught him watching the goings-on up there in the balcony."

"Is that right?" Paul asks. "Well, how did ya like it, then? The song and all?"

"I *loved* it," Yoko says. She appears from somewhere backstage with Lily. The resemblance is uncanny.

"Crikey, you two could be twins," John says.

"Yeah, double the fun," Paul chimes in.

"But she's American and I'm British, so not exactly," Lily says. "You'll always be able to tell us apart."

"You're from the States?" John asks Yoko.

"Yes," Yoko answers. "We're both from New York, and we're big fans of yours."

Suddenly, Lily has a flash of recognition in her eyes as she looks me over. "I know you," Lily says. "We met at the Ad Lib a few years ago. Remember, John? This is the guy you were chasing around that night?"

"Yes, I remember," John says. "So where's your tiny phone-camera thing?"

Paul says, "Yeah, he's been going on about it ever since. Can you show it to me?"

"I don't have it," I lie.

"Search him, boys," John says to the security guards. "Christ, I always wanted to say that, just like an American copper: 'Search him, boys.'" John chuckles.

It takes the men all of five seconds to find not only my smartphone but my iPod, as well.

"There it is! That's it!" John says, taking if from the security guy and showing it to Paul.

"How does it work?" Paul asks.

I take the smartphone and tell John, Paul, Yoko, and Lily to stand together. "Yeah, like that. That's good." I snap the photo and take a look. "Let me get another. Hang on. Smile please."

They all take direction very well. I look at the photo. Not only are John and Paul in the shot but Yoko is there, standing next to the grandmother who died when she was four. Incredible!

"This one's a keeper," I say.

I show it off to them. John's seen how the camera works, but Paul and Lily are stunned.

"How'd ya do that?" Paul asks. "That's the smallest camera I've ever seen, smaller than the one in the Bond films. Are you a spy or something?"

"I asked him the same thing," John says proudly. "What's that other picture you took of you and me? What did you call it?"

"A selfie," Yoko says.

"Yeah, a selfie," John agrees. "Take one with Paul."

I hand the camera to Yoko. "Why don't you take it of you, Paul, and Lily, Yoko?"

John does a double take. "What did he call you?"

"Yoko," she says.

"Yoko?" John asks. "That's a bit of a coincidence. I've just met another bird named Yoko. Common Japanese name, is it?"

"Yes, I guess it is," Yoko says. "Although, I'm Chinese." She smiles at John, then looks to Paul and Lily. "Okay, let's all stand close together," she says, taking the photo and showing them.

"Bloody hell," Paul says. "How can it take photographs and develop them so fast? And so sharp? I've never seen anything like it."

They are gobsmacked and turn the smartphone over like little boys with a new toy, until Paul notices my iPod. "And what do you call this, then?" he asks. "Another type of camera?"

"I guess you might call it a music maker," I say.

"Officially, we call it an iPod," Yoko says. "It's like a portable record player, holds thousands of songs."

Now even the security guards perk up.

"Thousands of songs, you say? How does it work? Show me," Paul says.

Everyone is crowding around now. The security guys, the stagehands, even the other dancers. It feels like we are revealing too much all at once. I'm getting nervous about all the attention. I look at Paul and John. "Do you mind if we talk someplace else? Someplace quiet where we can show you."

John turns to Paul. "What d'ya think?"

"Sure, let's go to my place," Paul says. "You lot look harmless enough. I'm going to the theater later with Jane, but I've got a bit of time now."

"I've gotta run," she tells Yoko. "I'll give you my address in Knightsbridge. Come over for tea at four, okay?"

"I would love that," Yoko says.

Lily writes down her address on a piece of paper, air kisses Yoko on both cheeks, and runs off. When we step outside, a group of fans rushes toward us. John and Paul sign some autographs quickly, and then we all get into John's infamous Rolls-Royce, painted in psychedelic swirls and colors.

"We're off to Paul's," he tells the driver.

Yoko pinches my arm, and I know exactly what she's thinking. Here we are in the backseat with two of the greatest songwriters of the latter part of the twentieth century.

"Tell me about this iPad?" Paul says.

"No, it's an iPod," Yoko answers. "An iPad is different. You use that to write."

"They have these in New York?" Paul asks. "I've never seen one and I've been in New York lots of times."

"They claim to be from the future, Paul," John says.

"Really? Can you tell me what's for lunch tomorrow?" Paul jokes.

It's a short ride over to Paul's house across from the Abbey Road Studios. It's a modest house surrounded by a big black gate, not that it does much good. As soon as we open the gate and park the car inside, two women rush over, one blonde and one brunette. I'd forgotten what hippies look like, but now I remember. They're wearing pants with huge bell-bottoms, peasant blouses, and have flowers in their hair. Their eyes become saucerlike when they spot Paul and John. The rest of us might as well be invisible.

"Paul, Paul, I ironed your shirts," one of them says.

"That's nothing. Paul, I cleaned your house *and* prepared you a snack. I would have made you dinner, but you're going out, aren't you?"

"Thanks, love," Paul says, putting his arms around both of them. "Sorry, but I can't have you stay today because, as you can see, I have company. I'm afraid I need my key back now."

He puts out his hand. The blonde slips her key out of her pocket and passes it to him. Then, as though she can't hold herself back anymore, she hugs him tight and kisses him on the cheek.

"There, there, Molly. Thank you, thank you. You too, Victoria. Thank you."

"Paul, I almost forgot, there is this American bird who came by for you this afternoon."

"Oh, did you get a name, love?"

"Linda," she says. "Linda Eastman."

I smile to myself. Paul has no idea that Linda Eastman will become his future wife, his soul mate. He's rushing out tonight to meet his girlfriend Jane Asher, but that relationship won't last. Ah, the power of knowing the future.

"Oh, sorry I missed her," says Paul. "Did she say when she'd be back?"

"She said she'd try you tomorrow."

"Great, thanks, Molly. Goodbye now."

We go inside, and he locks the door behind us. "Friendly neighborhood," Yoko says.

"Paul lets all manner of birds inside his house. I tell him he's daft, but he won't listen," John says.

A sheepish-looking Paul goes through his mail. "No

matter what I do, they get in anyway, so I give 'em a key on the condition they not let any of the others in. Best security team I've ever had. They keep the rest away, that's for sure. Tough birds. So come on, then, tell me about this iPod."

He leads us into his living room. There are guitars all over the room. I switch the iPod on with both Beatles watching over my shoulder. Yoko is quiet, taking in the unbelievable scene playing out in front of her—me, John, Paul, and an iPod of all things.

"Here's a list of songs," I say, spinning through it very fast so they can't make out any names. A lot of these groups do not yet exist and nearly all were influenced by John and Paul.

"Do you have any Beatles music in there, mate?" Paul asks.

"Sure." I put on "There's a Place" and put an earbud in each man's hand. "Put these in your ears."

"What d'ya call these?" he asks.

"Earbuds."

I want to wow them, so I turn up the volume. No chance of them time-travelling since I'm not involved. I'm pretty sure the time travel is happening because of me *and* the iPod, not the iPod alone. And Dr. Robert did seem to know that something was up, so it's gotta be connected. It's the only explanation. Grandpa had it for years and never left New York.

"Christ," John says.

"This sounds better than the studio," Paul says. "How do you get this kind of quality, and where is the record? I've never seen anything like this. It's revolutionary. How can I get one of these? Did you invent it?"

"He didn't invent it," Yoko explains. "Where come from, most people have one of these lying around. They're cheap, less than a hundred dollars, and they're kind of passé, to tell you the truth. Most of us keep songs on these now." Yoko holds up her smartphone.

"Wait, that thing holds music, as well? And plays it?" Paul asks.

She takes a breath and smiles. She's enjoying this. "This camera is actually what we call a smartphone. It does a lot of things. It's a camera, sure, but we also use it for making phone calls, listening to music, and a bunch of other things."

Yoko shows him a list of Beatles songs and some Rolling Stones songs, as well. She hands each man one of her earbuds next and starts "Paint It Black."

"Bloody hell," Paul says.

"This is the strangest trip I've taken yet," John says.

"It's no acid trip," I say. "I told you. We're from the future."

"Oh that's right, you did say that," Paul says. "Okay I'll play along. What year in the future?"

"The year 2015," Yoko says.

"And you say everyone there has these?"

"Pretty much."

"You're a cheeky bird, aren't you?" John chimes in.

"Cheeky? No one's every called me that before, but maybe I am," she says. "Lenny, I'm dying for a Starbucks right now, aren't you? I'm beginning to miss the future."

"And what, pray tell, is a Starbucks?" John asks.

"It's a place to get coffee," she says. "But the first one won't open for another thirty years or so."

I laugh because I know Yoko is just having some fun with John. She's figured out that our best approach is to just tell the boys the truth because they consider it so outlandish they'd never truly believe us. "Don't mind her," I say. "She's kidding around."

"Well, we don't have any coffee, but we have tea,"

Paul says. He calls into the kitchen to have some prepared. Then, all of a sudden, he turns serious. "Give us the truth, mates. You say you're from the future, but that's impossible. You must be inventors. What do you want for one of these iPod things? I've gotta have one. These things are going to change the entire industry."

"Bollocks," John says. "Music is meant to be played loud, not in yer ears where you're the only one's gonna hear it. That's no fun."

"But just think— You say you can fit thousands of songs on this tiny thing? What a blast in a car trip or on a plane," Paul counters. "It works on a plane?"

"In a plane, in a car, wherever you like," Yoko says.

"I prefer records," John says. "You can't fit any liner notes or lyrics on this iPoop."

John loves word play, an earmark of many of his songs. Even in casual conversation, he can't help himself, which is endearing in a way. We all just let it go.

"Oh that's all available on the computer," Yoko says. "You just google it."

"Google, goggle," John jokes. "Goo goo g'joob."

"How much for your iPod? I'll buy it from you," Paul says. "Name your price."

"This one is special, I'm afraid," I say. "It's not for sale. Besides, it doesn't exist on its own. You need a computer, a way to download songs, the Internet, and a charger. It's running on a tiny battery right now, and it will be useless here in a day or so."

But Paul won't give up. "If there are thousands of songs on that thing, play us something from the future," he says. "Something we'll write in a few years."

"Oh God, I can't do that," I say.

"Oh, come on, then," Paul says. "Prove to us you're from the future."

"Isn't this enough?" Yoko asks, holding up the iPod.

I think for a second. "What if I play you a song from the future by some guys who were compared to you at one time. How about that?"

They both lean forward. I cue up the Electric Light Orchestra, whose lead singer, Jeff Lynne, later played with George Harrison in the Traveling Wilburys. Lynne had always been a fan of the Beatles and would, in fact, meet his idols the following year, in 1968. He famously said his aim was to pick up where the Beatles left off, and John later called ELO "the Sons of the Beatles." But none of that has happened yet.

I cue up "Mr. Blue Sky" and press "play" so the boys can hear.

"They're terrific," Paul says. "What did you say they are called?"

"The Electric Light Orchestra, better known as ELO."

When the song ends, a light goes on in Paul's eyes. "Hey, I have an idea. What say you take us to your future so we can see the new bands for ourselves?"

"I can't do that."

"Why not?" Paul asks. "I'm ready to go right now. I'll even cancel my plans with Jane for ya."

"No, I'm sorry, but we can't," I say.

Paul waves his hand in disgust. "I don't know how you got your hands on this music player, but I do know one thing: you are not from the future."

I don't know if I'm pleased or upset that he doesn't believe me. I shrug. "Suit yourself."

"Well give us some proof, then," Paul keeps on.

I am happy to have them not believe me, but Yoko seems to love a challenge. "What if we told you about a project you're working on that no one knows about yet?" she asks.

"Like what?"

"Well, you just released *Sgt. Pepper* last year, right?"

"Right."

"And *Magical Mystery Tour* has not been received too well, has it?"

"Yeah, but anyone who reads the papers knows that," John says.

"Tell you what, let me read your aura," she says to Paul, putting her hands around his head. Yoko is only putting on a show because she knows Paul and John believe in signs and auras and all that stuff. John may be a cynic, but he's a gullible cynic.

"You are thinking a lot about a fruit," she tells Paul.

"A fruit?" Paul laughs. So does John.

But she is just warming up. "It's an apple, and it's on both of your minds a lot lately."

"Well, yeah, it's the name of our new company, but anyone who reads the papers knows that, too, love," Paul says.

"Okay," Yoko says. "Then how about this, Paul? You've already got someone in mind to sign to the label, a woman with a great voice—Mary Hopkin, and there's a single you're thinking about called 'Those Were the Days.'"

Paul's eyes get wide.

"Am I close?" she asks.

Paul looks stunned. "John, there is no way they can know that. I haven't even told you about this bird I'm thinking of for the new label. I only heard her sing this past week."

John narrows his eyes. He heard me explain all this before at the Ad Lib, and I would bet anything he's reliving that conversation now in his mind.

"Last time we met, I remember you would not answer a question I had," John says.

"What question is that?" Paul asks.

"This Lenny fellow told me the band would break up. He said our music would survive, but he wouldn't tell me any more about what happened next. That's when you ran out of the Ad Lib," he says. "I'd been drinking, but now it's all come back to me. So I'm gonna ask you again: what happens to us after the band breaks up?"

Then I get an idea. I don't have to tell him everything. A little is more than enough. "Okay, okay." I take a deep breath. "The band breaks up, and you and Paul go your separate ways. You record as solo artists, as do George and Ringo," I say.

"And who sells the most records?" Paul asks.

"Well, actually," Yoko says, "Ringo has the most hits!"

"What?" Paul and John say together.

"Yeah, and George produces a three-record set," I say.

"The future sounds bleak," John jokes. "Three records of George material would make me kill myself."

We all laugh.

Paul is still examining the smartphone and the iPod, turning them over and probably thinking about what he can do with them. Yoko nudges me.

"We really have to get going," I say. "And I need to take those with us."

"You're not off to show your gadgets to the Stones, are ya?" Paul asks.

"No way."

"We're off to visit Lily in Knightsbridge," Yoko says, holding up the paper with her grandmother's address written on it. "There's so much I want to talk to her about."

"I need to get going, as well. I'll drop you at her apartment," John says. "I'm going to see an art thing by the other Yoko."

"Will you visit us again?" Paul asks.

"Sure, if you like," I say, trying to sound nonchalant.

"Next time you come back, bring me one of those iPod things."

"I'll try, Paul."

"Tell you what? I saw you eyeing me guitars."

"Well, that's because I'm left-handed like you," I say.

"Really? You, me, and Jimi, eh? Okay, here's the deal, I give you one of my guitars now, and in return, you bring me an iPod next time we meet. Which one do you fancy?"

I cannot believe what I'm hearing. Paul McCartney is going to give me one of his guitars! I'm almost ready to just give him the iPod right now. I take a look at the collection of about a dozen guitars jammed into his living room. I don't play bass, so they're out, and I'd prefer an acoustic to replace the one that was stolen.

"That one's nice," I say pointing to a vintage Taylor.

"Ah, good taste." He gets up, grabs it, and then hands it to me. "It's yours."

"Mine? But I can't give you *this* iPod."

"That's okay. You look like a trustworthy bloke. Bring me one next time."

I take the guitar. "Do you think you could sign it?"

"Sure." He flips the guitar over and signs the back in black ink. "There ya go. It's all yours. Signed, sealed, and delivered. We have a deal, then?"

I can barely speak so I just nod. I look at the guitar and hope to God I can get it back to 2015. "Thanks so much, Paul," I manage to get out.

"Come on. We need to get going," John says.

Then Yoko and I walk out to his Rolls-Royce.

◀◀ TWELVE ▶▶

John is quiet as we drive toward Lily's place in Knightsbridge. He stares out the window for a while, almost like he's forgotten we're along for the ride. Yoko has her head on my shoulder as I rub my hand over the guitar Paul gave me. This day could not have gone any better. I almost feel like it's my birthday, even though it's Yoko's. I don't know that I'll ever be able to repay Paul with an iPod, but I plan to try if I ever get back here again.

"That was so nice of Paul," Yoko says.

"Unbelievable." I lean over to whisper in her ear. "Can you imagine how much this is worth?"

"Yeah, but you'll never sell it."

"No effing way."

Out of nowhere, John asks, "Have you two ever heard of the artist Yoko Ono?"

Duh! But we can't say that. "No, I haven't," I say. "Is she any good?"

"Don't know," he says. "I saw this one show she had at a friend's gallery. It had something to do with bags. Not sure I got the significance, but she also had one piece there that was just an apple for sale, an ordinary apple, selling for two hundred quid, and I thought that was great. It's funny, you know. Two hundred quid to buy an ordinary apple and watch it decompose. D'ya get it?"

"That is funny," Yoko said.

"Let me ask you something darlin'," he says. "You fancy this Lenny guy?"

Yoko laughs. "Thanks for putting me on the spot. He's okay."

"Hear that, Lenny? Sounds like she's crazy for ya," John says. "Sounds like you might have yourself a girlfriend if you play your cards right."

"What about you John?" I ask, thinking it might be fun to turn the tables on him. "Fancy this artist named Yoko?"

"Lenny," he says in mock surprise, "I'm a married man."

"Yeah, I know."

"But she's okay," John goes on. "She makes me think, and God knows I need someone to make me think. Paul's been controlling my brain for years now."

He smiles like he wants me to know he doesn't mean it, not really. "Paul's a mate, but Yoko is okay, too. Who knows what the future will be, right, Lenny? You know that more than most. So tell me one more thing about the future, something juicy you think I should know."

I think about it, and I know Yoko is turning it over in her head, as well. "There's so much to tell, but I don't want to interfere. Just don't give up on Paul, no matter what happens."

"I told ya, Paul's a mate."

"Yeah, but there will be times you guys will fight. Just remember, he's your mate, no matter what."

"I can't imagine I'd ever think otherwise."

"Imagine," I repeat. "That's a great word, isn't it? Full of possibilities. Maybe even a song title."

"Yeah. Imagine," he says and writes it down in a little book.

The Rolls comes to a stop. "This is Knightsbridge," John says. "Lily's building is right there across the street with the awning out front."

"Thanks, John."

I shake his hand, and Yoko kisses his cheek. "Will I see you again?" he asks.

"God willing," I say.

. . .

As we walk to the front door of Lily Chang's house, Yoko waves her hand at the scene. "Best birthday ever!"

"Yeah?" I ask. "You're having a good time?"

"The best. A crazy good time."

"And it's not over yet," I say.

Lily lives in a third-floor walk-up in Knightsbridge. She greets us at the front door and pulls us inside. "I'm so happy you could make it," she says to Yoko. "You too, Lenny."

Her apartment is small but elegantly decorated with Chinese art. She's already prepared the tea, and she makes a point of telling us that her tea set is Chinese, not English.

"It's beautiful," Yoko says.

"So," she says, "are you are boyfriend and girlfriend?"

We look at each other. "Not really," I say. "More like very good friends."

"But that can change, yes?" Yoko adds with a wink.

I blush.

"And you came here to find the Beatles, like many other Americans?"

"That's true," I say.

"Did you have a nice time with John and Paul?"

"They were great. Look what Paul gave me," I say, showing off the guitar.

"He's so generous. Do you know how to play?"

"Yeah, want to hear something?"

"Absolutely."

"You up for singing along, Yoko?"

"Of course. Why don't you play something by the Beatles?" she says. "Maybe 'Blackbird'?"

"'Blackbird'?" Lily asks. "I don't think I know that one. Is it new?"

Uh-oh. Time-travel mistake. It was bound to happen. "Blackbird" is on *The White Album*, which hasn't come out yet. I don't know if they've even recorded it. "Oh yeah, it's new. Paul played it for us when I was over there. Here, I'll give you a preview."

The truth is "Blackbird" was one of the first songs I even played on guitar with Terry the shrink, so I know it pretty well. I play the beautiful melody and let Yoko do most of the singing. When we finish, Lily applauds enthusiastically.

"I love it. Paul writes such beautiful melodies," Lily says. "I can't tell you how happy I am to meet you, Yoko. I love meeting other Asian women. My parents came here when most of their friends went to America to build the railroad. For whatever reason, they thought they'd have more opportunities here and moved to Liverpool, so they could more easily import items from China. Then my father died and Mum got a job working for Mr. Epstein, who felt sorry for her. She was his personal assistant. That's how I met the Beatles.

Mum would never have let me hang around with them if not for Mr. Epstein."

"What do you do when you're not dancing with the Beatles?" Yoko asks.

"I'm a singer. I've been singing since I was a child, and then John heard me one day and he's been trying to help me. We've even worked out a few songs together. They're mainly my tunes, but John always has great ideas about how to improve them."

I know Yoko is dying to hear more.

"Have you recorded any?" she asks.

"Not yet. It's not so easy for an Asian woman to record her own album, you know." There is sadness in Lily's eyes when she says this, and Yoko and I both see it, but she shakes her head and changes the subject quickly. "We will see. So where are you staying in London?"

We look at each other. "Nowhere really," Yoko says. "We've been crashing here and there on couches."

"Oh, well, if that's the case, why not stay here tonight?" Lily says. "I have plenty of room. I have to go out soon, but you can make yourselves at home here . . . unless you want to come? Yes, you should come."

"Where?"

"Mick and Keith are having a party, and all sorts of stars are expected. It will be fun. Why don't you come along?"

"The Stones?" I ask.

"Yes, lots of beautiful people, and a grand time is guaranteed for all." She laughs.

"We'd love to go," Yoko says.

"Absolutely," I agree.

. . .

135

That night, we take a taxi to the British nightspot the Scotch of St. James, better known as the Scotch, where we are guests of Mr. Mick Jagger. I'm so paranoid about losing Paul's guitar that I've brought it with me to the club. I know, stupid move. Who brings a guitar to a noisy club where everyone is drinking? But my time here is finite. I have no idea when we're going to try to return, and I don't want to risk not having the guitar with me when we do. Lily even lends me a guitar case so it will be protected. She tries to get me to check it with the coat check girl, but I feel more secure hanging on to it.

The music is very loud, and the people, as promised, are beautiful. All the Stones are there and so are lots of other famous musicians—Pete Townsend, Keith Moon, and Roger Daltry of the Who, blues guitar legend Eric Clapton, and Eric Burdon of the Animals, just to name a few. I am on overload. Yoko keeps poking and pinching me to look at one rock star after another. She can hardly speak, either. A lot of kids our age might not even recognize these guys, but Yoko and I dig the classic rock scene and can name every one.

I don't think I can take much more when Ringo walks in, followed by his best girl, Maureen. George Harrison and his model girlfriend, Pattie Boyd, follow close behind.

I nudge Yoko, and Lily notices. "You want to meet George and Ringo? Come on, I'll introduce you."

I've already met both of them, but I don't say a word. Ringo is cool, but I'm a little worried about meeting George again, since the last time we saw each other I was kicking him in the shin back at the Ad Lib. I follow along behind Lily and Yoko and try to keep my head down, hoping he won't recognize me in the dark club.

"Hey, guys," says Lily. "These are my friends, Yoko

and Lenny. They're Americans."

They greet Yoko warmly, but then George takes a closer look at me. "Have we met?"

I open my mouth to answer, but Ringo jumps in. "You were the guy running around the Saville Theatre today. Looked like you made the security boys work a bit harder than usual."

"Right. It all worked out in the end, though," I say. "We met John, Paul, and Lily."

At that point—just as I think George might remember me from the Ad Lib when I kicked him—he's distracted by Keith Richards, who comes over to say hello. Keith notices me holding the guitar. "Whatcha got here, mate?" he asks.

"It's a Taylor. Gift from Mr. McCartney," I say proudly.

"You don't say? May I?"

"Sure." I remove the guitar from the case and hand it to Keith.

"Oh yeah, I've seen him play this. It's a good one. I'd show you some moves, but it's left-handed. Keep your eye on it in this place, mate."

"I will. Uh, would you mind adding your signature?"

"Sure, got a pen?"

"Yeah."

I'm about to ask George to sign it, too, but someone pulls him away. I guess I'll have to "settle" for one Beatle and one Rolling Stone. I still can't believe my good luck. I'm about to ask Ringo to sign when Maureen chirps, "Let's dance." She pulls Ringo onto the dance floor, and Lily grabs Yoko and motions for me to join. Before I do, I place my guitar in a spot where I can keep an eye on it, and then hit the dance floor. I find myself squeezed between Mick Jagger and his girlfriend, singer Marianne Faithfull, on one side and Ringo and

Maureen on the other. I couldn't make up a story like this if I tried. I think of that song, "I'm In With the In Crowd." Boy, am I ever!

We move through all the popular dances of the sixties until three a.m. when I nearly pass out from a combination of exhaustion and excitement.

I pull Yoko aside. "We should probably be getting back. At some point your parents are going to expect you home, right?"

"Okay, yeah. We'll leave soon."

Just then, Lily asks Yoko to go with her to the loo. "When you get back, we gotta bounce!" I shout over the music.

"You worry too much," Yoko says. Then she gives me a peck on the cheek before she walks off with Lily.

I suddenly realize I haven't eaten in forever, and I have no idea how long I've been up without sleeping. No wonder I'm so tired.

I look across the room for my guitar, but it's not there. I feel sick, desperate. This cannot be happening. I scan the room, and there, in a corner, is a black guy in a hat playing my guitar. I rush over to him. "Hey, man, that's my guitar."

He looks up at me. It's Jimi Hendrix, only one of the best guitarists on Earth. He gives me a big smile and plays a riff. "Hey, man, it's cool. I just needed to play. Listen to this." He plays an instrumental version of "The Wind Cries Mary" and finishes with a flourish. He hands me the guitar. "Nice."

"You're Jimi Hendrix."

"Yeah, that's right. What's your name?" He puts out his hand for me to shake.

I want to say, *I'm a dummy for not recognizing you right away,* but I settle for "Lenny."

"Nice to meet you, Lenny."

"Hey, Jimi, would you mind signing the back of my guitar?"

"Sure thing, man."

Jimi adds his signature to Paul's and Keith's. I am riding a wave of adrenaline and feel like I might float away. "Have a good night," Jimi says as he walks away.

The crowd is dwindling. Most of the celebs are already gone, but Mick, as host, is still there. He and Jimi exchange a few words before Jimi heads off into the night, followed closely by Mick. At that point, the house lights come on, and I am one of three people left in the club.

"Shove off, mate, time to close," a bouncer tells me.

"I'm just waiting for my girl. She's in the loo."

"No one back there, mate. Just checked, so move along like a good lad."

"What do you mean there's no one back there? She said she'd be right back."

"Yeah, well, wish I had a quid for the number of times I heard some poor bloke say that to me. Run along now, Yank, will ya?"

I walk toward the exit, but then make a break for the small hall where the bathrooms are. I push into the ladies' room and yell for Yoko. The bouncer is right behind me, but I have time to see some writing on the mirror in lipstick.

Sorry, Lenny, I need to stay. Please come back for me. XO Yoko

A moment later, the bouncer is on me. "Come on now, friend. We don't want any trouble now, do we?"

He puts one hand on the back of my shirt collar and the other on the back of my pants and rushes me right out of the club. I make sure to protect my guitar as the door slams behind me. I look around, but the street is deserted. Everyone is gone, including Yoko. I can't believe it, but it makes perfect sense. Her grandmother died when she was four years old. The chance to hang out with her, talk to her, be with her, was too much of a temptation. I just never saw it coming. Stupid, stupid, stupid.

Out on the street, in the cool summer air, I consider my options. There's only one thing to do. I drag myself back to Lily's apartment in Knightsbridge and bang on her apartment door, but there's no answer. Clearly Yoko's mind is made up. I slump down inside the building's front door to catch them when they come in. I wait there an hour, then ninety minutes, but there's no sign of them. It's nearly dawn. They probably stayed at someone else's place. My only real play is to head back to 2015 and figure out what to do next.

I spot a park bench across the street, pull out my iPod, and cue up some Taylor Swift. Then I wrap my arms around Paul's guitar and pray I can bring it along for the ride.

◄◄ THIRTEEN ►►

I wake up and look at the ceiling. I'm back in my bedroom. I never know where I'm going to be when I get back. I chuckle. Time travel is so inconsistent! But I do know from the surroundings that it's 2015 again. Normally, I hate to stay in bed once I'm awake, but today I pull the covers over my head. I don't want to face the world or think about what might be happening with Yoko back in London. How exactly is this going to play out? What will her parents say? And can I get her back? Damn, my mind is muddled. It seems impossible that Yoko has run out on me to live out her life in some parallel universe in London circa 1967. At least for now. She did ask for me to come back for her.

Even though I know she's back there, I text, call, and e-mail her just in case. No response. I force myself out of bed and spot the guitar case on the floor of my room. Paul McCartney's guitar! It made it!

I open the case and lift out the guitar gingerly. It looks no worse for wear. I flip it over and see the autographs and can't help but smile. I think of the Grateful Dead lyric, "what a long strange trip it's been" and think that truer words were never written. I strum a few chords, forgetting all about where I am and what I'm doing. When I look up, the door to my bedroom is open and the Joes are staring at me.

"Where did you get that guitar?" Grandpa asks.

Where *did* I get this guitar?

"My friend Marlon."

"Well, come on. Join us for breakfast," Joe says.

Joe happens to be a great cook and has baked some special muffins that he serves with blueberry jam—homemade—and hot coffee, which I sorely need.

"Any plans for today?" Grandpa asks. "We were thinking maybe you'd want to come with us to see the latest Travolta movie later tonight."

"Um, not tonight, thanks. I thought I'd practice some new songs."

"You sure? He's supposed to be back in fine form with this one," Grandpa says.

"Yeah, I read something about it, but I hope you don't mind if I pass."

"Still enjoying the iPod?" asks Grandpa.

"Great songs," I say. "That's why I want to practice. There's a bunch on there I barely know."

"Great, I'm glad it comes in handy. How's the sound?"

I think of McCartney remarking on how it sounded so much better than the speakers at Abbey Road Studios. "Perfect, actually," I say.

If only they knew how perfect.

"How's the head feeling?" Joe asks.

"Uh, it's fine. I just need this coffee."

"Does your mother know how much of that stuff you drink?" Grandpa asks.

"Oh yeah. She got me hooked when I was twelve."

Grandpa smiles. He and Joe putter around the apartment for another couple of hours before they're out the door. They tell me they're going to some friend's apartment before heading to the movie.

"That's cool," I tell them. "Have fun."

And then I blissfully have the house all to myself.

I go to the computer and look up every article I can find about time travel, thinking about what to do next now that Yoko is still back in 1967. There's a lot to read and I spend hours surfing many different theories. Scientists are split—some think it's possible, some don't. No one knows how to do it, despite many attempts to build time machines. I am just starting to read about how the brain controls memory when the doorbell rings. I check the time on the computer screen; it's now nearly four o'clock. I figure it's some kind of package delivery, but when I open the door, two beefy men—one black, one white—are staring at me.

The white guy is holding up a badge. "Are you Lenny Funk?"

"Yes?"

"I'm Detective Morelli, and this is Detective Moore. Mind if we come in and ask you a few questions?"

"Is this about my guitar? Did you find it?"

They look at each other. "We don't know anything about a guitar. Let's talk inside," he says.

If it's not about the guitar, I wonder if they caught Giant Annoying and want me to identify him. I swing open the door.

Just then, I see a neighbor walk by, a good friend of the Joes. "Everything all right, Lenny?" he asks.

Detective Moore whips around. "Who are you?"

"I'm a neighbor, and I know this boy."

"Keep walking. This is police business."

"Okay but . . ." says the neighbor.

"Didn't you hear what the man said?" asks Detective Morelli.

I'm beginning to get nervous. These guys are serious. If they aren't here about the fight, I wonder what it is they want. I can't think of any other reason they'd want to talk to me.

"You wanna call his grandfather, go ahead, but we're done talking to you," Morelli tells the neighbor. Morelli seems to be the alpha cop and has a much more threatening air to him than Detective Moore.

Morelli turns back to me. "So can we come in?"

"Uh, sure," I say. It seems the only response anyway.

I close the door as the neighbor hurries down the hall. I wonder if he'll call the Joes. I walk the detectives into the kitchen, and we all sit around the table. I don't offer them anything to drink.

"Nice place," says Moore.

"Thanks. So what's this about?"

"You know a girl by the name of Yoko Peng?" he asks, looking down at his notebook.

My heart sinks. "Yes, she's a friend of mine."

"Girlfriend?" he asks.

"I don't think she would say that," I answer.

"Do you know where she is?"

Yeah, in London a few decades back, I want to say.

"No, I don't," I say. My voice squeaks a bit, and I know enough from television that I have just revealed a tell that announces to the detectives that I am lying. Stupid, stupid.

"Her parents say you were with her last night celebrating her birthday," Moore says. "They say you are the last person they saw her with, and she didn't come home. We told them it's a little early to worry about her—she's a teenager, after all—but her father has some juice. Seems he's one of our lawyers. The captain asked us to check it out and that road leads to you. I'm sure there's a logical explanation for where she is, so save us all a lot of trouble and just tell us."

"I don't know where she is," I say, and technically, that is true. I have no idea what Yoko is doing at the moment.

"When's the last time you saw her?" Morelli asks.

I'm a terrible liar. I think back to all the police shows I've seen. I hear some character saying, *Stick to the truth, because it's hard to remember a lie.* That's what I decide to do . . . mostly. There is no way I can tell them the whole truth.

"It was about two a.m. We were out kinda late. I walked her to her door and that's the last I saw of her," I say.

Moore is writing down what I said, but Morelli never takes his eyes off me. His stare is more than a little unsettling.

"Lenny," he says, "do you have any idea how many times boyfriends and husbands tell me a variation of that exact same story?"

"No, I don't."

"And you know what else?"

I shake my head. "What?"

"It's always bullshit," he says evenly. He seems to be raging inside, but his voice is so calm that it scares the shit out of me. "Never once has someone told me that story and it turn out to be true. Not once. You know what that means?"

"No."

"It means—" he pauses for effect, I can tell. He wants to make me nervous, and he's doing a good job "—that odds are you're lying, too, because what are the odds that you'll be the very first person to have that story turn out to be true?"

"I-I-I don't know," I stammer. God, I hate how weak I sound.

He smiles. "Why are you stuttering? You guilty of something?"

"No."

"Well, the girl's parents are upset. Who wouldn't be? Yoko's only seventeen years old. Her mother is crying just a few blocks from here. Her father is wearing out a path in his rug pacing back and forth. Just tell us where she is, okay? If she's with a boyfriend or girlfriend or whatever, it's better her parents know. This way they can stop worrying, you understand that, don't ya?"

"Yes, I understand, but there's nothing else I can tell you. I really don't know where she is." My voice breaks again. Ugh.

"Well, she never made it home, so you better hope she surfaces," Moore says. "Look, you strike me as a good kid. You're not a criminal. Think about how worried your parents would be. If this girl doesn't surface in a couple of days, you're going to be our prime suspect."

What?! "You've got this all wrong. I'm telling you, I would never hurt Yoko in a million years."

"Mind if we take a look around?" Morelli asks.

"Sure, look anywhere you want. I've got nothing to hide."

"Attaboy."

They go off on their search, but I don't care because I know there is nothing to find. I follow a few steps behind them.

"This your room?" Morelli asks, standing in the doorway of the guest room.

"Yes."

They look through my room, and they're just about to leave when Morelli picks up my guitar. "Nice, I used to play," he says, strumming it once. "Oh, you're left-handed. The strings are reversed. Too bad. Maybe I would have played you something. It's a nice guitar."

He turns it over, looks over the signatures, and whistles. "Whoa, these are some big names. McCartney, Richards, and Hendrix. Are they real?"

"Yeah, they are."

"Where did you get this? It must be worth a fortune."

Shit. I never thought he'd ask about the guitar. I can't tell him the truth, and I'm sure my hesitation makes it seem like I'm hiding something—again.

"From a friend."

"Nice friend. What's his name?"

"Is this important?" I ask.

"Just making conversation," Morelli says. He puts the guitar on my bed and takes a photo of it with his iPhone.

"Why are you taking a photo?"

He smiles at me. "Why not? I don't see one of these everyday."

The rest of the search is uneventful and they're finally about to leave for real. "We're going now, but I hope for your sake that this Yoko chick shows up," Morelli says. "If she doesn't turn up and Yoko's parents file a formal missing persons report, we're going to have to put it out to the media to ask for the public's help. Once we do that, they're going to start asking questions about the last person to see her. And guess whose name is going to come up? The *Post* and *Daily News* are gonna be camped outside your front door twenty-four seven."

He turns and walks away. Detective Moore gives me his card. "If you think of anything, call. We know you're lying about something. You seem like a nice kid. Do the right thing. Don't try to protect her if she's run off with someone. Don't try to be cute, don't try to protect her. Just tell the truth."

Except how exactly am I going to make the truth sound reasonable?

They leave, and a second later, my cell phone rings. I look down in the unlikely event it's Yoko but, just as I've feared, it's Joe.

"Hi, Joe."

"Lenny, what's going on there? Mr. Felling just called and says two police detectives are questioning you?"

"Yes, they're looking for Yoko. I think she may have run away."

"What?"

"I don't know where she is. I saw her last night, but I left her at her house. Her parents might file a missing persons report, but right now the cops are just asking questions. I'm the last one who was with her, though."

"Is that true?"

"I guess so, but I left her at her front door." What else can I do? I have to keep my story straight now. I'm stuck with it.

"And you told them that?"

"Yes, but they asked to search the house and I let them."

"Did they find anything?"

"No, because there's nothing to find."

"Of course," Joe says. "I know that, but did they take anything? Anything at all?"

"No."

"Okay, good. Did you get their names?"

"Yes, one of them gave me a card."

"Tell me the contact information."

"Do not talk to them again," Joe says once I've given him the info. "You are a minor and they shouldn't have spoken to you without an adult there. I'm going to call a lawyer, but do not talk to them or let them in again, do you understand?"

"Yes, absolutely, but . . ."

"What else?"

"They say once Yoko's parents file a missing persons report, the press will get my name and be waiting outside our front door."

"Shit. The press?" He pauses. "Yoko's parents haven't filed a report yet?"

"Not according to the detectives."

"They're probably bluffing," Joe says. "You're a minor, and they probably wouldn't release your name officially, but they can leak it for sure. And they will because, from their point of view, you're suspicious because you were the last one to see her. The press will eat that up. Lenny, you're not covering for her, are you? Do you know where she is and protecting her out of some false sense of loyalty?"

"No, Joe. I swear I'm not."

I feel horrible. I have to go and bring her back. I have to. "Okay, okay. Lie low and don't answer the door or talk to anyone. Got it?"

"Got it."

"Okay, I'll get Joe and we'll be back soon."

I get dressed quickly and fly out of the house. I figure the best way to avoid answering questions from cops or reporters is to not be home in the first place. I take as much money as I have and get out of there. Where I'm going I have no idea, but I make sure I have the iPod and a charger.

As I walk up the block, a guy steps out from between the parked cars to block my path. I freeze. I've never been mugged, but this feels like it just might be it. Every nerve in my body is telling me to run, but the guy takes me by surprise. He grabs my shirt and shakes me.

"Where is she?"

"Who?" I ask.

"You know who."

"No, I don't."

But when I notice all the product in his hair and hear his Russian accent, I realize I do know who he is: Dmitri, Yoko's ex-boyfriend.

"She broke up with me because of you. She showed me your picture on Facebook and told me you were her new friend and was talking about you all the time. I knew you were trouble."

"I'm not trouble."

Dmitri pins me against a tree and wraps his other hand around my neck. "You think you're smart? I'm gonna show you where smart gets you. Tell me what you did to her. I just went to her house and her mother said she was out with you last night. So where is she?"

"I don't know."

He punches me in the stomach, and I double over. That really hurt, and I feel like I might throw up.

"Well?"

"I don't know! I left her outside her house last night."

"Her parents told me she never came home. They called me for help, and I'm going to help them. Now where is she?"

"I don't know," I say again.

He punches me in the stomach again, too, and my gut starts to cramp.

"Give me the iPod," he demands.

"What iPod?"

Another punch. "I'm not a fool. She told me she likes your iPod because it has good music. I'm going to copy it and make my own iPod just like this, and then I'm going to give it to her as a present. You will be, how you say, history. Now give it to me."

It's not a terrible plan, but I can't give him the iPod. It's too important. How will I find Yoko if I give it up? "There's no iPod, just my phone. Here!"

I give him my smartphone. The iPod is in my back

GET BACK: imagine...saving John Lennon

pocket and so small I'm hoping he won't find it.

"Yoko said it was an iPod."

"She was wrong. I keep all my music on my phone. See for yourself."

He takes the phone and punches me again, even harder this time.

"This isn't it. I know what you're doing. I'm going to say this one more time: give me the iPod."

"There is no iPod," I say through gritted teeth. I can barely talk.

Dmitri puts his hands in my pockets and finds it for himself. "Ha, no iPod, huh?"

He gives me another punch, and this time I do throw up. All over his Nikes.

Some guy walking his Rottweiler sees what's going on. "Everyone all right over there?"

"Yeah," says Dmitri. "Everything is just fine."

"I'm calling the police," the dog walker says.

But then he does something even better. He lets go of his dog's leash. The Rottweiler chases Dmitri up the block. But Dmitri is pretty fast and strong. I see him get into a waiting cab and they speed off.

Shit.

Donovan Day

◀◀ **FOURTEEN** ▶▶

I assure the dog walker that I'm all right and then begin walking the streets aimlessly. I'm not all right. Far from it. I'm screwed and so is Yoko. Without that iPod, she's gonna be stuck in the past forever. And what about her parents? If she disappears, they'll be heartbroken. What was a great night has turned into a nightmare. Yoko's capricious decision not to come back with me is having big consequences in the present. I wonder if I can track Dmitri down and get that iPod back. It's the only way.

But before I do anything, I think about calling my mother. She always has good advice, but explaining everything to her means having to explain that I've been lying to her and the Joes for the past week. She'll be upset, and what are the odds that she'll even believe me? I wouldn't believe me. Everyone will assume the concussion did some serious damage to my brain. I have no proof of what I'm saying. But what about the guitar? Isn't that proof? Those signatures. *No, Lenny,* my inner voice says, *"that proves nothing except that maybe you stole the guitar from a memorabilia dealer somewhere.*

Ugh. I can't think straight.

I am getting a serious headache and that makes me think of Dr. Robert. He said I should call him if I wanted to talk. I decide to walk to his office and, in an hour, I am in his waiting room.

"Do you have an appointment?" the receptionist asks.

"No, but I think he'll see me."

"Well, he's very busy today."

I look around. There are all of two people in his waiting room.

"Can you please just let him know I'm here? I'll wait," I tell her.

She looks dubious but does what I ask. Within minutes, she gives me a snooty look. "Go right in."

I can feel the hate coming off the two patients who've been waiting, but I push my way through the outer door. Dr. Robert is standing there waiting for me.

"Lenny, what's up? Are the headaches back?"

"Can we talk somewhere private?" I ask.

"Of course," he says, ushering me into the office where I looked at the scans of my brain.

"The last time I was here you told me you just want some truth, remember?" I ask.

"Of course."

"What I'm going to say is going to sound very strange, but I swear it's the truth."

"Okay, wait a moment. I have a feeling this is going to take some time, am I right?"

"Yes. For starters, my girlfriend, Yoko, has disappeared, and the police are looking at me like I'm the prime suspect. I know where she is, but . . . well, it's going to take some time to tell you everything."

"Whoa, whoa, whoa. I need to see these two folks, and then I'll be free. You can wait in here, okay?"

"Sure."

154

The last two patients take about an hour, but then he rejoins me. "Okay, Lenny, I'm all yours. What's going on?"

I tell him everything, all about the time travel and Jim Morrison and Daisy and James Taylor and, finally, all about the Beatles and Lily Chang and how Yoko decided to stay back in the past. He asks a lot of questions about Lily and Yoko, in particular. When I'm finished explaining everything, Dr. Robert gets up and looks out the window for a long time. Then he turns around and smiles. "Lenny, this might sound strange, but I believe everything you just told me. I always suspected time travel was possible. To tell you the truth, it's why I study the brain."

"The first time you examined me, you asked if anything strange was happening or if I was having unusual dreams," I say. "You saw something in that MRI."

"Exactly. I told you, the portion of your brain that seems unusually large has to do with memory," he says. "People have been writing about slipping back in time for decades, and I've always suspected it had something to do with a birth defect or an injury they received to their brains."

"And you think something happened to my brain when I got into the fight?" I say. "It changed somehow? That's when all this began."

"Yes."

"When you say people have been slipping back in time for decades, what are you talking about?"

Dr. Robert pulls a book off his shelf. "I first read about it in this scientific journal published the UK in the 1970s. Maybe it's just a coincidence, who knows for sure, but the preeminent example of this whole phenomenon happens to have occurred in Liverpool, where, as you know, all four Beatles were raised."

"No way."

"It's true. There is a shopping area there called Bold Street where, over the years, people claim they have time-slipped backward. One minute they are walking on Bold Street in the current day, and the next they are back on the Bold Street of the 1950s. Some of them, upon their return, are able to give detailed and accurate descriptions of stores that have been shuttered for decades. There are other instances of this, as well. There are people alive today who remember events differently than anyone else, almost as if they lived part time in an alternate universe. I can give you the perfect example. That story you just told me about you and Daisy saving Jim Morrison's life? Well, I don't have any memory of Morrison dying when he was twenty-seven," the doctor says. "In my world, he's been alive for decades."

I get a chill when he says this. "This is spooky, Doctor."

He shakes his head. "Not spooky, just biology. Memories seem to lie on top of one another in the brain so, for me and for most people, the memory of Morrison being alive is on top of whatever memories we had of him dying. You changed the past and our collective memories at the same time."

I nod, following him carefully.

"But once in a while, because of brain chemistry changes within an individual, the memories that are underneath come to the surface. We call those remnant memories. They are disconcerting because remnant memories don't correspond to what's generally accepted by others in society. It's very common among Alzheimer's patients—their brain chemistry shifts their memories and they recall things no one else does.

Whether those remnant memories are real is what's unclear. Maybe someone just like you—someone with the ability to time-travel—changed something that happened in an earlier time. There are cases I've read about where people recall the Titanic arriving successfully in New York harbor, people who can't seem to recall it sinking. Did someone like you go back in time and change that reality so that now all we remember is the Titanic sinking? It's a possibility."

"Wow, and you think it all has to do with me hitting my head on that subway beam?" I ask.

"Yes, of course. I've examined some of the brain scans of those Liverpool folks from Bold Street, and those scans look very much like yours, Lenny, except your memory area is much bigger. I had a feeling you might be time-slipping. That's why I believe you."

"But if it's all in my brain, what about the iPod? And why can I bring people back in time with me?"

The doctor smiled. "You're a bright kid, Lenny. Without realizing it, you've figured out a way to control that section of your brain. By listening to a specific song related to a specific time period in history, you can steer your brain to that specific moment in the past when the song was relevant. It's just a theory—"

I interrupt him. "No, it's not a theory. That's exactly what I was doing. I figured it out on my own. I think I understand what you're saying, but even so, how did I manage to take Daisy and Yoko back with me?"

"I think you know the answer, don't you?"

"Well, we held hands . . ."

"Exactly. Basically, they came along for the ride."

"Wow."

"Wow, indeed. What's really incredible is that you've come up with all this on your own and in a very precise way. You're quite a kid, Lenny. I'm lucky your grandfather introduced us. I've been looking for someone like you for years."

"If you're right, then I don't need the iPod to go back," I realize aloud.

"I think you're wrong there," he says.

"You do?"

"Yes. On its own, the iPod is nothing more than what it's always been, a music delivery device. Your grandfather had it for years and he never time-slipped. It's true that the magic is in your brain, Lenny, but what's great about the iPod is that it's portable. You could probably sit in a room and listen to 'Hello, Goodbye' on a record player and achieve the same result, but how would you get back to the present? You'd have to find a record player and play a modern song, and that would get messy, wouldn't it? You'd have to carry a record from 2015 along with you. It's just not as practical as an iPod, so the iPod is important, or at least I think it is."

"So what should I do? I need to find Yoko and bring her back."

"I think you need to do what she asked you to do. Go back for her."

I snap my fingers. "You make it sound so easy, like ordering pizza."

"Well, in a sense, it is easy for you, given what you've told me. It's impossible for the rest of us, but you have a gift. Use it."

He's right, and I know it. "I'm going to do it."

"I do have one other thought."

"Yeah?"

"Take me with you," he says.

"Really?"

"Absolutely. I could help you navigate London, a city I know well. But to be honest, my request is selfish, too. I doubt I'll ever meet anyone like you again. This is a once-in-a-lifetime chance. When I was a young man in London, I met John and Yoko, hung around with them. It was different then, easier to meet celebrities, and I was their age. I studied auras and colors, New Age treatments, and they ate it up, especially Yoko. I was kind of like their medicine man. I'd love to revisit that time, knowing what I know now. It would be completely different. And the chance to time-travel? Lenny, you have no idea how much it would mean to me to relive my past in a sense."

"Did you go to medical school in England?"

He smiles. "No, I had a great life over there, but family pressure got to me and I traveled back to the States to attend a traditional medical school. But I miss those days quite a lot."

Just then, my phone rings. It's Joe. "I need to take this," I tell Dr. Robert, and he nods.

"Lenny, where are you?" Joe asks.

"I'm with Dr. Robert."

"Why are you there? Did your headaches come back?"

"No, nothing like that. He asked me to call him if I had any weird dreams so I did."

I'm beginning to tell lies to everyone, and it's making me sick to my stomach.

"Those detectives were here again," Joe said.

That's the last thing I want to hear. "What did they want?"

"Yoko hasn't come back, and her parents are going to file a missing persons report," he says. "Have you heard from her?"

"Not a word."

"Lenny, there's another problem," Joe says.

I can tell by the tone of his voice that something serious has come up. "What is it? What's the matter?"

"That new guitar you brought home . . ."

"Yeah? It's not new, but go ahead."

"The cops took a photo, and then showed it to Yoko's parents. The cops had noticed that memorabilia room in their house."

"All that stuff belonged to her grandmother. I told you about that."

"Yeah, and Yoko's mother said you two spent a lot of time in that room. That's the last place she actually saw you and Yoko. Now Yoko is gone and you have that guitar, which the police say is a priceless piece of rock memorabilia. You told us that Marlon gave it to you, but clearly that's a lie. So what's the truth Lenny?"

"I can't say."

"You can't or you won't?" Joe asks.

"I can't."

"Well, you better think of something, kid, because the cops think you stole it from that room over at Yoko's house."

"But that's not true!"

"That may be, but their theory is that you stole it. Where else would a kid like you get the money for something like that? It's worth a lot, Lenny. And you needed a new guitar. Everyone knows that, even the cops, because you reported yours stolen. They think you took this one, Yoko got upset, and you two had a fight. You want me to say the rest?"

I was shaking with anger. "They think I did something to Yoko over a stupid guitar?"

"Yes, they think you may have killed her, even if it was an accident."

"That's crazy! She hasn't even been gone for more than a day!"

"It is crazy, Lenny. We know you, and we know you would never do anything like that, but they don't, and to them, the pieces are all fitting together."

"This is insane. Paul McCartney gave me that guitar, and then Keith Richards and Jimi Hendrix signed it."

"Lenny, now you *sound* insane. Your grandpa and I got you a lawyer, one of the best. You should come home and talk to him with us."

"I don't need a lawyer," I say.

"Yes, you do. The police want you to go in for more questioning. The lawyer will protect you. No way are we going to let you talk to the police again without him."

"I cannot believe this," I say. "I would never, ever hurt Yoko."

"Lenny, you've got to tell the truth here," Joe says in his serious voice. "If you know anything, if Yoko has gone off with a boyfriend, you've got to tell us."

Just then, I have a flash of pure genius. "There is one thing, Joe. Tell the cops to ask her parents about her ex-boyfriend, a Russian guy named Dmitri. She just broke up with him, and he came to see me today and was really angry. He beat me up and took Grandpa's iPod. I'd like to get it back."

"Wait a minute, I'm writing all this down," he says. "When exactly did he attack you?"

"After the cops came to visit. When I left the house this morning, Dmitri was waiting for me and punched me in the stomach a few times. You know that guy with the Rottweiler on your block? He saw the whole thing. I have a witness. The cops should look at a guy named Dmitri Romanov. Yoko told me she just broke up with him."

"Are you hurt?"

"No." I laugh. "I actually threw up on his sneakers

after he punched me one too many times, so I kind of got my revenge."

Dr. Robert is listening intently. I know Dmitri had nothing to do with Yoko's disappearance, but he is violent and angry and he did steal my iPod. This will force the cops to chase someone else and give me a little more time to bring Yoko back.

"Do you know where this Dmitri guy lives?"

"No, just somewhere in Brooklyn. That's what Yoko told me," I say. "But maybe her parents know his phone number."

"Okay, I'll call them. Are you coming home now?"

"Yes," I lie.

"Don't talk to anyone on the way."

I hang up and look at Dr. Robert.

"What the hell is going on?" he asks.

I tell him the police theory about the guitar. "Jesus, for a teenager, you live one complicated life," he says.

"Tell me about it. Okay, doc, I want you to come with me, and I guess it's now or never. I can't let them lock me up."

"They have zero proof," he says.

"I know, but it's better that I just bring Yoko back. Better for her parents and everyone else, most of all me."

"You want to go back now?" Dr. Robert asks. "But how will we get back without the iPod?"

"I don't need the iPod. I have another idea." Thank God it came to me in time.

"What is it?" he asks.

"iTunes."

"iTunes?"

"Yes, it will take the place of the iPod. Who needs a record player?"

"God, I am so old-fashioned," Dr. Robert says. "You

are right, of course. Is your phone completely charged?"

"Yes. Are you ready?"

"Lenny, I've been ready for years."

I look at him and then at what I'm wearing. Neither of us are wearing twenty-first century sneakers, which would be a major tip-off, but the rest of our clothes seem passable. "Our clothes, what do you think? Will we stand out?"

He laughs. "In the London of the sixties? Anything goes . . . or went." He smiles. "We'll be fine."

"Okay. Let's do this."

I give Dr. Robert one earbud, and I take the other. "Hold my hands and concentrate on the London you knew, back when 'Hello, Goodbye' was a big hit."

Donovan Day

◀◀ FIFTEEN ▶▶

This trip, like the ones before, seems effortless. I'm not aware of any big physical change, but like all the other times, I know instantly something is different in the atmosphere around me. I'm sitting in a leafy park under the cool shade of large maple trees, and I hear soft British accents floating all around me. As always, I take a minute or two to acclimate myself. Dr. Robert, if he has made the trip, is nowhere in sight. I stand and stretch my arms over my head.

I look around and note that I'm in a neighborhood park surrounded by rows of well-kept houses. It looks a bit like Knightsbridge where Lily Chang lives, but for all I know, every residential neighborhood in the city looks this way. I walk the periphery of the park, keeping that bench in sight in case Dr. Robert is around. That's when I spot him, looking in the front window of a dress shop.

I call out to him, and he smiles and waves me over. "Listen," he says.

The Beatles song "Hello, Goodbye" is playing on a radio inside the shop. "That's why we wound up here?"

I say.

"It seems so." He throws his hands up. "It's all a guess really, and at this point, I don't really care, because it worked, Lenny. It worked! We're in Swinging London in the 1960s. Extraordinary."

"We should check the date to see exactly where we wound up," I say.

"I already checked in today's *Times*. It's December 7, 1967."

"Does that date mean anything to you?"

"Not to me, but to the Beatles it does," Dr. Robert says. "The newspaper has a story about the Beatles' Apple Boutique. It opens today."

"What's the Apple Boutique?"

"It's a store the Beatles opened when they started Apple Records. They were getting killed by taxes, and someone convinced them to open a store. So that's what they did."

"I never heard of it," I say.

"That's because it didn't last long. It was a crazy idea. The Beatles had no clue how to run a retail shop, and it was a giant money loser. In the end, they let the fans take anything they wanted for free."

"And today is the opening?"

"Yes."

"We have to go," I say. "We can try Lily's apartment later, but something tells me Yoko will want to go to this. She loves clothes."

"Yes! Good idea, Lenny. It's only a few blocks away, which may be another reason the time gods dropped us here. Amazing how this whole thing works."

"I'm still trying to figure the whole thing out. When I was home this morning, I looked up the date they made the film *Hello, Goodbye*. It was in early November of 1967, so that means Yoko has been here for about a month."

Dr. Robert thinks about it. "But from your point of view, she's been here less than twenty-four hours?"

"Right."

He pulls out a little notebook and writes something down. "I'm taking notes on everything. It would be nice to understand all this a bit better."

"You're telling me."

True to his word, Dr. Robert does know his way around London, and within fifteen minutes we are on the corner of Baker and Paddington Streets where a huge crowd is assembled, all jostling to be among the first to buy the Beatles' idea of fashionable psychedelic clothing. The crowd has spilled into the streets, and the bobbies are struggling to control traffic. It looks very much like a scene out of *A Hard Day's Night* and the crowd is, as usual, heavily female. We have zero chance of getting in the front door.

"Now what?" the doctor asks. "Got any ideas?"

"Yeah, I do," I say. "The same thing happened in Paris. We couldn't get in the front, but we got in through the kitchen."

"This place doesn't have a kitchen."

"No," I say, "but it's sure to have an employee entrance. Follow me."

I lead the doctor down an alley where, sure enough, there is an employee entrance. Dr. Robert and I take advantage of the chaos and barge ahead as though we belong. He especially has an air of authority and uses it well. In a few moments, we are inside where the crowds are just as bad.

"See anyone you know?" Dr. Robert asks.

"Not yet."

"Keep looking."

It's hopeless. There are women everywhere, and

it's hard to pick a particular face out of the hundreds crowding together. I would bet money that Yoko is in here with Lily, but I need to find them. I do have one idea. Without saying a word, I stand on a chair, climb onto a counter, and yell, "Ladies, ladies! We need to form a line. Everyone please queue up on the right to pay the cashiers."

The crowd looks at me and then does exactly what I say.

"If Yoko is here," I say, "she just spotted me. At least that's what I'm hoping."

A moment later, someone shouts out my name. "Lenny! Lenny! Over here!"

I see Yoko standing on a counter across the store. "Stay put," I shout. "We'll be right there."

I have to fight my way across the store, but in five minutes, I'm hugging Yoko. "You came back for me," she whispers into my ear. "Thank you, Lenny."

"You scared the shit out of me."

"I'm sorry. I had to stay," she says. "I couldn't run out on my grandmother only hours after meeting her for the first time. I hope you understand."

"I do. Is she here?"

Yoko waves her arm. "Somewhere around here," she says.

I suddenly remember Dr. Robert is standing next to us. "Yoko, I want you to meet Dr. Robert. He's the neurologist who examined me. I thought it was a good idea for him to join me this trip."

"Hi, Yoko. I've heard a lot about what you and Lenny have been up to, and honestly, I am very jealous."

"Dr. Robert studies time-slipping, as he calls it. He's an expert," I say.

"It's nice to meet you. Oh, look, there's Grandma."

Dr. Robert laughs when he sees Lily Chang, who is

only a few years older than Yoko. "Grandma? Wow. I'd forgotten how pretty Lily was, and she does look very much like you . . . or you look like her."

Yoko looks a bit confused. "You two know each other?"

"Well, not yet. She won't know who I am at this point," he explains. "But we'll meet a couple of years from now."

Yoko shakes her head. "I think I get it, but this time-travel thing is so confusing."

Tell me about it, I think.

"Come on. I'll fetch her, and we'll talk outside. We need to keep our stories straight. All Lily knows is that I'm an American who's traveling overseas. She has no idea I'm her granddaughter . . . or that I will be one day."

"Got it," Dr. Robert says.

We push our way through the crowd, Yoko whispers something to Lily, and we manage to force our way out.

"Hey, Lenny. Good to see you again," Lily says. "Sorry we ditched you at the club."

"Yeah, that wasn't cool. You scared me to death," I say.

Yoko puts her hand on my arm. There's no way I can stay mad at her. "It's okay. I'm just glad everyone is all right. This is a friend of mine, Lily. His name is Dr. Robert."

"Like the song," Lily says, referring to the song "Dr. Robert" from the Beatles' *Revolver* LP.

"Exactly," he says.

We head out of the store, and Lily leads us to a nearby pub. She is as charming as ever. Everyone orders beer, and the women tell us what they've been up to since I saw them last. "Lily has introduced me to everyone who's anyone," Yoko says.

"I had to," Lily says. "Once I heard Yoko sing, I had to show her off to my friends, including the Beatles, of course."

"You sang for the Beatles?" I say. I'm so jealous, but I keep my mouth shut.

"Yes," Yoko says. "Well, really only George, Paul, John, and Yoko. Ringo was somewhere else that day."

"You know the Beatles?" Dr. Robert asks.

Lily smiles. "Of course, they're my friends. I've known them since the beginning. I'm from Liverpool."

"It's been a blast," Yoko says. "Lily took me around to other bands that need backup singers, and I recorded a song with Mick and Keith. It was an acoustic version of 'You Can't Always Get What You Want.' Mick liked what I did but said he might substitute a full choir later."

Dr. Robert writes everything down in his little notebook.

"Why are you taking notes?" Lily asks.

He smiles at her. "Because I'm a doctor—of the human body and of the human spirit."

"Lenny, I know you want Yoko to go back to the States with you, but believe me, she'll get a ton of work here now that the Stones have given her a shot," Lily says.

Yoko steps in. "I really appreciate all you've done, Lily, but I need to get back to my family. They'd freak if I stayed."

Yoko, you have no idea.

"Well, you can always come back," Lily says. "I'll be here, and my door is always open for you."

"Thank you."

"What about me?" asks Dr. Robert. "London is happening these days. Maybe I should stay."

Yoko and I both look at him. Now I know why he

was so anxious to come back. He's looking for a second chance.

"Are you thinking of relocating to London, Doctor?" Lily asks.

"It is tempting," Dr. Robert says. "I love it here, and I'm sure I can find work."

Suddenly, Lily looks at her watch. "Oh, hey, you guys, I'm late for an appointment, but Doctor, if you do decide to stay, give me a call. I'm in the book. Any friend of Yoko's . . ."

She turns to Yoko and gives her a long hug. "You'll need to come by the apartment for your things, so I'll see you later, honey," she says.

"Okay," Yoko says, though I'm pretty sure she knows we're out of here. "Thank you so much for spending so much time with me. It really meant a lot."

Lily waves her off. "My pleasure. Anytime." She smiles and then turns and walks away.

There's an awkward silence after Lily leaves.

I look at Dr. Robert. "Are you really thinking about staying?"

Dr. Robert laughs. "Yes! Can you blame me? I miss all this," he says, waving his hands around. "Everyone here is so much more alive than in the present. Can't you hear the conversations going on around us? No one is wasting time on his or her goddamn devices. They're engaging with one another. We've lost this. All you have to do is listen for a few moments, and you'll see it. Everyone here is more alive."

"What about your family, your practice?"

"I never had any children and I'm twice divorced. Who will really miss me?"

"Your patients."

"In New York? There are a thousand other doctors just as qualified."

"You're serious, aren't you?" Yoko asks.

"You should understand more than anyone, Yoko. You stayed!"

"Yes, but only for a month. I never meant it to be forever, and . . ." She hesitates.

"What?" Dr. Robert asks.

"Well, I hate to be rude or anything but you're in your sixties! Are you sure you're going to fit in here?"

He laughs. "Oh, I'll be all right, don't worry about me. I have a huge advantage, just knowing what I know."

"But how are you going to survive here, doc?" I ask. "Your credit cards are no good. You have nowhere to live, no job. Do you even have any cash?"

"I'll crash with Lily at the start, and I've got about a hundred bucks in my pocket, but you know what? That's enough," he says. "I've seen the future, and I'm not impressed. Lenny, you know I've been thinking for a long time about the past and present and how they interact and how we can change the future by affecting the past. It's mind-blowing, life changing. I have a chance to do some great things here."

"Like what?"

"Well, a lot of things. Just think about all knowledge you possess that these people don't. Anyone from the future has to be considered a genius. You can lead a revolution in fitness. Tell them about AIDS and the HIV virus and how they can protect themselves with condoms. Hell, maybe prevent AIDS from even happening. There are a million things," he goes on. "And frankly, money is immaterial. I can make a lot of money overnight just by betting. Remember, I know who the next prime minister is going to be, the next US president. The English bet on everything so I won't have to worry about earning a living. I can even become a record consultant. Who could pick out which songs will be hits better than I could? There are a million possibilities."

"Sounds like you've been giving this some thought," Yoko says.

"Only for years." He laughs. "But never seriously until I met Lenny." Dr. Robert then turns Yoko. "But you *must* go back, Yoko. You need to for Lenny's sake. He's in trouble."

"What happened?" she asks.

"Your parents are worried about you, and they're going to report you missing. And guess who's going to be the prime suspect? Me!" I say.

Yoko put her hands over her mouth. "Oh my God! I can't believe it. I was only thinking of myself. That's horrible."

I look down. I am still pissed at Yoko, but every time I look into her eyes, my anger dissipates. She's just too cute. "You had your reasons," I say. "I didn't think of the consequences, either, until the cops showed up on my doorstep."

"We need to go back right away," Yoko says.

"You should," Dr. Robert agrees. "And don't worry about me. I'll be okay."

He has a weird look in his eye.

"Is there something else you're not telling us?" I ask.

"Yeah, there is," he says. "I didn't know if I should tell you, but the real reason I wanted to come back is to save John Lennon."

"What?!" Yoko and I say at once.

"You gave me the idea, Lenny. Remember John kept asking you about his future, what happens after the Beatles and everything?"

"Yeah, he was really focused on that."

"That's because John always had a feeling that

173

something was going to happen to him. It started when he said the Beatles were more popular than Jesus. That brought out the fanatics, and the Beatles, especially John, got tons of death threats. One of the reasons they quit touring is because John was afraid someone would shoot him when he was performing."

"Yeah, I do remember that now that you mention it," I say.

"I know what I have to do. I'm going to stop Chapman before he has a chance to get close to John. You can count on it."

"How can you even think of doing that?" I ask. "There are always consequences when you change the past. We've seen that in the last twenty-four hours."

Dr. Robert is excited now. "Lenny, you've proven that you *can* change the past. You did it with Jim Morrison. You told me he originally was supposed to die in 1971, but you prevented it. All I know is that Morrison is alive and he's a freaking shaman! You did that, Lenny. You and Daisy! And if you can do it with Morrison, I can do it with John Lennon. This is personal for me. John wasn't just a Beatle to me. He was a friend. Only good can come from me stopping his killer. I'll keep Mark David Chapman far away from John, I promise you that."

Yoko and I look at each other. Of all the crazy things that have happened, this just might make the most sense in a weird, wonderful way.

"Maybe you're right," I say.

"I know I'm right, Lenny, and it's because of you. I'm going to change history . . . with your help."

"But doc, we don't know what else happened because we kept Morrison alive. We have no idea of the dozens, maybe hundreds, of changes that occurred because of it," I say.

"I know that, Lenny, but this is John Lennon we're talking about."

I need to think. It's too much all at once and I can feel a headache coming on. Suddenly, I'm aware that we're in an English pub, which is filling up with a lunchtime crowd and getting noisier. I don't know what to say, and that's when Yoko touches my arm.

"I think he should do it," she says.

"You do?" I ask.

"Yeah, I do. I think you should stay, doc," she says. "And save John."

I scratch my head. It's hard to keep track of all the moving pieces. If Dr. Robert stays, what else happens? There's something nagging at the back of my brain. "Wait a minute, there's one other thing," I say. "When we went back with Daisy, her younger self was there. We saw her. Somewhere in this city, the eighteen-year-old Dr. Robert is going to show up. What about that?"

He laughs. "Yeah, I thought of that, too. I'm not going to do anything to him or about him. He'll live his life just like always, and I'll live mine."

"I can't believe it's that simple," I say. "You're the same person."

"Are we? You just said yourself that you and Daisy saw the young Daisy when you went back. Didn't they both exist at the same time? I think it's possible. I'm not going to interfere with the young Dr. Robert's life."

Yoko laughs. "I think he's got you, Lenny."

I'm not so sure. Something is still bugging me. "How old are you now, doc?"

"Sixty-five."

"That means you'll be seventy-seven in 1980 when John gets shot. How do you know you'll live that long?"

The doctor's expression grows serious. "You're right. That's why I'll need to get to Chapman earlier. Once I get settled, I'll go to Hawaii where he lives. If I play this

175

right, he'll never make it to New York."

"What are you planning to do?" I ask.

He takes a long drink from his beer. "I don't know. I'll figure it out when I see him. There are a lot of possibilities. You don't need to worry about that part."

"Lenny, we need to get back," Yoko says.

"I hope this works, doc."

"Me too," he says.

"Well, I've made my argument," I say reluctantly. "Are you sure? Are you *really* sure?"

"I'm sure," he says with a smile. "Now you two get out of here and go home. If you don't show up soon, Yoko, the cops are going to come down on Lenny hard."

Yoko hugs Dr. Robert. "Take care of yourself, doc."

"Go on now, I'll be okay."

I look back as we leave the pub. He's striking up a conversation with a guy next to him.

"I can't believe we're leaving him here," I tell Yoko.

"He's made up his mind. He'll be fine, Lenny," she says.

"It was really okay for you being here?"

"More than okay. It was fabulous. I'm going to miss it," she says. "Let's go before I change my mind."

We walk over to Hyde Park and find a quiet bench. I pull out my smartphone.

"Where's your iPod?" she asks.

"That's another story for another time. I'll tell you when we get back. What d'ya want to hear?"

"Ed Sheeran?"

We close our eyes to the sounds of "Thinking Out Loud" and blast off.

◄◄ SIXTEEN ►►

wake up in my bed tangled up in the sheets with Yoko. Both of us are fully dressed. I am mortified but calm down when I realize Yoko is still sleeping. I watch the rise and fall of her breasts under the sheet and feel myself growing hard. I don't want her to wake up to *that*—talk about a creeper. I slip out of bed and wait for things to settle down, if you know what I mean. Then I shake her arm. She looks alarmed before realizing where she is.

"Lenny?"

"Yeah?"

"Where are we now?"

I take a swallow. She is so beautiful. "In my room . . . in my bed."

She smiles up at me. "I'm glad I picked you up that day in the subway."

"Picked me up?"

"Uh, yeah," she says smiling. "If you remember, I came over to you and started singing."

"I remember."

Our faces are just inches from each other. I notice her

eyes change ever so slightly as she touches my chest. "I'm feeling very warm here," she says.

I swallow. Oh God. "Me too. Very warm."

I move my face a little closer to see if I'm reading her right, and she reaches up that very second, pulls me down to her and kisses me.

I part my lips slowly, and this time, she opens her mouth. Now we're making out for real, and she kind of moans a little, like *mmm*. I move on top of her and shift my hips. She moans again.

This goes on for what seems like a very long time. We're both moving our hips gently and kissing like we're getting air from each other's mouths. But then she pulls away and moves so we're side to side.

"This is nice," she says.

"Yes."

"But we need to get up," she says. "I'm sorry, but we do."

There is nothing I want to do more than stay in bed the rest of the day, but I know that at any moment, one or both of the Joes will swing the door open to wish me a cheery good morning. I don't know how they'll react to finding Yoko here, and I don't want to find out.

I force myself to sit up. "Okay. How do we explain your disappearance?"

"I'll just tell them I was with Dmitri and you didn't know anything about it."

"Um, that's not going to work," I say.

"Why not?"

I tell her about Dmitri confronting me and taking my iPod, and how he's already been to Yoko's parents asking where she was. Then I tell her about the cops and how they thought I stole Paul's guitar from Lily's room.

"But that's your guitar."

"Yeah, but I couldn't tell them where I got it. I said 'a friend gave it to me,' which sounds like complete BS. They're convinced you caught me taking the guitar from Lily's room and that I did something to you in retaliation. That's their theory anyway."

"That's insane."

"I know, I know. The Joes have even hired a lawyer for me. I'm just glad you're back."

"Me too," she says. "But where was I?"

"Does it matter? They'll see you're alive and you'll tell them I didn't steal the guitar, that you lent it to me, and I think this whole thing will go away."

"You're probably right," she says. "If they really press me, I'll tell them I asked you to cover for me, that I met some boy and we rode the Staten Island Ferry all night and I've been at his place over there."

"What if they want his name?" I ask.

"They'll have to drag it out of me and they won't. I'll stop talking to them. There's nothing they can do. Like you said, my parents will see I'm fine and that's all they'll care about."

"Sounds like a plan," I say.

"Hey, do you have a T-shirt I can borrow? This one reeks of smoke. Everyone back then smokes all the time," she says. "I never thought people smoked that much."

"Didn't you watch *Mad Men*?" I joke.

"Yeah, but I thought they were exaggerating."

"Apparently not!"

"So we good with our story?" Yoko asks.

"If you can sell it, I'm fine, but how did you wind up here?"

"We'll tell them I showed up in the middle of the night last night and you were nice enough to let me stay till morning."

"You ready for the granddads?"

"Sure, let's do it."

As if on cue, my bedroom door opens and the Joes are standing there with a plate of pancakes.

"Lenny!" says Grandpa, "Who is this girl? Are you Yoko?"

"Yes, I'm Yoko," she says before I get the chance. "None of this is Lenny's fault. I texted him in the middle of the night, and he snuck me in. He had no idea where I was before this."

"Young lady, you have no idea how much trouble you've caused," Grandpa says.

"I'm really sorry," Yoko says. "I stayed out very late and was scared to go home, but Lenny had nothing to do with that. He didn't know, I swear."

Grandpa doesn't say anything, but Joe jumps right in. "Lenny, here's what's going to happen," Joe says. "First of all, Yoko is going to call her parents. Then, we're going to walk back into the kitchen and put these pancakes on the table, and you two are going to wash up and tell us the whole story. Then we're going to call the lawyer I got for you Lenny. Do you understand?"

"Yes, sir," we both say at once.

. . .

How are your parents doing?" Grandpa asks when Yoko walks into the kitchen holding her cell phone. Yoko makes a face. "Well, they're not happy but they're glad I'm okay. Here, they want to speak with you."

Grandpa takes the phone and has a brief conversation with Yoko's parents, assuring them that she's fine.

"Okay, I'll send her over right after breakfast," he says, handing the phone back to Yoko.

Then, we tell the Joes the story we made up in bed only moment before. They seem to buy it.

"So Lenny did not steal that guitar from your grandmother's collection?" Grandpa asks Yoko.

"No, sir."

Grandpa turns to me. "Then where did you get it, Lenny? It's obviously worth a lot of money."

I take a deep breath. How am I going to explain this?

"I lent it to him," Yoko jumps in. "It used to be my grandmother's, but I know that Lenny needed a new guitar so we could practice for our return engagement to the subway platforms of New York, so I said he could borrow it."

"Why didn't you just say that Lenny?" Joe says.

"Because," Yoko says deliberately, and I can tell she's making this up on the fly, "I made him promise not to. I thought my parents would be upset. It's just a loan. Once he gets a new guitar, he'll give it back. You can't play that kind of guitar in the subway anyway."

"You kids . . . Okay, let's call the lawyer," Joe says.

"I think I should go home to see my parents," Yoko says.

"Yes, you're right. You go, but Lenny, I want you to stay here," Grandpa says.

"Okay."

I walk Yoko to the door where we kiss ever so briefly on the lips. "Text me and let me know what's going on," I tell her.

"Okay, bye."

I go back into the living room where Joe is on the phone with the lawyer. "Yeah, I see," he says. "I don't understand. What does Lenny have to do with that?"

There's a pause on his end, and I wonder what

could be wrong now because, judging from Joe's face, something is definitely wrong.

"What's up?" I say to Grandpa.

"I don't know, but I think something else has happened," he says.

"Like what?"

Grandpa shushes me and tunes in to Joe's conversation. "Okay, we'll meet you at the precinct," we hear him say. "We'll bring him there. Okay, thanks." Joe hangs up.

"What now?" I ask.

"Lenny, you went to see Dr. Robert yesterday, right?"

"Yes, I told you that."

"Well, he didn't show up for work today, and he had a full slate of patients scheduled. Everyone at Mount Sinai says that's not like him. A colleague went to his apartment at the Plaza Hotel, and there's no sign of him. They're still looking, but his receptionist called the police and told them you were the last patient yesterday. Said you came in demanding to see him and the doctor agreed, and then rushed through the rest of his appointments. Then he sent her home for the day. According to her, it was very unusual, and now no one knows where he is."

"Jesus," Grandpa says.

My head is spinning. I knew there was another reason I didn't want Dr. Robert to stay in the past, and now I know what it was. Damn! How could I have been so stupid not to think of it? But, of course, I don't say any of this to the Joes.

"Well, all that is true, but I didn't do anything to him," I say. "We just talked."

"Do you have any idea where he is?"

Shit. Here we go again. These lies are draining.

"You understand how this looks, Lenny. First Yoko disappears and now Dr. Robert, and both times you were the last person to be with them. What's going on with you? Is there something you want to tell us?"

I look at the Joes and consider telling them the truth, but I know they won't believe me. I wouldn't believe me, either. "There's nothing to tell," I say. "Just really bad karma, I guess. Bad coincidences. What time do we need to be at the precinct?"

"In an hour."

"Okay. I'm gonna take a shower."

...

I don't even text Yoko before the shower. I need to think. My life is getting away from me. I'm tired of time travel. What began as a kick has turned into nothing but problems. I almost wish it never happened, none of it. As the hot water runs over me, I think about disappearing myself. Maybe I should just go back and live in the past. Like Dr. Robert, I know what all the hits are going to be, I know what bands will matter and which ones will fizzle out. I'll be able to predict the future with uncanny accuracy. It will be fairly easy to turn that skill into a job somehow. If I do that, all these problems will go away.

I think about that for five minutes, and then I think about my mother and the Joes. They'll never stop looking if I disappear, and they'll be heartbroken. I can't do that to them. I have to man up and fix the problems I've created, and once I do, I'm through with the past. I'm not going back ever again.

I shut off the water, change into fresh clothes, and turn on my computer. I can't believe I've waited so long to check this, but with making out with Yoko, dealing with the Joes, and my legal problems, I took my eye off the ball and now I need to know: What happened to John Lennon? Did Dr. Robert succeed in saving him?

Every article I pull up tells the same depressing story. John was fatally shot by Mark David Chapman on December 8, 1980 in front of the Dakota. That means Dr. Robert failed.

I look up Dr. Jonah Robert next. It's not that uncommon a name but none of the entries seem right. Maybe just Jonah Robert? I have to dig and dig because he has a common last name, but then I find something that gives me chills. The story is about a plane crash back in 1973. The article says forty-five people died when the plane crashed near Kauai and one of the victims was a man named Jonah Jones "who lived in London and was on vacation." That has to be our Dr. Robert. He must've been on his way to find Chapman, who grew up in Hawaii.

Just then, my phone announces that I've gotten a text. I jump at the sound. It's from Yoko.

John is still dead

I know and so is Dr. Robert

What happened?!

He died in a plane crash in 1973 on his way to Hawaii

OMG!!!! That's awful!

Yeah, poor guy. He had me convinced he could do it.

So if he died in '73, that means John still died at the Dakota?!

Yeah, I looked it up already.

Shit. Now what?

Gotta think…meanwhile, how did it go with your parents?

All is forgiven. How about you?

Ugh, I'll call you.

When I do, I tell her about the disappearance of Dr.

Robert and how the cops are after me—again!

"Maybe you were right. Maybe we shouldn't screw around with the past," she says. "Too many things could happen."

"It does feel like it's fighting back, doesn't it?"

"I wonder. Hey, you want me to come with you to see the cops?" she asks.

"No, I'll weather the storm. The Joes will be there and my lawyer. It'll be okay. I'm a minor, and our lawyer is going to let me answer some questions but not many. I'll tell them the truth up to a point. You know, even if I told them the God's honest truth, they'd think I was nuts."

"Yeah, you're right." She pauses. "So Dr. Robert did not save John . . . What do you want to do about that?"

"I think I need to go back and get Dr. Robert, tell him what's what, and bring him back."

"You think he'll listen?"

"I hope so," I say. "Who wants to die in a plane crash, right?"

"What about John?"

"I don't know. Haven't figured that part out yet."

"I want to come," she says.

"Not this time, Yoko," I say. "Your parents will freak if you go missing again, not to mention the cops. This time you stay."

She sighs. "Okay. Hey, I almost forgot. I got your iPod back!"

"You did? How?"

"Dmitri came by with his tail between his legs. He gave me the iPod to return to you and he apologized."

"And?"

"And what?"

"I know he didn't just come by to say hello," I say. "He wants to get back together with you, right? What

185

did you say?"

"I told him I didn't want to go out with him anymore, that I'd met someone new."

"Oh? Do I know the lucky guy?"

She laughed. "I think this is a conversation we need to have in person. Go talk to the cops, and we'll see each other later."

"I can't wait."

"Me neither," she says, and then the call disconnects.

I look up and the Joes are standing in my doorway. "Come on, Lenny," Joe says. "We need to talk to the cops."

. . .

My lawyer's name is Reggie Redford, a former football player for the New York Jets. He's big, strong, and takes no prisoners. I've seen him on television a bunch but never in person. He's waiting for us in the lobby of the First Precinct where he's joking around with the desk sergeant. He spots Joe immediately and comes over.

"You must be Lenny," he says, taking my small hand in his giant one.

Reggie is easily six foot five and looks like he could still play football. His hair is a bit gray, but that's his only concession to age. He's got a take-charge attitude that's hard not to admire. I like him immediately, and I'm glad he's on my side.

He tells the desk sergeant to call Detectives Morelli and Moore and let them know we're all here, then turns to me. "So here's the drill, Lenny. You talk if I say you talk. Other than that you don't say anything, not even hello. You got it?"

"Yes, but—"

"There are no 'buts.' There's only Reggie's law. I don't need to hear your whole story or anything else. You tell your grandpas whatever bullshit you want. I'm here to protect you, and in order for me to do that you can't do much talking, so get used to keeping your mouth shut. You got that?"

"Yes, sir."

"Good boy. Let's go."

Morelli and Moore come out to the lobby area and beckon for us to follow as they lead us into a conference room.

"We being taped in here?" Reggie asks them.

"Yes," Morelli says.

"Okay." He turns to us. " Totally legal but I wanted to double-check and now you know, too. So, detectives, you got any questions?"

Morelli looks at me and directs all his questions to me, none to Reggie. It's like Reggie's not even in the room as far as Morelli is concerned. But Reggie is having none of it.

"Were you with Dr. Jonah Robert yesterday afternoon?" Morelli asks.

Reggie puts up his hand. "You can answer that."

"Yes."

Reggie winks at me and leans toward me. "Good, I like that," he whispers in my ear. "One word answers are the best."

Morelli establishes that I visited Dr. Robert's office and spoke to him there for a considerable amount of time. I tell him I left the office around four o'clock, and that's true, but there's so much more that remains unsaid.

"And when you left, where was Dr. Robert?"

"In his office."

"Did you hurt him in any way?"

"Don't answer that, Lenny," Reggie says.

I stay quiet.

"Did you kill him?"

"Don't answer that, either."

"You're impeding this investigation, counselor."

"Come on, Detective. You know we're not going to answer those types of direct questions. Lenny is a minor. You've got nothing. Lenny, do you know where Dr. Robert is? That's all Detective Morelli really wants to know."

Ugh. Time to lie again. "No, I-I-I don't know."

"Why are you stuttering?" Morelli asks.

Now that's a good question, but Reggie steps in. "Don't answer that." He turns to the detectives. "This boy can stutter, bark, vomit, whatever. Don't mean nothing in a court of law, detective, and we both know that. Anything else?"

"Oh, I got a bunch more, but you won't let him answer anything. I'd love to know why people seem to disappear when he's around. First that Yoko kid, now this doctor."

"I believe that 'Yoko kid,'" Reggie says sarcastically, "has returned and she's just fine."

"Yeah, yeah," Morelli says and then turns to me. "You better be careful, Lenny. This guy's gonna walk you right into jail."

"Okay, that's it. This interview is over. Lenny, let's go. Have a nice day, detectives."

It's nice to have a huge ex-football player on your side. We leave and meet up with the Joes outside.

"You know where the good doctor is Lenny?" Reggie asks me.

"No."

"Detective Morelli is a bulldog. Lie low and don't break any laws. Don't even jaywalk. He may have you followed. In fact, he probably will."

. . .

I have a quiet dinner with the Joes. Yoko's parents have grounded her, I can't see her tonight after all. Grandpa does agree to walk over and get my iPod from her place, though, so I at least get that back. I know I can travel without it, but it's like a security blanket. I feel more comfortable with it.

By eleven o'clock, everyone is asleep and I'm lying in bed wide-awake. I know what I have to do. In our conversations while walking around London, Dr. Robert told me that Lily had sung on one Beatles song, but she didn't get credit. Ironically, it was "Across the Universe," a composition by John that he first recorded with female backing vocals, one of them Lily's. That version is not the popular one that was later featured on the *Let it Be* album, but you can hear the women's voices on the group's *Rarities* LP.

I'm happy to have my grandfather's iPod back, even if I don't *need it*. I scroll through the songs and find that early version of "Across the Universe" and close my eyes.

Donovan Day

◀◀ SEVENTEEN ▶▶

I find myself in a hallway sitting on the floor. Everything is quiet. There's no one around, so I stand and walk down a long white corridor. There's a door marked STUDIO 2, and I walk in. I'm in a recording booth with a big soundboard, but it's empty. Below me, on the very large recording room floor, I spot John and Yoko Ono side by side. I remember the stories about her crashing the Beatles' recording sessions and staying by John every moment, even sitting outside the loo when he went to relieve himself.

There are instruments everywhere—Ringo's drum kit, dozens of guitars, a couple of sitars, and a grand piano. But no music is being played even though the other three Beatles are in the room. Paul, now sporting a full beard, is fooling around on his bass with earphones on, George is talking to two men in the back of the room, and Ringo is staring at a chessboard. They are all are smoking cigarettes. I get the sense that everyone is waiting on John, who seems to be consulting with Yoko about the song. Two women sit nearby, and one of them is Lily. She's talking to Dr. Robert, whose gray hair is now quite long.

I smile to myself. If this had been my first trip back, I would have been blown away, but now, it's strange to say, I'm used to seeing the remarkable. I know I'm very lucky. People would kill to be exactly where I am standing, watching the Beatles mill around during a recording session. I know from the bios I've read that, at this point, the Beatles are more or less sick of one another, and tired of John and Yoko, but despite the bitterness, they are still together.

I see a button on the walk that reads "TALK" and hold it down. Now I can hear what's being said in the room below. Everyone has stopped talking except for John and Yoko, but they are speaking so quietly to each other, I only hear murmuring.

"Okay, then," John says at last. "Let's have a go at it, boys. Where's Geoff?"

A clean-shaven guy in a white jacket stands up on the recording room floor and starts climbing the stairs toward the booth I'm standing in. Dr. Robert is right behind him. I let go of the "TALK" button. I know I'd surely be kicked out if I was on my own, but I'm gambling that once Dr. Robert vouches for me, I'll be allowed to stay. I stand my ground. Geoff comes in first. "You can't be in here," he says politely. "This is a restricted area, sir."

"I know," I say. "I'm looking for Dr. Robert."

Dr. Robert spots me, and his eyes light up in surprise. "He's with me, Geoff. It's okay. John knows him, too. This is Lenny. Lenny, this is Geoff Emerick."

"Fine, you can stay, but be quiet. And there's not to be a word to anyone on the outside about what you see or hear."

Dr. Robert takes me by the arm and places me in the back of the recording room while Geoff pushes the

"TALK" button . "All good, John."

"All right, then."

John steps in front of one microphone while Lily and the other woman share another. All three of them are wearing headphones so they can hear the music track. They are recording the vocals for "Across the Universe."

John counts it down and begins singing, "Words are flowing out like endless rain into a paper cup . . ."

I sit there with my mouth open. This is gold—John Lennon laying down a vocal track to one of his classics. They do take after take, some because John forgets the words, some because his voice cracks. It goes on for thirty minutes until John is satisfied with one of the takes.

"Play that one back for me, Geoff."

Geoff pushes a few buttons, and the music and vocal tracks are paired so everyone in the studio can hear. When the song ends, Paul claps. "It's a keeper, mate."

"Yeah, it's not bad," John says. "What do you think, Mother?"

Yoko Ono has barely moved and could be asleep, but she immediately sits up. "You can do better. Try again tomorrow."

The other three Beatles, as well as Geoff, look disgusted, but John nods. "Tomorrow, then, lads."

They're calling it a night, and Dr. Robert looks over at me. "Let's split. Thanks, Geoff."

"You're welcome. Remember, not a word," he says to me.

Dr. Robert and I step into the white hallway.

"Why are you here?" he asks.

"To save you."

"From what?"

"A plane crash."

I tell him the whole story, including the part about the cops now looking at me because he vanished. "What a mess," he says.

"Tell me about it. How's it been here?"

"Good. With Lily's help, it was easy to meet John and Yoko. And they dig my aura as much as they ever did." He laughs.

"You've become quite the hippie, doc."

"Always was, Lenny."

I remember that Dr. Robert said he actually met John and Yoko when he was a teenager.

"What about the younger version of you. Is he here, too?" I ask.

He laughs. "No. He won't show up for another six months."

"Listen," I tell Dr. Robert. "I want you to come back with me. Now. You're not going to save John. He dies just like he always did because you went down in that crash and never got to Chapman."

Before Dr. Robert can react, John and Yoko come out of the studio and John sees me. "You again, Mr. Time Traveler?"

He claps me on the back. Yoko Ono is staring at me. She is just as small as she appears in photographs, but her features are softer and she looks more feminine in person. I can sort of see what John sees in her, though she is dreadfully thin and pale as a ghost.

She looks at John and then at me. "Who is this?" she demands.

"Yoko, this is Lenny, the bloke I've been telling you about. Remember? The man from the future. Paul and I met him back in London."

"And you know Dr. Robert, too?" she asks me. Yoko's eyes are vacant and threatening at the same time. I get a chill just looking at her.

"Yes, we go way back," Dr. Robert says.

Yoko smiles for the first time, and her demeanor goes from chilly to warm. "Lenny, it's nice to meet you after all these years. John always talks about you. What year did you say you are from?"

"2015."

John laughs. "I told you, Mother. Hey, Lenny, how's your little music maker?"

I can't help but laugh.

"Did you bring it?"

I decide to keep the iPod out of sight. "Not this time, sorry."

"What about the phone camera?"

I pull it out of my pocket and take a photo of John and Yoko, then show it to her. I can see she's impressed and might even believe that I'm from the future. She does seem open to the possibility.

"Where is your Yoko?" John asks.

"Yes, I liked her when we met," Yoko Ono says. "Is she back in London?"

I'd forgotten that my Yoko had met the Yoko back when she was staying with Lily. "No," I say, "she didn't make the trip this time. I came here to speak to Dr. Robert." I glance at Dr. Robert.

"Is he from the future, too?" she asks.

I decide this time to go with the truth. "Yes."

"I need to talk to you," Yoko Ono says. "Come with us."

The four of us walk out of the studio and into the alley, and we get into John's flamboyant Rolls-Royce. Once we are settled, Yoko Ono gets right to the point. "What can you tell me about the future?"

She acts as though she meets someone from the future every other day.

"Well," I start, "the future is pretty big topic. What

do you want to know?"

"Tell me about the war," Yoko says.

"What war?"

"Vietnam," she says immediately.

Of course, she asks about Vietnam. In 1969, the fighting rages on.

"It's all over," I tell her.

"So there's peace?"

"Not exactly," I say. "It's complicated.

I tell them both about 9/11 and the wars in Afghanistan and Iran, and I try to explain George W. Bush's reasoning for invading Iraq. They are aghast.

"Sounds like Vietnam all over again," John says.

"The one in Afghanistan lasted much longer," I explain.

"What about the kids? The protests?" John asks.

I tell him there are plenty of people against both wars, but since the US government eliminated the draft, things aren't quite the same.

"College is so expensive now," I say. "It's different. Students think more about getting jobs than worrying about a distant war."

I tell him how war has disappeared from the everyday American conversation because nearly all the people serving our country are largely from the working class, the heartland outside the big media cities, and the poor.

"Doesn't seem fair," he says.

"It's not, but it is what it is."

"What does that mean?" Yoko asks. "'It is what it is'?"

"It means people accept it and don't try to change it."

"I'm glad I don't live in your future," Yoko says.

"I know what you mean," I say.

Then Yoko, ever the businesswoman, asks about changes in the music industry. I give them a rundown about the changes ahead, how people stop buying records in favor of tapes, and then CDs, and then MP3s and digital files. I tell them no one makes much money from selling records, but that touring has become incredibly lucrative.

"Maybe Paul is right," John says. "He always says we should keep touring."

"Paul does love touring," I tell them. "It's like he's on one big tour."

"Just a minute, mate. You can't be serious. You don't mean to tell me that Paul is still playing live and going out on the road in 2015, do ya? He'd be over seventy years old!"

"Well, he seems much younger. He sounds and looks great."

"He's still playing gigs at the age of seventy? You must be joking."

"He's seventy-three and still rocking."

"Bollocks! Does he have his hair or is he bald as an egg now?"

"He's got his hair," I say, "but I'm sure he dyes it."

John can't stop laughing. Of course, Yoko joins in, more than happy to deride Paul, her nemesis.

"And Linda, is she still trying to sing?" John asks.

I stop smiling. "No, Linda dies of cancer sometime in the late nineties."

"I'm sorry to hear that," John says. "I know Paul really depended on her. She is the new John. And me other mates? George and Ringo?"

"Ringo is sometimes with a group he calls the All-Stars, a bunch of guys from other groups, like the Eagles."

"Good old Ringo. He's a survivor. And George?"

I look at the carpet. "George is gone, I'm afraid. Cancer got him back in 2001."

"Is it the fags that got him?"

"Yeah, lung cancer."

"I warned him. That's why I only smoke pot. Much healthier."

The conversation seems to stop. I'm not sure why, but something is up. John glances at Yoko, who nods, and then at me. "Listen, mate, Yoko wants me to ask you something else . . . What happens to the two of us?"

John's eyes search mine. I don't really know how much to say or if I should say anything. So I stay silent for a few moments.

"Why are you hesitating?" Yoko asks.

"She's right, mate. You have an easy face to read," John says. "There's something in your eyes. What is it? Do the bastards finally get me?"

They're waiting to see what I'm going to say. I weigh my words carefully. "Appreciate your time. Every moment."

Dr. Robert is looking out the window.

"Tell me what happens," John says. "Whatever it is, I want to know."

"No, it wouldn't be fair to you. My only advice is to live your life to the fullest. You'll do that anyway. You'll make a lot more great music."

"Can you promise me I have more time? That's it not going to happen right away?"

"You have time," I say. I'm getting emotional. My voice cracks just a bit.

"What else?" John asks. "How will I die?"

"I can't tell you how or when, John. You'd always be looking over your shoulder. Just know that you have time, more than a decade. Follow your muse, enjoy your life. That's all I can say."

"All right, Lenny, all right," John says. "Mother, we can't wait for death and be all afraid. We must live our lives doing what we think is best and that's that."

"No," Yoko says. "Lenny can help us and he will, won't you Lenny."

She gives me a look so powerful that I shudder. There is something about her. Her stare is piercing but I can't look away. I almost feel like she's reading my mind. It's eerie. I feel something welling up inside me. Maybe Dr. Robert was on to something. He just didn't go about doing it the right way. And he ran out of time. It will be different for me. As I come to this realization, Yoko nods imperceptibly.

"What do you want to say, Lenny?" John asks.

I shift my attention to John. "I'm going to do everything in my power to save you," I say. "That's all I can say. Now, please, let me out. Dr. Robert and I must be going."

John orders the driver to pull over, and he and Yoko get out and hug me. Her attitude has changed and I can feel it as much as I felt her power moments before.

"We have faith in you," Yoko says. "We are in your hands. No more words."

They get back in the car, and I watch it speed away.

"Do you think that was wise?" Dr. Robert asks.

"I had to do it. Now let's get out of here," I say, spotting a small neighborhood park.

We sit down and Dr. Robert wants to talk, but I stop him. "Not now. We have to get back. Listen. Please."

We split the earbuds, hold hands, and listen to the latest from Florence and the Machine.

Donovan Day

◀◀ EIGHTEEN ▶▶

The moment I regain consciousness, I see the light coming through the blinds in my room. Dr. Robert is sleeping next to me. I shake him, panicked. "Get up! You've got to get out of here. Now!"

The clock reads 6:00 a.m.

"We've only got a few minutes before my granddads wake up. You've got to split, and I mean now. Come on."

"Okay, okay. I feel like I'm hungover," he says.

"You'll get over it. Hurry."

I open my bedroom door, and there's not a sound in the apartment. The Joes are still sleeping, but one or the other will be up at any moment. They always get up early. "Come on," I whisper to Dr. Robert. "It's now or never. Just go home and tell the cops you were on a bender or something."

I unlock the door and he scoots out, then I sneak back into my room and lie down on the bed. Another crazy night in a series of them, and this time, I've really done it, telling John I would save him. How the hell am I going to do that?! And why did I say it?

Then I notice my headache is back. It's not as bad as the early ones I had right after the fight. It's a milder version, but similar, a throbbing pain. I close my eyes and do my best to put everything out of mind.

. . .

My cell phone is ringing somewhere in the distance. I hear it, but it sounds so far away that I let it ring and ring. At some point, I manage to force my eyes open to look at the time. The clock says it's eleven thirty. Good, I needed to sleep, and I'm not done yet. I fluff my pillow and turn over. The day can wait. I'm exhausted. I don't want to talk to anyone. I close my eyes, but five minutes later, the doorbell rings. I hear muffled voices, and then a knock on my bedroom door.

"Yeah?"

Grandpa opens the door a crack and sticks his head in. "Lenny, are decent? Yoko is here to see you."

"Yeah, I'm good," I say, throwing the cover over me. "Tell her to come in."

She enters, looking as pretty as ever.

"How's our favorite doctor? All good?" I ask.

"Yes, he's fine. He told the cops he was on some kind of bender and phoned the cops himself to tell them to stop looking and to stop harassing you. You're in the clear."

Ah, some good news for a change.

. . .

The summer is coming to a close, and over the past few days, Yoko and I have gone back to practicing a few songs. The guitar Paul gave me has a sweet sound. I wish I could repay him with an iPod, but that's just not in the cards. Even after a couple of days of singing and playing together, Yoko and I can tell we have some special chemistry, at least musically.

Romantically, we still flirt around each other, but with the exception of a peck on the cheeks or lips, we've not kissed passionately since that day we woke up in each other's arms. I'm not sure why exactly. Dmitri is a thing of the past, but I sense Yoko is keeping a part of her to herself. Maybe she just thinks it's better for the music. I'm not ready to ask her outright or to make another move. For the moment, I'm content the way things are, although I want a lot more.

The big news is that Yoko and I have been working on some of the songs her grandmother wrote with John Lennon. One in particular, a tune called "Can't Get Enough of You," sounds fantastic when she sings and I play. To my ears, it sounds like it could even be a hit.

A week has passed since my last trip back, and we're sitting in my room in the Joes' apartment. My mother is still nursing her cousin back to health. Yoko and I are playing this new song for the umpteenth time, and it sounds great. "I think we're ready to go back into the subway," I say.

"Or somewhere even nicer," she says. "I don't want a repeat of what happened the last time. Why don't we try for a coffeehouse this time?"

"There is a wine bar around the corner that features live music once a week. The owners know the Joes. Maybe they can ask him about us playing there."

"I'm up for it," she says.

"Do you think we should open with your

grandmother's songs?" I ask. "Something original? Or do you think they'll want something they've heard?"

"You know how audiences are," Yoko says. "I think we open with some upbeat stuff they know and then sprinkle in the original stuff. I still can't get over that Lily never made a record of her own."

That's the last thing I hear her say before my head feels like it explodes. I drop the guitar and fall backward on my bed.

"Lenny! Lenny, are you okay?" I hear her say the words, but I can't seem to respond. "I'm going to get your grandfather."

I grab her wrist. I'm able to talk again and manage to sit up. My head is still hurting, but the acute pain has passed. "Wait, don't call him," I say. "He and Joe will just worry. We need Dr. Robert."

. . .

That afternoon, Yoko and I are in Dr. Robert's office as he looks at the latest MRI of my brain. My head is pounding. It has not felt this bad since the night of the accident.

"Doc, my head is really getting bad. The headaches are more frequent, too. "

He looks over the scan and then shines a light in my eyes.

He looks worried. "There's been a significant change. Look at this scan. It's from the first time you came here. You see this area?"

"Yes, that's the memory part of my brain, right?"

"Yes, that's right. Now look at this one we just took," he says.

"It looks smaller," Yoko says.

"Yes," he says. "I have no idea why, but it appears to be heading back to normal size. It's still twice the size of a normal person's, but there's no doubt it's smaller than it was."

"Is that why his head is hurting?" Yoko asks.

"Most likely. Lenny, your brain is changing, and any change can cause headaches. Your brain has been through a trauma, and now it's shrinking back to its normal size."

"But that's a good thing, right?" I ask. "Don't I want a normal-sized brain?"

"Do you?" he asks.

"What do you mean, doc?"

Dr. Robert sits behind his desk. To me, he seems the same as always, but I detect a little sadness in him, and I have to believe it's from visiting the past. I think he wanted to stay and probably would have if I hadn't convinced him to come back.

"Well, I have a theory about that," he starts, "but you probably don't want to hear it."

"What is it?"

"As this segment of your brain goes down—as your brain becomes more 'normal,' if you will—there's a good chance you won't be able to time-travel anymore," he says. "None of us will."

"You miss the old days still, don't you, doc?" Yoko says.

"I'm afraid I do, but I especially miss John. I almost can't hear a song of his anymore. It's too painful," he says.

"You think I should go back and try to save him?"

"Lenny, I don't want to tell you what to do," he says. "The three of us know better than anyone that it's not easy to change the past and that things can go wrong. It doesn't always work out the way you think it's going to work out, and yet . . ."

"Just say it, doc," I urge.

"Lenny, you have a gift, but it's temporary, so you need to decide what you want to do quickly because it's going to be gone soon."

"So time's-a-wastin', is that what you're saying?"

He nods. "This time it really is."

"What do you think, Yoko?"

"Only you can decide, Lenny."

"I'll think about it."

. . .

Tonight, I'm going to have dinner with the Joes again, just us. Yoko does the same with her parents. If we are going to do this, we both thought it made sense to say goodbye. I can't guarantee anything, not that I ever could. But with my apparently rapidly shrinking brain, everything feels more serious, like there is a good chance that if we try again we could get stuck in the past.

The Joes have no idea anything is wrong. They are in very good spirits, and Joe is holding a bottle of Champagne when I walk into the kitchen.

"Hey, there he is," he says. "Just in time for the celebration."

"What are we celebrating?" I ask.

"You, Lenny. We're celebrating you," Joe explains. "When the summer began, we didn't know what to expect, but you've made us proud. You've done all right, kid. And I have great news. The owner of the Commerce Street wine bar says you can try out for him anytime this week. If he likes what he hears, he'll let you play one night."

"That's fantastic, Joe. Thank you."

"Better than the subway, huh?" he says.

"And safer," Grandpa chimes in.

"Thanks for letting me stay here," I tell them. "None of this would have happened if you guys hadn't agreed. Are one of those glasses for me?" I say pointing to the three filled champagne flutes on the counter.

"For one night only, yes!"

I pick up a glass, as do my granddads. "Here's to Yoko," I say. "The summer wouldn't have been the same without her."

"To Yoko," they agree. "You should have invited her."

"Well, I didn't know we were celebrating. Anyway, she wanted to have dinner with her parents."

We sit down to dinner, giddy from the Champagne. "What do you guys think of time travel?" I ask.

They both look up from their plates. Joe laughs. "Time travel? What brings that up?"

"Oh, I don't know. I guess I was thinking about the Beatles and how great it would be if I could go back and see them in action, at the height of their career."

"Now that is a great reason to time-travel," Grandpa says.

I look at him, then at Joe and back again. "Do you think time travel will ever be possible?"

"I don't know. Seems unlikely," he says.

"I think this world is the only one we've got," Joe adds.

"You're probably right," I say. "But it makes you think. Like, what if you could go back in time and see the Beatles at the Cavern Club or Jimi Hendrix at Woodstock?"

"Sign me up. If you do figure it out, I'm in," says

Grandpa. "If only, right?"

"If only," I say. "Let me ask you another question . . . What do you remember about the day John Lennon was shot?"

"Worst day of my life," says Joe. "I was always a 'John man.' He was my favorite Beatle, and he was just getting his life together again when he was killed. So unfair. I went over to the Dakota when the news broke and spent the whole night there."

"Your mom was a teenager, but we stayed up all night playing Beatle songs. That was a long night," Grandpa remembers.

"Another reason we need better gun laws," says Joe. "The Brits blamed the Americans for our proliferation of guns, and I can't say I blame them. For New Yorkers, it felt like a double blow. John had become a New Yorker. He was always walking around the Upper West Side and Central Park and all that. He chose this city to settle in and raise his family. I hate that he was murdered here."

"What do you think of Mark David Chapman?"

"He is sick in the head," Grandpa says. "Just like all these assassins and mass killers. They should never get their hands on guns, that's number one. And we should do more for the mentally ill. That's another thing. What's really sad is how nothing has changed, like that Adam Lanza kid who killed all those children in Newtown and the guy in Colorado at that movie theater. They are mentally ill, but they got guns anyway."

"So if you could travel back in time, if you could stop Chapman or Lanza from doing what they did, would you?" I ask.

"Man, I'd love that," Joe says. "Who wouldn't want to save John? I always thought if he'd lived, he and Paul would had gotten back together to write songs again.

Maybe the Beatles were over, but not their songwriting partnership. Of course, Yoko was in the way, too."

"Yeah, you're probably right," I say.

"But we'll never know," he says.

"No, I guess we won't, but it's nice to think about." I raise my glass. "Here's to time travel and dreaming of the impossible."

We clink our glasses.

After dinner, I call Yoko. "Let's do it. Tomorrow."

Donovan Day

◀◀ ◀ NINETEEN ▶ ▶▶

’m in my bedroom the next afternoon when the doorbell rings. The Joes are at work and I let Yoko inside. She is carrying a small backpack.

"What's in there?" I ask.

She pulls out a vinyl copy of Lennon's *Double Fantasy* album. "I don't know. I just like the idea of having it with me. I also have this." She showed me a little canister.

"What's that?"

"Pepper spray, every girl's best friend."

"You're gonna pepper spray Mark David Chapman?"

"You never know."

Actually, we talked about all this with Dr. Robert this morning. He wanted to come, but I convinced him he'd be more helpful to us in the present, just in case. At the very least, he could tell our families what happened to us, not that they'd ever believe it.

"We have a pretty good plan. Anything else?"

She pulled out a stuffed rabbit . "Good luck charm," she mumbles. "Don't make fun. Let's go."

I unplug my fully charged iPod, and we sit on the bed.

I cue up "Double Fantasy," and we put in the earbuds and hold hands.

"Here we go."

. . .

When I come to, I am on a park bench. I sit up and open my eyes. We are on Central Park West across from the Dakota. Yoko is sitting next to me, and I nudge her.

"We're here."

We both look up at the Dakota.

"Is it just my imagination or does that building look pissed off?"

"Yeah, it's not your imagination. I feel the same way." I have a bad feeling.

It's still light out, so I know we have time. We walk west on Seventy-Second Street past the entrance to the Dakota. I look at it closely as we pass. Is this the right day? Everything seems so . . . ordinary. Up on Broadway, I buy a copy of the *Daily News* to check the date—December 8, 1980.

Yep. It's the day John Lennon was murdered.

It is approaching three thirty when we walk by the building again. I spot a woman in black leaving with her entourage. I recognize her immediately as photographer Annie Leibovitz. She's with a group of assistants and they've just been inside the Lennons' apartment. One of those photographs—the one showing a naked John hugging Yoko like a fetus—will run a week after his death on the cover of *Rolling Stone*.

Leibovitz later remembered that she tried to get a photo of John alone, but he insisted that Yoko be included. Leibovitz was unhappy because she knew her bosses did not want Yoko in the shot. A week later, the photo became one of the most famous pictures ever taken.

By four thirty, a group of fans are in a small huddle near the stone arch driveway waiting for the former Beatle to exit. I spot Chapman immediately. The hairs on the back of my neck stand up. I want to punch him in the face. It's eerie to know what's going to happen, like watching a movie the second time around.

Chapman is standing just feet from me, as ordinary as ever, a pudgy loser. He has on a scarf and a nerdy winter jacket and is clutching a copy of the *Double Fantasy* album in one sweaty hand. I join the group, nodding at Chapman who smiles weakly.

I also spot Paul Goresh, a passionate Lennon fan and amateur photographer whose claim to fame is that he once sneaked into John and Yoko's apartment posing as a repairman. Incredibly, John forgave him and the two struck up a casual friendship. Chapman and Goresh are making small talk, and Yoko and I join in.

"Any sign of him?" I ask Chapman. I need to feel him out.

"Not yet," he says.

"It's always a waiting game. Sometimes you get lucky, sometimes not," Goresh interjects.

"You here a lot?" I ask Goresh.

"Oh yeah, I'm a regular. John's a good guy. Most times he'll sign autographs or say hello. If he's in a really good mood, he might pose for photographs."

I nod, my teeth chattering slightly. It's winter, and for all my preparation, I am not dressed warmly enough. Yoko seems to be cold, too, and we break away from the group to stand closer to the building, to block the biting wind.

Just then, there is a commotion, and John and Yoko appear. I have to make sure they don't see us. This is serious, and I don't need John and Yoko Ono quizzing me again. I turn my Yoko around so our backs are facing John so they don't recognize us. I know Yoko gets in the car ahead of John, and then he stops to chat with Goresh. I can hear every word.

"Paul, have you been here long?" John asks good-naturedly. Their bond is clear to everyone who is there. I'm sure Goresh is quite proud of it. As they joke around, a flustered Chapman, face-to-face with his idol, sticks out John's album but doesn't say anything.

"You want that signed?" John asks.

Instead of saying yes, Chapman clumsily asks the question John has already proposed: "Would you sign my album?" He hands it and a pen to John, and he signs the LP.

Then something weird happens. Instead of leaving it at that, John hesitates before getting into his car. I thought maybe he'd seen Yoko or me. Instead, he looks right at Chapman. "Is that all you want?" It is a very odd question. What else would Chapman want, and what else can John give him?

"No thank you," is all Chapman says.

John gets into the waiting limo and speeds away.

Goresh starts to squeal and tells Chapman he's gotten a photo of him talking to Lennon.

"They'll never believe this in Hawaii," Chapman says.

Then Chapman places the signed album, a prize he'd come all the way from Hawaii for, on the ledge of the Dakota. "Do me a favor," he says to the doorman. "Remember where I put that, because you'll want to know."

The doorman, probably used to crazy Beatles fans,

just smiles. We rejoin the group. Goresh says he has to get home to New Jersey, but Chapman suggests he stick around. "You never know, something might happen and you'll never see him again."

Goresh gives him a look but clearly doesn't take that as a warning in any way. He says good night to us and walks in the direction of the subway. Everyone goes his or her separate ways, all except me, Yoko, and Chapman.

"So what's up?" I ask.

"What do you mean?"

"I mean, what are you gonna do now?" I ask. I can't shake my overwhelming desire to punch him in the face.

"Don't know."

"Well," I say, "there's the Christmas tree lighting ceremony at Rockefeller Center. Do you want to see that? I heard you say you're from Hawaii. You've probably never seen it. It's a pretty big deal. Tourists flock there."

"No thanks. I want to be here later when John comes back."

I enjoy toying with him a little. I want him to think I am on to him, and of course, I am. "Why?" I ask. "You already got his autograph."

Chapman looks pissed. "What do you care?" he hisses. "Quit listening to my conversations. If I wanted to tell you I am from Hawaii, I would have. Now get lost."

He turns to Yoko. "Your boyfriend is a jerk," he tells her and then stomps away.

"I think you're the jerk," Yoko says.

"Fuck off."

We watch him leave. "That went well," I say. "We are definitely on his radar." I motioned to him, meaning we should follow.

She puts her hand on my sleeve. "No, we don't need to," she says. "We know exactly where he'll be at ten fifty tonight."

She's right, but I'm anxious and hate the idea of waiting another five hours. We walk until we find a nearby diner. I order the open roast beef sandwich; Yoko gets a Denver omelet.

"We need to be right in front of the Dakota tonight as John is getting out of his car," I say. "We can't be late."

Yoko nods. We talk about the plan again. There are probably a lot of things we can do, but the safest seems to be that we are in place a few moments before the shooting. I am planning to tackle Chapman at that moment and ruin his aim. I don't want the bullets to hit anyone else so my plan is to grab Chapman's arm and point it straight up, that or tackle him before he can even get off a shot.

"We'll stop him, don't worry," Yoko says. "But . . ."

"But what?"

"This is big, Lenny. Even if we do stop Chapman, we don't know what's going to happen next. There are always consequences."

"Do you think we shouldn't go through with it?"

"I didn't say that, but sometimes it almost feels like the past is alive, like it knows we're here."

"We can't think like that."

"I know, but we gotta be very, very careful, then. Promise me."

"I will."

At 10:15 p.m., Yoko and I are back in front of the Dakota. We see the usual group of Lennon fans. Goresh is gone, but Chapman is present and accounted for, looking as sheepish as ever. There is no way anyone would suspect what is about to happen. Chapman looks like all the rest, a little anxious to see his hero in the flesh, but otherwise unremarkable.

I keep my distance because I don't want him to become too paranoid about me. I have to be quick. I am burning up with anticipation. I see tiny black dots in front of my eyes. For a second I feel as though I might faint. I begin breathing deeply.

Stay calm, Lenny. Stay calm.

I continually move my feet back and forth, ready to spring at Chapman, keeping him in my sight at all times.

And then it is 10:50 p.m.

A limo slides to a stop outside the Dakota. Yoko Ono steps out first and heads inside. John steps out next, carrying the tapes from the recording session, the final mixes of Ono's voice on her song "Walking on Thin Ice."

The small crowd surges forward. Everyone is watching John except me and my Yoko—I am watching Chapman. Adrenaline shoots through me as I see Chapman's hand go into his pocket. He is making his move. There is no time to think. I am within feet of him and the only one who sees what he is up to. It's now or never.

He pulls out his gun. I launch myself at him and body-slam him to the ground, but he still manages to get off one round. Everyone looks in our direction. I hear a woman scream.

"He's got a gun," someone else shouts.

I stay on top of Chapman and keep my eyes on that gun, slamming his arm over and over into the sidewalk. Finally, someone steps on his hand while another guy pries Chapman's fingers apart and takes the gun away.

Chapman is squealing and crying out, but he's not making any sense. I am overcome with emotion and slug him in the face. His glasses go flying. His nose begins to bleed. In the doorway, there is a commotion. John is standing there, watching the scene and he looks like he's all right. I can tell in a flash that he recognizes me and knows what is happening. He nods and then turns away quickly, bending over someone on the ground.

Someone has yanked Chapman to his feet and has him in a headlock. Another guy holds one arm behind his back, threatening to break it off. Chapman is a lamb, not putting up an ounce of resistance. There is a crowd near John. I can't get close enough to see what's happened, but people in the crowd are shouting that someone has been hit.

"Is it John?" I ask.

"No, he's fine. It's a woman."

"Yoko?"

"No, I think it's a member of her staff."

Somewhere in the distance, I hear a siren. Chapman is crying, his nose a bloody mess.

"Hey, man, you're a hero," someone says to me, slapping me on the back. "You saved John's life."

I don't react. Everything is moving quickly now. I need to know who has been shot. I push through the crowd toward John, knocking people out of my way. Someone puts his hand on my arm. "Hey, man, you need to talk to the cops."

I ignore him. At that moment, I find myself standing next to John. He is tending to a woman lying on the ground, her eyes glassy. "Come on, Lily, hang in there, please," he says.

My eyes widen, panic seeping into my chest, my heart clenching. I put my hand on his shoulder, and he looks up.

"Thanks, mate, but the bullet hit her. Bloody mess."

I just stare blankly ahead. I can't make myself

understand . . . until I do. John is okay, Yoko Ono is okay, but Lily Chang has been hit, and it looks dire. I look around for my Yoko and begin screaming her name. People in the crowd look at me funny.

"She's okay, man, she's upstairs," one guy says.

I mean *my* Yoko, but I can't tell him that. She is nowhere. And then it hits me. Lily Chang is dying and will likely die here on the sidewalk, and that means my Yoko will never be born. I let out a ferocious cry. The gargoyles on the Dakota look down at me, angrier than ever. Yoko is right. The building does look pissed off. And now it is. The past has taken its pound of flesh.

The sirens are getting closer. The police are closing in.

I touch John on the shoulder. "I need to go."

"When will I see you again?"

"I don't know."

My headache is back, and it's more painful than ever before. I have to get out of here. I don't need the cops asking me a bunch of questions about who I am and where I live. I don't exist in this time. I don't want to get stuck. I'm not sure what to do, so I turn and run through the crowd into Central Park. I'm not needed here anymore.

I run and run until I am nearly through the park. I stop at the Tisch Children's Zoo to catch my breath. No one is behind me. The zoo is eerie at night. Every shadow is a menace. I feel vulnerable. It is easy to hear the sound of the animals in the dead of night, even in a city like New York.

I sit on a bench and think about what has just happened. I've done the impossible. I have saved John Lennon. But at what cost?

Donovan Day

◀◀ TWENTY ▶▶

I walk east to the Plaza on Central Park South, sneak in through the service entrance, and take the elevator up to the tenth floor where Dr. Robert's apartment is. We made arrangements that I would come here after we saved John's life. But I thought Yoko would be with me. I can't wrap my head around the fact that, in this new world, she does not exist. I find a quiet stairway in the Plaza where I hide and replay images of the past hours over and over. I have no idea how long I stay there, but at some point I hear someone in the stairway and exit to a hallway, where I can see that it's morning, and I hope I'm back in the present.

I take several deep breaths and knock on Dr. Robert's door. As soon as I see him, I know I've made the trip back. He smiles at me and hurries me into his place. "Congratulations. I've been waiting. How do you feel?"

"I have a headache, but it's bearable."

"Rough night, huh?" He smiles.

"You have no idea."

"Oh, I think I do. Come look," Robert says.

I cross the room to look at his computer. The

Wikipedia entry for Lennon is already open. The first thing I notice is that his life has no end date, which means he's still alive in 2015. I exhale and scroll down to the entry called "The Attempted Assassination of John Lennon."

John Lennon, a member of the Beatles, survived an attempt on his life outside his residence at the Dakota on December 8, 1980 when a Hawaiian man named Mark David Chapman pulled a loaded handgun out of his pocket.

A Good Samaritan, who has never been identified, spotted the gun and tackled Chapman before running into Central Park. There has been speculation for years that Lennon's savior is somehow attached to Chapman, but Chapman has denied it and investigators never found evidence that Chapman had an accomplice.

Chapman got off one shot as he was brought down. The stray bullet hit a member of Lennon's staff and former backup singer Lily Chang, who died hours later at Roosevelt Hospital. Chang had been working as Yoko Ono's personal assistant when the murder took place. A year after the shooting, Lennon wrote a song dedicated to Chang called "Lily," which became a #1 record.

After the shooting, the Lennons moved out of the Dakota and back to London because, they said, they were "upset by the proliferation of guns in America." Lennon has campaigned for years for more gun control laws in the States, a move that has not endeared him to millions of Americans who value their right to bear arms.

Lennon has since received thousands of death threats and has stopped performing. However, he continues to enjoy a

*successful studio career and his 1995 reunion album with
Paul McCartney,* John & Paul, *became the greatest-selling
record of all time and spun off six #1 singles.*

*Chapman was convicted of the murder of Lily Chang
and received a sentence of twenty-five years to life. He was
released from prison in 2012 and moved back to Hawaii.*

*Lennon and Ono divorced in 1990, which enabled
Lennon's reunion with McCartney, a partnership that
was regularly blocked when Lennon was married to Ono.
The divorce cost Lennon an estimated $150 million. Ono
moved back to Japan soon after the breakup, where she still
exhibits her art. Lennon has not remarried, though he's lived
on and off with a string of high-profile women including
Madonna, Sheryl Crow, Katy Perry, and Rashida Jones.*

The entry goes on to describe John's career and how
the Beatles eventually reunited for one glorious concert,
a benefit for cancer research after George learned he
was dying from the disease. It notes that George was
weak but played every note while Eric Clapton waited
in the wings to fill in if needed.

"Impressed?" Dr. Robert asks. "You changed history
and we're all better off for it. Not many people can say
that."

"What about Yoko?"

"She's still in Japan."

"No, *my* Yoko."

Dr. Robert's face changes immediately. "I didn't say
anything because I wasn't sure you'd remember," he
says.

"Of course I remember. I kissed Yoko, held her. How
could I forget?"

Dr. Robert touches my arm. "I remember her, too. I

was just trying to save you some pain in case you had no memory of it. Once Lily was killed, Yoko never existed."

"She disappeared from the Dakota that night, just disappeared," I say.

"Yes, that makes sense, Lenny. You understand, right?"

"But you remember her even though, in this 2015, she never was born," I say. "I'm confused."

"I remember because the three of us time-traveled together," he says. "We exist in a kind of alternate universe."

"So those who time-travel remember everything?"

"It seems that way, yes," he says.

"Will John remember her?"

He scratches his head. "I don't think so. Chances are your Yoko has been wiped from his memory."

"So I saved John but killed Yoko," I say.

"Well, more accurately, she was simply never born," Dr. Robert says. "I've checked. There's no sign of her on the Internet and her parents do not live in the Village. Her mother didn't exist, either, once Lily died."

I hold my head in my hands. "So I killed two people?"

"Don't beat yourself up, Lenny. I know it's hard but try to look at the positive side. John Lennon is alive, and millions of people adore him. He's written tons of new music. He and Paul have collaborated again, and it's all because of you!"

"But it's not worth it, doc. If all lives are truly equal, what have I done? Who am I to play God? What would my Yoko say if she know what we did? How can you tell me to just forget her, to look at the bright side?" I yell.

"I'm sorry, Lenny."

I ask Dr. Robert to get me some water. I return to the

computer to read more about John. I google an image of him as a seventy-five-year-old man. It surprises me because I've never seen him past the age of forty. His hair is now thin, but it is the same old John with that slight sneer on his face. Seeing him makes me wistful. Have I done the right thing or not?

"Yeah, age caches up with all of us," Dr. Robert says. "I know you don't want to think about this, but . . ."

"What?"

"Lennon's in town. He would love to see you. He's hinted many times over the years that he knows the man who saved him. He even wrote a song about you called 'Time Stranger.'"

"Really?"

"Yeah. Journalists tried to pry more of the story out of him. Yoko, too. She has let on that she knows your identity, but they never say a word. He'll be overjoyed to see you."

"He knows I'm here?"

"Yeah, I told him I was expecting you. We're in touch. He's in New York for a charity function. I did a little checking, and he's over at Peter Brown's apartment at the Langham, next to the Dakota."

"Peter Brown, the Beatles former go-to guy? That Peter Brown?"

"Yeah, it's another weird coincidence, but . . . they're just across the park. John's leaving tomorrow, so this is your chance."

"But . . . what do I say to him? I don't even know how I feel about everything."

"Talk to him about it. Who better to tell how you feel? He knows the whole story. He knew Lily well, and he mourns her to this day. He told me so himself."

"But what do I say? 'I'm glad you're alive, but I'm bummed because I killed my girlfriend in the process'?"

"I don't know what you're gonna say and neither do you until you go over there and talk to him. You'll figure it out. He wants to see you. He's been saying as much in all the interviews published over the years, how much he wishes he could thank you in person for what you did."

I don't think about it for long. How can I not go? "Okay. Let's go before I change my mind."

Dr. Robert rides with me in a cab over to the Langham, but he insists on waiting downstairs. "This is your time, not mine."

I hesitate at the building entrance. The Dakota, right next door, seems to be watching me. It doesn't look angry anymore, as it had that night.

"How do I get in?"

"Just tell the doorman you're here to see Peter Brown and give them your name. I guarantee the door will open wide."

"Okay."

"Oh, and Lenny, one more thing—John is up there with his new wife."

"What new wife? Wikipedia didn't say anything about a new wife."

"Yeah, well, Wikipedia doesn't know everything. He just got married this past week. It's a surprise. The happy couple is about to leave on their honeymoon. She's up there with him."

"Who is she?"

"Go find out for yourself."

"Please tell me it's not Katy Perry."

He laughs. "No. You'll see."

I turn and speak to the doorman, who calls upstairs. "Go right up," he says a moment later.

When I get to the second floor, the door to Brown's apartment is already open. John is standing there waiting for me. "I can't believe it. It's really you, Lenny Funk!"

He wraps his arms around me. Before I know it, I feel another set of hands embracing the two of us.

"Lenny, I'd like to introduce you to me new wife . . ."

I look at the beautiful woman standing next to us. She doesn't have makeup on and is dressed casually in jeans and a T-shirt, but there's no mistaking who she is.

"Shakira?"

They both laugh. "You didn't know?" Lennon asks.

"News travels slowly."

"I'm happy to meet you, Lenny. John has told me a little about you," Shakira says in beautifully accented English.

I'm speechless. John Lennon married Shakira? She's short, like Yoko, but she couldn't be more different. Shakira is an exotic beauty, even more so in person than in her striking videos.

They usher me into the apartment as I try to process everything. Weirdly, it all makes perfect sense. Shakira is a star in her own right. But she's also a humanitarian who builds schools for poor children in Colombia and other parts of South America. She cares about the common people, something that Lennon no doubt admires greatly. Well, I think, she's a way better fit than Katy Perry.

The two are all over each other as they lead me into Peter Brown's apartment. They introduce me to Peter, and we all sit at a big round table in Brown's dining room. Everyone is smiling.

"Where have you been all these years, mate? I always thought you'd turn up, but didn't know when."

"Well, I wasn't born until 1998."

"Right, right."

"John always told me about you, but I never believed

him," Brown says. "I don't how this happened, but I'm glad you were there at the right time."

"Yeah, don't ask me how it works," I say.

"Who cares? John wouldn't be here if not for you," Shakira says.

John claps me on the knee. "I can't believe we're meeting again, mate. Why did you run off that night?"

"Because I didn't belong to that time. I thought the cops would ask too many questions I couldn't answer. I had to go."

John accepts my explanation, and we move from topic to topic. I have loads of questions about his life. He answers each one thoughtfully and seriously. Brown offers me food, drink, pot—anything, it seems, is on the menu.

"We want to do something for you, Lenny," John says. "Just tell us what we can do."

"Tell me about Lily Chang," I say.

"Yeah, that was a drag. That crazy bloke got off one shot, but it was enough. Got Lily in the chest. It was horrible. She died in my arms. I testified at his trial. Big circus, you know."

"That's why I wanted to see you, why I came here today. Lily was my girlfriend's grandmother."

"But Lily never had children."

"Not in this world, but in my world—the one where Chapman's bullet killed you, the world that existed before I changed everything—Lily lived a much longer time and had a granddaughter named Yoko. Now she doesn't exist."

"Sorry, mate," John says, thinking.

John falls quiet, like he's trying to process something. "What is it?" I ask.

"Lily was pregnant when she was shot," he says.

"You're kidding?! She was?"

John shakes his head. "Yes. What a drag, right? She told me a couple of nights before she died."

Maybe I can solve at least one riddle. "Who was the father?" He looks up quickly and meets my eyes. "She wouldn't say. She went to her grave with that secret. So if I'm following you, what you're telling me is that Lily's daughter would have been your Yoko's mother, is that right?"

"Yes. And Lily made her daughter promise that when she had a child, she'd name it John if it was a boy and Yoko if it was a girl."

"Oh man, Lenny, that terrible."

"Yoko loved you," I say.

John shakes his head again. "I wish it hadn't worked out this way, believe me."

"The whole thing is so messed up, John, but I'm glad you're all right. I just wish no one had gotten hurt, that's all. I'm feeling lost without her, you know?"

"I know, Lenny," he says. "You saved my life, man, and I'm forever grateful. Anything you want, you tell me."

I can't come up with anything except the obvious. All I want is my Yoko, and not even John Lennon can bring her back. The rest of the afternoon goes by in a blur. It seems John is still great friends with Ringo and misses George very much. He is as witty as ever and gracious, as well. The old Lennon temper does not surface once. I ask about Sean and Julian. He tells me how he's made up with Julian and saw Cynthia before she died. He and Sean have been writing some songs together.

"And how is Paul?"

"Ah, Paul is the same bloke as ever. He cannot stop touring. It never gets old to him—never. I love the guy. He's my mate, and I see him all the time. But I'm not going back on the road. It was good when we teenagers, but man, I've had it. I have to tell you something funny, though. You showed that iPod to Paul, and he never forgot it. He went on babbling about it for years to everyone he knew, but everyone thought he was daft.

"Well, I'm happy you guys are on good terms."

"Yeah, we had a bit of rough patch there, but it's water under the bridge."

Everything has worked out . . . almost. Is it worth it? Millions will say a resounding "yes" and so does a part of me. The other part desperately misses my Yoko. But I can't think about it anymore. My head is pounding, so after three hours, I tell John I have to go.

"We're off on our honeymoon, mate. It should be a good one. Hips don't lie and all that, right?" He and Shakira laugh.

"Where are you going?"

"We're having a bed-in down in Colombia to raise awareness for Shakira's schools."

He pauses. "Say, would you give me a moment, Lenny?" John asks.

He goes into another room, and I pass the time talking to Shakira. In a few moments, John is back. He hands me an envelope. "I want you to visit us in London when we get back. Here's my private cell phone number and address in London and some other information that might help you. When you're ready to come, just read it, okay?"

"Okay, thanks, John." I fold the envelope and stuff it in the back pocket of my jeans.

"And of course, it's on me," he says at the door. "You tell me when you want to come. I'll get someone to make all the arrangements. You'll never spend another quid when you're with me. It's the least I can do."

John sees me out. He touches my face with his hand.

"I know you're in pain but you'll do the right thing, Lenny. I know you will."

I give him a big hug and hurry down the hall before he can see me cry.

Donovan Day

◄ ◄TWENTY-ONE► ►

Dr. Robert is waiting outside the Langham.

"So?"

"Let's walk. I need to process everything. John is married to Shakira?"

Dr. Robert laughs. "Yeah, she's a honey, isn't she?"

"I guess it makes sense. They seem happy."

"He's a very lucky guy."

"I'll say. He doesn't seem to miss Yoko Ono at all."

He raises an eyebrow. "Would you?"

"I guess not. Not if Shakira was my wife. Wow."

"The rumors are flying that they're making an album together. He say anything about that?"

"Nothing about that, but he was in great spirits and happy to see me. You were right about that."

I don't say much as we walk across the park toward the Plaza.

"You're quiet. What are you thinking, Lenny?"

I'm thinking something no one wants to hear. I'm wondering if I can undo what I've done. "It seems wrong to deny my Yoko her very existence. It's not right."

"John didn't remember her?"

"No, I don't think so, but when I told him that my Yoko was Lily's granddaughter, he looked different somehow. For a second, I thought he was going to tell me he did remember her, but then all he said was that Lily was pregnant when she died."

"She was?!"

"Yes."

"What else did he say?"

"That was all about that, really. Nothing else. Doc, I'm thinking…"

"Don't torture yourself with what-ifs, Lenny. You made your choice."

I stop and look him in the eye. "Not really. I never knew that Yoko was the price. And if I knew *that* was the price, I don't think I would have saved John. I know that sounds horrible."

He smiles. "No, it sounds human. But what can you do about it now?"

"What if I went back again?"

"You've got to be kidding. What would you do differently?"

"I'd do nothing."

"Nothing?" he asks.

"That's right, nothing. I love John and his music, but Chapman did what he did. I had nothing to do with that. But killing Lily Chang and changing things so Yoko is never born? That's on me, and I can't live with that. I'd let history play out the way it did the first time and not interfere. I'd do nothing."

"Lenny, I know you by now. You're not just talking. You want to do this."

"Yes."

"How are your headaches?"

"Terrible, worse than ever."

234

We're nearly at the Plaza. He stops and puts both hands on my shoulders. "Lenny, I'm worried. Maybe you shouldn't go. What if you can't get back? We know from that last scan that your brain is likely shrinking every day. At some point soon, it will be back to normal size. You're taking an enormous chance."

"I know, but it's the right thing to do. I have no choice."

. . .

When I get home, both Joes are sitting in the kitchen, only they're not eating or preparing any food. "What's going on here?" I ask.

"Lenny, we need to talk," says Grandpa.

"Sure. About what?" I ask.

"Sit down."

"We just got a call from Dr. Robert."

I can't believe it. He wouldn't . . .

"Oh?"

"He told us some things," Grandpa says.

"What kind of things?"

"About you, about your headaches coming back."

"They're not coming back."

"Lenny, don't lie to us. We know Dr. Robert did another MRI. He told us everything. The thing is, you need to rest."

"Okay, I'll rest."

"No, we mean it."

"Okay, I get it."

"No, you don't," Joe says. "We called your mother. She's coming home tomorrow to take you to Ohio with her. We think you'll rest more there without all the distractions of New York."

"Come on, Grandpa, I've been good. You said so yourself just last night."

He puts up his hand. "We thought you were being good, Lenny, but Dr. Robert told us a lot of stuff you've been doing, and he's worried your brain is taxed, that there's a possibility you could have a stroke."

"A stroke? I'm seventeen years old! That's not going to happen."

"You don't know that," Grandpa says. "Your mother is coming and you're going to Ohio with her tomorrow, so you best start packing tonight."

"But I have plans to go out tonight."

"They're canceled. You're grounded."

"That's not fair. You can't do that."

"We can and we will. You're not to leave this house until your mother arrives tomorrow. Then we'll see what she wants to do. Tonight, you're going to rest whether you like it or not."

"I cannot believe Dr. Robert called you guys."

"He had to, Lenny. He's a doctor and you're a minor," Joe says.

I turn around and storm into my room, and I slam the door as hard as I can. For the first time in a very long time, I feel all my old demons returning. I'm pissed and I see black dots in my peripheral vision. I throw things around my room until the Joes burst in.

"What do you think you're doing?"

"I'm giving you the Lenny you want—the bad kid. Right? Isn't this what you really want from me? The Lenny you think I really am?"

Grandpa's face drops. "Lenny, no one thinks that. We're worried about you, that's all."

I stuff my hands in my pockets, and that's when I feel his old iPod. I throw it at him and immediately regret it. "Here, take this. I don't want it. Get out of my room."

They leave, and I sit on the bed, barely able to focus. I cannot believe I gave him that iPod. Stupid, stupid, stupid.

As I calm back down, I make a decision. I'm going back to December 8, 1980 *tonight*, and if the Joes happen to look in my room and I'm not there, I'll have to deal with the consequences. My head is pounding, but I can't afford to put it off any longer. My brain is shrinking. I know it and I don't need another MRI to tell me. I'm sorry I threw the iPod at Grandpa, but I don't need it. Whatever allows me to time-slip is in my brain. I just need to take advantage of it while I can. If I never come back, then I never come back.

I sit there stewing until there's a knock on my door. I open it to Grandpa holding out the phone. "It's your mother, and then it's time for dinner."

I take the phone but don't look at him. I just hear his footsteps walking away. "Mom?" I say into the phone.

"Lenny, what's going on there?"

"Nothing. Everything was going great until tonight. Grandpa told me I have to go to Ohio and I kind of lost my temper."

"Did you hit him, Lenny?"

"No! I would never hit Grandpa. Mom, everything's been really chill here until tonight. I guess Grandpa is worried about my concussion."

"What concussion?"

Oh no. They didn't tell her. What a bonehead I am tonight.

"I'll tell you when you get here. It's nothing. I've been having headaches, and the two of them are worried. You know how they are. They're old men."

"Lenny, don't talk about the Joes like that. *Is* there

237

something wrong with your head? I'm beginning to worry."

"No, it's fine. I got into a stupid fight on the subway a couple of weeks ago, but it's over."

"A fight? With who?"

"Some kid. He stole my guitar, and I was fighting to keep it. Would you rather I just gave it up? I couldn't do that, Mom."

"Oh, Lenny. I'm sorry. I know how much that guitar meant to you."

I can tell I'm near tears. "Only because you bought it for me. That's why it was special. I love you for that, Mom."

Now she's crying. "Now I'm really glad I'm coming. I'll be there tomorrow around eleven. Grandpa is going to pick me up at the airport. I want you to come, too. We need to talk. Everything will be all right."

"Okay, Mom," I say, my voice tight.

"You be good, Lenny."

"I am good."

"I know you are, honey. I love you."

"I love you, too. Remember that."

I hang up before she can say anything else. If I never get back, she'll remember that last part. Talking to my mom always calms me down, but I do some of Terry's breathing exercises, anyway, and then I go into the bathroom to wash up.

"Hey," I say to the Joes when I enter the dining room.

"What did your mother say?" Grandpa asks.

"She wants me to go to the airport with you tomorrow."

"We're leaving here at ten."

"Okay."

I help set the table, and we all sit down for dinner. I am jumping out of my skin the entire time. Everything moves in slow motion, and I can barely focus on anything the Joes are saying. The fact is, I don't much care. I have a ton on my mind, and yes, my head is throbbing, but I can't let on. They insist I watch some dumb reality show with them on Bravo. Each minute seems like forever, but I suck it up until eleven, when I tell them I'm going to sleep.

"Hey, I'm sorry we fought," I tell them. "I love you guys. I hope you know that."

Grandpa gives me a hug—he is so emotional—and Joe just gives a small smile and nods.

"Good night, Lenny," they both say.

"Good night."

I wait in my room until I'm sure they're asleep. Then I start listening to "Double Fantasy."

This has to work.

Donovan Day

◀ ◀TWENTY-TWO▶ ▶

My eyelids flutter open. I'm on that same park bench. I look around and pray it's the right day. I walk around the corner to the front entrance of the Dakota where the first person I see is Mark David Chapman. He's walking toward me, wearing the same coat and same scarf with the same *Double Fantasy* album tucked under his arm. He seems to be in a hurry, and it's no wonder—it's 4:45 p.m. He is minutes away from finally meeting his idol.

I want so badly to punch his pudgy face, but I need to stay chill. Something inside me gets the better of me, though, and I bang into his shoulder hard as he passes.

He stops. "Watch it."

"I think *you* should watch it," I tell him.

He puts his right hand inside his jacket pocket. I know what's in there. I can tell he's thinking about pulling the gun out to scare me—or maybe worse, shoot me—but I stand my ground and stare him down. "I don't have time for this," he says, spinning around and heading for the entrance of the Dakota.

Breathe.

I am letting my temper take over again, something I can't afford right now. Tonight is critical. The important thing is that I've made it back. I've been given another chance. This time, I promise myself, everything will be simple. All I have to do is . . . nothing. It pains me to think that, but I've made up my mind. The events must play out as they did in history. John Lennon will die, Lily will live, and Yoko will be born. I tell myself that John has already lived a life like no other, and truly, I'm not doing anything to alter the reality that happened long before I was born. I'm not changing the past. I'm fixing it.

And I'm restoring life to my Yoko. I take comfort in that.

I join the small group of fans in front of the Dakota where Chapman is chatting with Paul Goresh. Chapman ignores me, and I leave him be, too. At five o'clock, John and Yoko come out. I turn away, but this time, I'm a hair too late. I feel a hand on my shoulder.

"Hey, mate, is that you?"

I turn and am face-to-face with John. Chapman and the other fans are staring. I'm sure they wonder why John has picked me out of the crowd. So much for my seamless plan. I've only been in the past for half an hour and I've already screwed things up.

"It is you," he says. "Great to see you again."

"I, um, wasn't sure you'd recognize me," I say.

"You think too little of me, mate. I'd recognize you anywhere. Still . . . traveling, I see."

Everyone is listening, especially Chapman, and this is not a conversation I want to have in front of the others.

"Yes, still traveling. What are you up to?"

"We're making a Yoko record tonight. Why don't you come along?"

I don't really have much choice. John nudges me

toward the car and the rest of the scene plays out as it always had. He signs the album for Chapman while Goresh takes their photo. Then John is back in the car with me and so is Yoko. She moves quietly and I am barely aware of her, but here she is.

"So good to see you, man," John says. "You disappeared last time before we got a chance to say goodbye. Where's your Yoko anyway?"

"She didn't make it this trip. How's the new record doing?"

Anything to change the subject.

"Great. Mother was right."

"I told John he should record again," Yoko says.

Yoko is so soft-spoken, but she is not to be underestimated. The other Beatles learned that lesson the hard way. She is not just another bird. She has a will of steel and the determination to get her way, and she is far savvier at business than any of the other Beatles, though Paul will catch up to her one day.

I smile at her and hold out my hand. "It's good to see you again, Yoko."

Yoko takes my hand. She has a way of looking at me that makes me think she can read my mind, that she knows why I'm here. I have to admit, I'm a little afraid of her. John doesn't notice any of this. He's in great spirits, talking about the band he's put together for the recording that night.

"Why have you come back again?" Yoko asks out of the blue. "Is something going to happen to John? Is this the night?"

She's caught me off guard, and I don't have the words to lie. "Yes, it's going to happen soon."

Now John is paying attention. "What?"

But I can tell Yoko knows the answer by the look on her face. "Your death, John. That's why he's here."

John's face drops. "Bloody hell! Why now?"

I feel horrible, but I have to lie to them. "I will do what I can."

Yoko is stone-cold. "Did you come back to keep your promise?"

"Yes, I told you I would try, and that's what I'm planning to do. But from this moment on, even I don't know what's going to happen."

I hate myself, but there is no way to explain why I'm here or what I plan to do, which is to let history take its course.

John looks ashen now. What am I doing? Nothing is going the way I thought it would.

"Are *you* the killer?" Yoko asks me suspiciously.

My jaw drops. "Of course not! I would never hurt John, ever."

"It's okay, Yoko," John intercedes. "I trust Lenny. He will try. That's all anyone can do, but I need to be prepared."

"Don't say that," she says and then turns to me. "When exactly is this going to happen?"

"No, Mother, don't ask Lenny that. We have to face this head-on. Thank you for coming to tell me yourself, Lenny, and thank you for trying. I know you'll do what you can, but I believe you. You don't know what's going to happen the rest of the night, do you?"

"No. Things are different because I'm here with you, so we have to wait and see."

"I'm grateful you've given me the chance to say some goodbyes. Let's finish up the record tonight, Mother, and then I need to make a few calls."

"Will you tell them you're about to die?" she asks.

"Not in so many words. Don't want to freak 'em all out, but I need to call Aunt Mimi and Paul, George, and Ringo. Julian and Cyn, too. Poor Julian. I've been such a shitty father Lucky I had the chance to get it right with Sean."

I keep my mouth shut. I've said too much already.

. . .

That night in the recording studio, I sit with John and Yoko as they supervise Yoko's vocals on the track, "Walking on Thin Ice." Talk about irony! I can barely breathe watching what I know are John's last hours. He appears calm, relaxed. He seems to have gained something, some acceptance. He seems ready to face death. He is especially loving toward Yoko and kind to everyone in the studio. At one point, he goes in to work on a guitar lick, and that's when I see it—the blue guitar pick. He really did use it that night as my Yoko had said.

Watching John strumming contentedly, I know he'll never get a chance to make those last phone calls, never see Sean again. I am in agony, but I can't say or do anything more.

Yoko picks that moment to slide next to me.

"Tell me when," she says.

"I can't."

"So you're just going to let him walk into his death, simple as that? How can you live with yourself?"

"There are no easy answers."

"But you can help him. All you have to do is tell us when it's going to happen and we can be somewhere else."

"And then what? Did you ever stop to think what might happen instead? Maybe the killer's bullets will hit you. Maybe he'll leave here tonight and go after

Ringo, maybe Paul, or maybe a school full of innocent children. I can't live with myself if any of that happens. I can't play God. Can you? Are you willing to trade one life for another, even if it's to save John? Are you prepared to sacrifice Lily Chang for John?"

She doesn't answer.

"I didn't think so. You can't do it and neither can I. Everything must happen the way it's meant to happen. I'm just here to change the dynamic."

She swallows audibly. "All right."

"All right?"

"Yes, I know you are right. Thank you for changing the dynamic, as you say. Whatever happens, John is at peace."

She leaves, and soon I watch John collect the tapes from that night's session. He slips the pick into Yoko's pocket, and we get back into the limo for the final ride back to the Dakota.

Yoko asks John if he wants to go to dinner.

"No, I need to say goodbye to Sean."

I turn away, tears forming in my eyes.

The limo moves silently on, closer to the moment of John's death. I am so torn up. There are no right answers. Why am I the one who has to decide? Second thoughts creep in. Can I really stand by and watch John be murdered? It's inconceivable, but I have seen the future. I am a mess. My head suddenly starts pounding as it never has before. I'm seeing stars.

And then, we're there, outside the dreaded Dakota. This time, I have a view from inside the limo and see the small crowd of fans. Chapman is there but barely visible. It's heartbreaking to see how inconsequential he looks, given how he is about to make worldwide headlines by killing a man loved by millions. It's sick. The world is about to change because of one mentally ill man with a gun, a formula that repeats itself far too often in America.

And that's when I get the idea, just as the limo is only a few feet from the building entrance. What if no one has to die? Not John, not Lily. Maybe I can stop Chapman cold, stop him from firing a single bullet. Maybe no one will die tonight. I have to try. I am here to change the dynamic, after all.

The moment the car stops, I push by John and Yoko and get out first.

"There's something I need to do," I mumble.

Yoko is the next one out of the car as John takes a moment to gather the tapes on the backseat. Chapman is right there. He recognizes me and looks a bit panicked. I get in his face and wrap my arms around him before he can reach for his gun.

"What are you doing?"

"Shut up, I know you have a gun."

He doesn't say anything. His face is filled with rage. "Get off me!"

I haven't counted on Chapman being so strong. I've underestimated the adrenaline flowing through his body. He breaks free of my arms and throws me to the ground, pulling the gun from his pocket. By now, John has passed. He is moving toward the entrance of the Dakota. Chapman raises the gun and goes into a shooter's crouch.

I have one more chance. I push Chapman hard, but he still gets off that damned first shot. This time, I see the bullet whiz by John's head and crash through a second floor window. No one's been hit. Chapman looks in my direction for a split second. His eyes are wild. I think he might turn the gun on me, but instead, he slams me in the head with it. I lose my balance as he resumes his pose and fires off four more rounds. From the ground,

I see John fall. People are screaming, especially Yoko. I got up and rush Chapman, and this time, I knock him over.

"You stupid, stupid man," I say, holding him down.

"Don't hurt me," he squeals.

"Forget that, you loser." And then I let him have it, hitting him as hard as I can in the face. Blood flies out of his nose. The doorman comes over and grabs the gun from him.

"Do you know what you've done?" he asks Chapman.

"Yes, I just shot John Lennon."

"Why?"

"I don't know."

We pull Chapman to his feet. Something drops from his coat pocket. It's his copy of *The Catcher in the Rye,* the book that convinced him John was one of those phonies Holden Caulfield is always talking about.

"Can you please pick up my book?" he asks.

"You will burn in hell," someone yells.

He ignores everything but his stupid book. Someone finally picks it up and hands it to him. Incredibly, he sits down and begins reading. Police cars are pulling up to the main gate. I watch as a cop rushes over to John, while another slaps handcuffs on Chapman, who beg them not to hurt him.

"No one's gonna hurt you," the cop says.

No one except me. As the cop holds Chapman against the wall, I kick him hard between the legs, and he lets out an "oof."

The cop turns around. "Hey! Back it up!"

I watch a moment longer as the cops, who appear as stunned as anyone. The last thing I hear is the cop asking John, "Do you know who you are?" as he and another cop carry John's limp body to a police car that then roars off into the night.

Yoko has disappeared. Chapman is hustled into another cop car and driven from the scene. That's when I see Lily Chang. She has a hand to her mouth looking at everything from the archway. She is shocked but unhurt. Despite everything, I feel a glimmer of hope.

"Did anyone see what happened?" I hear a cop ask the crowd.

"He shot John Lennon," someone screams.

I put my hand, bloodied from Chapman's nose, into my pocket and move backward. It's time to go. Quietly, I move away from the chaotic scene. I know the rest of the story. I don't run because I don't want to attract any attention.

"Hey, that guy punched the shooter," I hear someone say just as I turn the corner onto Central Park West. "He tried to stop him."

"Hey, wait a minute!" I hear someone else shout.

I turn and run into the park. In minutes, I'm in the dark and there's no one around me. It would be easy to head home now, back to 2015, but there's one more thing I have to do.

I start walking in the direction of the Dakota, only this time I approach it from Broadway. At West Seventy-Second Street, I stop and take it all in. The street is closed to traffic and filled with thousands of people. People are singing "All You Need is Love" and "Give Peace a Chance."

I wade into the crowd, scanning faces. I don't think there is much chance I will see him, but he said he was here—my Grandpa's husband Joe. I look and look, but there are so many people. And then a spot opens up in the crowd and I see him. He's standing in a big circle with the others, holding hands and singing with his eyes closed. He's so young. I think about talking to him, but what am I going to say? That I'll know him thirty-five years from now? So I just watch him until I think of something I can do. I surreptitiously pull out my cell phone and take his photograph. No one notices a thing.

Now it's really time for me to go. Because I'm never coming back, I try to remember every detail, and then walk over to my bench on Central Park West. I sit down and close my eyes, listening to the choruses of "All You Need is Love" being sung over and over.

I love how the crowd sounds, but I need to get back so I tune the iPod to Fiona Apple's version of "Across the Universe" and let it take me home.

◂◂TWENTY-THREE▸▸

When I open my eyes again, my mother is standing over me.

"Mom?"

She is holding my hand. "Boy, you sure do sleep a lot."

"What time is it?" I grumble.

"Three in the afternoon."

"Sorry, I guess I missed your plane."

"I guess," she says, smiling.

"Lenny, what's going on? Are you okay?"

I sit up with an energy that surprises both of us. "Mom, I'm great actually."

"How's your head?"

I rub my hand over my head. The headaches are gone. "No more headaches. I really do feel great . . . and hungry."

Half an hour later, I'm finishing the biggest breakfast I've ever had—scrambled eggs, Belgian waffles, bacon, toast, you name it. The change in my appetite coincided with the change in my head. I know the concussion was making my head hurt, but I had no idea it was affecting my appetite, too. With all the excitement, I barely noticed how much weight I'd lost.

Everyone is being overly polite and walking on eggshells. I think they are afraid of another tantrum like the one I threw the night before. I don't know how to reassure them, so I broach the taboo subject of going to Ohio with Mom to care for her cousin.

"When are we leaving for Ohio?"

"You want to go?" my mother asks, as though I've just asked for another helping of waffles.

"Not really."

"I think you should stay here. I've talked it over with the Joes and they want you to stay until my cousin gets better. It should only be a couple more weeks."

The Joes both smile. "Yeah," says Grandpa. "He's okay. We love having him."

I feel a buzz in my pocket and pull out my cellphone. Excitement shoots through me. I've been afraid to call her, but this could be the text I've been waiting for.

Can we talk?

It's a text from Yoko, *my* Yoko. The world is good. Everything is back in its place.

"Yes!" I shout out loud.

"What's that all about?" Mom asks.

"My girlfriend. We were having a fight, but she's talking to me again. Can I go over to see her? Please?"

The Joes leave it up my mother. "Okay, but no disappearing acts," she says. "I want you back here in an hour. And bring her with you. I want to meet her."

"I will. Thanks, Mom."

. . .

Yoko's mom answers the door and gives me the once-over. "Hello, Lenny," she says.

"May I come in?"

"Lenny!" Yoko shouts from inside.

She throws her arms around me and pulls me farther into the house. "Mom, we're going into Grandma's room."

"Okay, but leave the door open."

"Lenny, Lenny, it's so good to see you. Where have you been? I've been trying and trying to get in touch with you."

I was hoping this would happen. She has no memory of the time she did not exist and I'm not about to tell her. "The last thing I remember is seeing Chapman point his gun—"

"Nothing after that?"

"No, nothing."

I shake my head. "Well, I'm just happy you're all right, but . . . I'm sorry Yoko. I tried to save John, but it didn't work. Chapman was too strong and the past too powerful. John is dead."

"I know that much. It's the first thing I checked when I got back," she says.

Suddenly, I sneeze and reach into my back pocket for some tissue when I feel the envelope John gave me when I visited him at Peter Brown's apartment. I'd forgotten all about it. I tear it open and see that it's not his address and phone number like he said it was. It's a handwritten letter.

"Holy shit," I say.

"What is that?" Yoko asks.

"It's a letter from John. He gave it to me when— Well, never mind, but he gave it to me and I forgot all about it."

"What does it say?"

And then I read the letter out loud:

"Dear Lenny,

I'm writing this letter from 2015. You just left the flat after our visit with Peter Brown and Shakira. I don't know if we'll ever see each other again, but there are a few thousand things I want to tell you. First off, thank you, mate! You gave me more time. I have a feeling you're going to take it away, though, and I want you to know that I understand. I understand all too well. When you told me that your girlfriend was named Yoko and she was the granddaughter of Lily Chang, everything fell into place.

I told you Lily Chang was pregnant, but what I didn't tell you is that I'm the father. It was to be my baby. Bloody hell, you say? Yeah, I know, but it's true. I asked Lily to keep it a secret. The baby was conceived in August 1980 when my Yoko was off on one of her trips to Japan. (Advice: never go to Japan without your man!) But the truth is, Lily and I had a few flings under the sheets here and there over the years. My Yoko <u>never knew,</u> if you're wondering. Had she known, well . . . Lily would never have been her assistant.

So you see, when you started talking about your Yoko and how she was Lily's granddaughter, I realized that—somehow, someway—you were talking about my granddaughter. Your Yoko is my granddaughter, I'm sure of it.

Lenny, I don't know how any of this works. I have no idea if you're real or some by-product of all the drugs, but I hope you're real, mate. The time-travel thing is a trip, but I believe in the unseen world. I'm glad I got to meet you, and I'm sorry I never got to meet my granddaughter. Please tell her that her grandfather says hello if you ever see her again!

One more thing: the song 'Across the Universe' came to

me after I met you back when we were filming 'Hello, Goodbye' (now that song is a still piece of shite). I always thought 'Across the Universe' was a good piece of work, and you inspired it. Thank you. Think of me when you hear it and know I wrote it with you, Lenny Funk, in mind.

Love and peace,
John"

"Oh my God," Yoko says.

"Can it be true?" I ask.

"My mother was born in May 1981. That means she was conceived in August 1980. The math works!"

"Holy shit!"

"I heard that, Lenny!" Yoko's mother calls from the other room.

I pop my head out of the memory room to look at her. "Sorry, Mrs. Peng. Wait, Mrs. Peng, can I ask you a question?"

"Of course, dear," she replies.

"This sounds a little weird, but do you remember your father?"

I see something cross her face, something not good. "I never knew my father."

"I know you never talk about him, Mom, but why not?"

"My mother would never tell me who he was," says Mrs. Peng. "It was a big secret. She wouldn't even tell me on her deathbed."

"But she made you swear to name me Yoko, right? You told me that," Yoko confirms.

"Right. Yoko if I had a girl, and John if I had a boy. She lived with John and Yoko, but you know that."

"Thanks, Mrs. Peng," I say as Yoko pulls me back to the memory room.

"Lenny, this is amazing."

I shake my head in disbelief. "I'm kind of blown away. It means John had a daughter, your mother, that no one ever knew about."

"Wow, my grandmother can really keep a secret. I've been through all her things in here and there's not even a hint."

I look around at all the Beatles memorabilia. "I don't know about that. Look at all this stuff. A lot of it is connected to John. Maybe she was telling everyone without telling, if you know what I mean."

"I do." Yoko looks at me, then her brow furrows. "Wait. But I don't understand. How did you meet John in 2015? And Shakira? And—"

"Yoko, please," I say. "I don't have the energy to go into it right now. Can we just agree that some things are better left unsaid?"

She pulls me in for a hug. "Of course, but someday I want the whole story."

I don't say anything. I'm exhausted. "Yoko, I want you to hold the letter for me."

"I can't. John wrote it to you."

"Yeah but . . . it belongs in this room anyway."

"Oh, Lenny."

We kiss as long as we dare until we hear her mother's footsteps outside the room.

"I want you to meet my mother," I say. "She's at my house."

"I'd love to, but what's she doing here?"

"Long story. Everything is okay now. I promised her I'd only be gone an hour, and I have something planned at home."

"What is it?"

"I can't tell you. It's a surprise."

◄◄ TWENTY-FOUR ►►

So you're Yoko. I've heard and read so much about you from my dad," my mother says, wrapping Yoko in an embrace. Mom looks over Yoko's shoulder at me. "See, the Joes keep me abreast of everything going on with my son."

"Best summer of my life," I tell her.

She releases Yoko and looks at her. "So Lenny tells me you're a very talented singer," Mom says.

"Ah, but your son is the arranger and musician. I'm only a hired hand," Yoko says.

"Now, we all know that's not true. Yoko makes every song better," I say.

"Well, let's hear something!" Mom pleads.

Yoko smiles. "Okay. Do you wanna hear a new one?"

Mom and the Joes sit back and listen. It's the song we've been practicing that Lily wrote with John—"Can't Get Enough of You." The lyrics alternate between male and female voices, and it's perfect for Yoko and me. She sings while I play the guitar Paul gave me.

There's much clapping when we finish. "Beautiful," Mom says.

"So . . ." I start. Everyone is looking at me. "I've got a little surprise for you all . . ."

"Dessert?" Grandpa asks with obvious excitement.

Mom rolls her eyes at her father. "What kind of surprise?"

"Well, it's not dessert. Sorry, Grandpa," I say. Then I take a deep breath. "I want to take you back in time."

"You were talking about that just the other day," Joe says. "Man, I wish you could."

"But I can, and tonight, I'm going to prove it."

"Okay, I'll bite," says Joe. "Prove it how?"

"I'm glad you asked." I pull my phone out and find the photo of him at Seventy-Second Street the night John was murdered. "You told me you were outside the Dakota the night John was shot, right?"

"Right."

"Well, I was there, too, and I saw you."

"Come on, Lenny. You weren't even alive then," Joe says.

"That's true, so explain how I took this photo."

I hand him the phone. His mouth drops as he zooms in on the photo. "How did you get this? That's me, but no one took my photo that night. At least I don't think anyone did. This is photoshopped, right?"

He hands me back the phone, but I tell him to look at the metadata, the information that says when the photo is taken. "It says it was taken yesterday," Joe says. "Obviously you manipulated it."

"You can't manipulate metadata," Yoko says.

"Come on, Lenny, quit it," Mom says. "It's not really funny."

"He's telling the truth, Mrs. Funk," Yoko says. "I've gone with him. We've met the Beatles. John is the charismatic one, Paul is as charming as he seems, Ringo is a party animal and a great dancer, and George, well,

I wish we'd gotten to know him a bit better."

"Seeing is believing, right?" I say before anyone can comment. "What if I can show you?"

"Well, I'm dying to go back in time," says Grandpa.

"Lenny, I think you're seriously losing your grip on reality, but fine. Try to show us so we can move on and get you the help you need," Joe says.

"Deal," I agree.

What I haven't told anyone is that I went to see Dr. Robert that afternoon for one more MRI. It showed my brain is still shrinking, but he told me it is still well above normal size. He again warned me against taking any more trips back in time but I'm willing to try it. I know it will work. I can just feel it. I've never felt more confident about anything in my life, and I'm going to give my mom, grandfather, and Joe the thrill of a lifetime.

"Can I have your iPod, please, Grandpa?" I ask. He retrieves it from the kitchen. "You remember how you gave me this right after my concussion?"

"Sure," he says slowly, nodding.

"Well, somehow the concussion made the memory section of my brain swell, and now, when I listen to some of the classics and really concentrate, I can go back in time."

"We're waiting," Joe says.

I hand the iPod to Yoko and smile at her. "Yoko, cue up 'All My Loving.' It's the first song the Beatles played in the United States. Okay, everyone, we're gonna hold hands, listen, and think about the Beatles' first glorious appearance on *The Ed Sullivan Show*."

"Is that where we're heading?" Grandpa asks, even more excited now than he'd been about the concept of dessert.

"No more questions, Grandpa. Close your eyes."

There's not enough earbuds for all of us, but the iPod is turned to its loudest setting. The music sounds tinny, but we can all hear it and that's the important thing.

· · ·

The roar of applause startles me. I open my eyes and look around. I'm sitting with Yoko, Mom, and the Joes in the audience, about halfway up from the stage. Everyone except Yoko looks shell-shocked.

And then I hear that distinctive voice. "Thank you ladies and gentlemen!"

I smile. Yoko squeezes my leg.

I did it. We are exactly where I want us to be. Up there on stage, right in front of us, is Ed Sullivan. We are sitting in the audience. It's the night of February 9, 1964. Ed is beginning his now-classic introduction in his now-famous cadence:

"Now, yesterday and today our theater's been jammed with newspapermen and hundreds of photographers from all over the nation. These veterans agreed with me that this city never has witnessed the excitement stirred by these youngsters from Liverpool who call themselves the Beatles. Now tonight, you're gonna twice be entertained by them. Right now and again in the second half of our show. Ladies and gentlemen, the Beatles! Let's bring them on."

The noise of girls screaming is deafening. The familiar guitar begins, and Paul McCartney sings the opening lyrics to "All My Loving."

I look over at Yoko. She is screaming her head off along with everyone else. Because the venue is so small, the sound is far better than at most of the early Beatles concerts. We can actually hear the lyrics, and we can see them shimmy and shake, showing us exactly why the girls love them so much. They are irresistible, all so thin, young, and handsome. Mom is going a bit wild, as well, cheering along with the Joes.

It's shocking to see what babies the Beatles were when they made it so big, barely out of their teenage years. Mom digs her nails into my arm. "This can't be happening," she screams over the crowd. "Did you hypnotize us? Drug us?"

"Nope. Go with it. Enjoy it!" I yell back. "It is happening."

The Joes don't say a thing; their eyes are glued to the stage. Forty feet away, the Beatles are introducing themselves to America with their brand of rock 'n' roll. It all feels so familiar because we've seen it a million times, but there's nothing like seeing it in person. I swear you can smell the pheromones in the theater.

After the first song, the band slows it down so Paul can sing "Till There Was You." The camera gets close-ups of each of them, telling the audience who is who. After this night, the names John, Paul, George, and Ringo will be etched into a generation's memory.

"This is so great," Yoko says. "Thank you, thank you!"

The last few days have been exhausting, and though I'm drained, this is just what I needed—a shot of pure, unadulterated joy. When the camera pans over John, the producers of *The Ed Sullivan Show* put up a caption: SORRY, GIRLS. HE'S MARRIED.

I still feel sick knowing how it will all end for John. He'll live a magical life, but it will end way too early. The irony, of course, is that most of what he sings about is love and peace. It's heartbreaking, but I hide what I'm thinking from the others who happily move to the music.

Yoko puts her arm around me as they began singing "She Loves You." This is my chance. I tell her to come with me.

"Mom, we'll be right back. Keep an eye on the boys."

Every face is focused on the Beatles, so it's easy to slip backstage.

"Where are we going?" Yoko asks.

"Shh. You'll see."

And there she is, right where I imagined. Lily Chang is backstage watching the performance. She can't be more than eighteen years old and, at this age, looks exactly like my Yoko.

Yoko sees her, too. "How did you know she'd be here?"

"John told me."

"Why?"

"He wants you to convince her to record the songs she writes."

At that moment, Lily looks over at us and sees my Yoko. She doesn't know us, of course—she'll meet Yoko in 1968—she's friendly and greets us immediately.

"Hi," she says in her British accent.

"Hi, are you with the band?"

"Yes."

"They're fabulous."

"Yes, but they look a lot sexier in leather," Lily says. "But I like the hair, and I love their music."

"Those haircuts will help make them legends," Yoko adds. "You might even call them 'the four mop tops.'"

"I like that. Mind if I steal it?"

"No problem." Yoko smiles. "I love their songs."

"Me too. No one is like them. They write their own material, you know."

Yoko doesn't hesitate for a moment. "I understand

you do, too."

"Who told you that?"

"John."

"You know John?" she asks, looking uncertain now.

"I've met him a couple of times here and there."

She looks skeptical.

"He respects you," Yoko tells her. "He thinks you should record."

"Yeah, he's told me that."

"You don't believe him?"

Lily shrugs. "Not really."

"He told me you're as talented a songwriter and as he and Paul are."

"That's crazy." Lily pauses. "Who are you, anyway?"

"What if I told you we're related?"

That surprises her. "How?"

"I'm your granddaughter."

Lily laughs. "Can I have some of whatever you're on?"

"It's true. I'm your granddaughter, and I'll find your songs sometime in the future. Songs like 'Can't Get Enough of You.' It's your first song, isn't it?"

Now Lily truly looks shocked. "H-how?" The noise is dying down because the boys have finished their first set, so we hear her clearly, even though she's whispering.

Then Yoko sings the song softly to her. "Won't you please record it so I can listen in the future? Have something to remember you by?"

"I don't who you are or what this is all about, but if I am your grandmother, I'll see you in the future," Lily says.

Yoko's eyes fill with tears. "No, you won't. You'll die when I'm only four years old."

"What are you talking about?" Lily puts a hand on her hip, reverting to her previous disbelief.

The Beatles are walking toward us and so is Brian Epstein. "Hey, who are you? You're not supposed to be here," Brian says to Yoko and me.

"We need to go," I say.

"Think of me," Yoko tells Lily. "And please, record those songs. Please. Do it for your granddaughter."

I pull her away, and we head back toward the audience. Lily is watching as we leave the backstage area.

"Do you think she'll listen to me?" Yoko asks.

"I don't know, but we did all we could. Let's get out of here."

When we get to our seats, I tell everyone to hold hands again, and I turn up the iPod as loud as it goes and we all hunch down, trying to huddle so we all can hear in the still-noisy theater. The next thing I know, we're back in 2015 in the Joes' apartment.

◄◄ TWENTY-FIVE ►►

Everyone is sitting on the sofa, already up and waiting on me to come to.

"Well?" I ask.

No one says anything.

"How did you do that?" Mom asks after a while.

"I told you. That concussion scrambled my brain. I don't actually need the iPod, but I'm superstitious about it."

Grandpa and Joe are looking at each other. "Holy shit," Grandpa says.

"Maybe it is all hocus-pocus, but it was exciting," Mom says. "I felt like I was there."

"You were!" Yoko and I yell at the same time.

She shakes her head. "Impossible."

"Let me read you a quote from John," Yoko says. "It's one of my favorites. 'I believe in everything until it's disproved. So I believe in fairies, the myths, dragons. It all exists, even if it's in your mind. Who's to say that dreams and nightmares aren't as real as the here and now? Reality leaves a lot to the imagination.'"

"So that's it? We're supposed to believe in fairies and

dragons?" Joe asks.

"Why not?" I ask. "Look, believe what you want. If you think I hypnotized you or gave you drugs or whatever, that's up to you, but I believe we time-traveled."

"Me too," Yoko says.

Grandpa smiles wide. "Me too."

"You do not!" Joe says.

"Yeah, I do. I know what I feel and what I saw. I was a kid again. I felt it in my body. That is not hypnosis and we didn't take anything, so what else could it be?"

"Oh, come on.. What do you think?" Joe asks my mother.

"Well, it did *feel* real. Those were the Beatles. The songs sounded slightly different than the records, and if it were hypnosis or whatever, wouldn't they have sounded exactly the same?" She pauses, biting her lip for a second. "Lenny, I think I believe you."

"And I think we should leave you guys to yourselves," Yoko says with a smile. "Lenny and I need to check out something at my house. Is that okay, Mrs. Funk?"

"Sure, Yoko, but call me Amity."

We get up, and I can hear my family still debating as we leave the house. I'm not sure if Joe will ever come around.

Yoko practically runs back to her house, dragging me with her.

"Mom, Lenny's here," she shouts when we get inside. "We're going into the memory room, and we'll keep the door open."

"Okay, honey."

We get to the door, but Yoko stops. "Well?" she says to me.

"Well what?"

"I'm too excited. You check."

"Check what?"

"To see if anything's different!" She looks at me like I have five heads. And then I realize why.

Duh, Lenny. Yoko's grandmother could've become a star!

I open the door and walk into the dimly lit room. It looks more or less the same—the walls covered with posters and photographs, the three guitars sitting where they always were. But then a glint catches my eye and, there, over the piano, I see it. The wall above the turntable is filled with gold records, dozens of them.

"Yoko!" She runs in. "Look!"

We rush to the wall to look more closely at the records and I take one down. "'This Gold Record signifies that "Can't Get Enough of You" has sold more than one million records as a single,'" I read off the plaque.

"Oh my God, she listened!"

The wall is filled with at least twenty-five Gold Records.

Yoko is so happy she's bouncing on her heels, and I can't stop smiling. She is so cute. We yell and give each other high-fives.

"What's all the noise?" Yoko's mother asks.

"These records . . ."

"Oh, those. You've seen those before, Yoko, what's the big deal?"

"Grandma recorded all these?"

"Yes, she was a very good pop singer. How do you think she bought this house? The money from those records!"

"And they've always been here?" Yoko asks.

"Always." She shakes her head. "You kids never notice anything," Mrs. Peng mumbles as she walks out.

Yoko and I burst out laughing. This time, I don't care if the door's open or not. I take her face in my hands and kiss her on the mouth for a very long time.

ACKNOWLEDGMENTS

Time-travel novels can be tough to keep straight and helping me negotiate the straits on this book were Danielle Rose Poiesz, a crackerjack content and copy editor who runs her own company Double Vision Editorial, and DVE copy editor Lorrie Grace McCann. Any mistakes that remain are my own. For the interior design of the book, I thank Libby Murphy of Book Alchemy, and for the fabulous, exciting cover design, credit goes to graphic artist Kit Maloney. I also thank Donna Eastman and Gloria Koehler for their suggestions and hard work. Finally, what would my life be without Susan, Alex, and Peter, the best family in the world. Thank you everyone.

Donovan Day

Made in the USA
San Bernardino, CA
15 December 2015